"You should have thought to ask."

"You wanted me to create an environment for Laura that would be acceptable to the St. Clairs." She straightened her spine. "I can tell you right now that if Winchester Falls doesn't get a church, it won't become a place the St. Clairs will consider suitable."

He sat there, staring at her. She would not look away.

"You still should have consulted me first. As an equal partner." He said the last few words quietly, so faint that she had to strain to hear them.

"You are right." And he was. She was barging ahead without thinking, but if he had done the same to her, she would have been furious. "I apologize."

"Apology accepted." He stuck his hand out down the length of the table. "They can have the land. Do we have a truce?"

She took his hand in hers. His was rough and calloused, the hand of a man who worked long, vigorous hours, using reserves of strength and vitality.

She pulled away sharply, suddenly aware that she had let her hand rest in his for longer than absolutely necessary.

Growing up in small-town Texas, **Lily George** spent her summers devouring the books in her mother's Christian bookstore. These books, particularly ones by Grace Livingston Hill, inspired her to write her own stories. She sold her first book to Love Inspired in 2011 and enjoys writing clean romances that can be shared across generations. Lily lives in northwest Texas, where she's restoring a 1920s farmhouse with her husband and daughter.

Books by Lily George

Love Inspired Historical

LILY GEORGE

Once More a Family

HARLEQUIN® LOVE INSPIRED® HISTORICAL

Recycling programs
for this product may
not exist in your area.

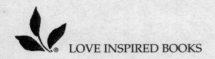

LOVE INSPIRED BOOKS

ISBN-13: 978-0-373-28364-4

Once More a Family

www.Harlequin.com

Printed in U.S.A.

"For I know the thoughts that I think toward you,"
saith the Lord, "thoughts of peace, and not of evil,
to give you an expected end."
—*Jeremiah* 29:11

For my tireless beta reader, Marie Higgins, and my fellow writers Kristin Etheridge and Belle Calhoune. Without your cheerleading and support, I would not have made it.

Chapter One

Winchester Falls, Texas
March, 1905

Heat radiated in waves around her. Who knew that Texas would be so terribly hot, especially so early in spring?

Of course, this was the uncivilized part, not the more well-established, genteel cities one heard about, like San Antonio or Austin. Perhaps scorching heat was befitting the rough-and-ready northwestern Texas town of Winchester Falls.

Ada Westmore stepped gingerly out onto the train platform, holding tightly to her hat as the wind threatened to tear it free of all its carefully placed hat pins. She caught a glance of her reflection in the train-car window as she struggled to keep the door from slamming shut. Her black hair, so tidily arranged this morning, framed her face in straggling locks. Her dark blue eyes were ringed with fatigue. Her dress, once a fashionable shade of dark green, had been dyed the requisite somber hue for mourning. Yet the color really didn't matter, for it was muted by a fine layer of sandy dirt that had blown through the train-car windows.

Ada straightened, shoving the hat pins more deeply into her coiffure to anchor her hat securely. Then she gathered her skirts in one hand while navigating the steps to the platform. A porter waited, extending his hand as she made her way down.

"Thank you," she said, grateful for the assistance. She scanned the length of the platform, but no one seemed to be expecting her. Surely Aunt Pearl would be here by now. The train was late, after all, having been delayed by a solitary cow that had refused to move from the tracks and had to be coaxed away by the conductor. "Is there a waiting room inside the depot?"

"Yes, ma'am," the porter replied. "But it's so hot right now most people wait out on the platform. At least that way, you can hope to catch the breeze."

Ada gave him a wan smile. This was no mere breeze, but a howling, scorching gust that made her feel as though walking might be a passing fancy but not something to be seriously attempted. She should probably offer the man a tip. She opened her reticule and removed a few precious pennies, the last of the small horde that she had managed to bring with her. He took them from her with a curt nod.

Ada burned with shame at the paltry sum, but what could she do? From her debutante days in New York, she could claim very little. Her home was gone, sold on the auction block, and all of the luxurious possessions with it. There had barely been enough for her two younger sisters to finish their semester in boarding school. In fact, unless she came up with a steady income, both her sisters would be turned away from the school for the next term. There was nothing to do but beg Aunt Pearl for assistance. With her aunt's help, she could either find a position or establish a home of their own. Either way, she had reached the limit of what she could accomplish on her own, and she needed to make things work so her sisters would not face disaster. Ada made her way down the length of the platform, peering curiously around her as she strode.

Winchester Falls was different from New York, no doubt about it. True, there were several tall buildings nearby and the train depot had a certain charm to it, but everything looked, well, raw. Small wonder, for Winchester Falls had only really come into its own in the past decade, or at least that's what Aunt Pearl had said in her last letter. She glanced around at the rugged landscape. Somewhere out there, the falls that gave the town its name rushed over a hillside and into a nearby river, or so she'd read in a newspaper. It was difficult to believe that a refreshing waterfall could play any part in this landscape.

Her valise had been unceremoniously dumped on the platform next to her trunk, and the porter had vanished. There was nothing to do but retrieve it and then have a seat atop her trunk. Aunt Pearl would be here eventually. She had to come. She was Ada's only living relative, save her sisters, and she had promised to help Ada start a new life out here.

Nervousness gripped Ada as she collected her bag, but she straightened her back and lifted her chin. Was this any way to feel, when she had faced far more dire situations? She had marched in suffragist parades and been pelted with rotten eggs from jeering onlookers.

She had padlocked herself to a police wagon when they had tossed her fellow suffragists in jail. No matter what Texas threw at her, she could certainly handle it.

"Miss, I'll take that bag," a voice drawled behind her.

Ada dropped her case and glanced up. A young man, quite tall and broad shouldered, stood before her. Though his straw hat was in his hands, arrogance and power emanated from him, from his stance to the slightly mocking light in his green eyes. There was something elemental in the impression he created. He was as much a part of this rough landscape as the boulders that ringed the depot. She was staring at him. She gave her head a quick shake.

Handsome men like this always made her feel inadequate, and feeling inadequate made her appalled at her lack of spine.

"I beg your pardon?" Her voice had a definite quaver to it. She cleared her throat. "I am waiting for my aunt. Surely I have the right to be here?"

He raked his hand through his thick blond hair. "Mrs. Colgan sent me to fetch you."

"Aunt Pearl isn't here?" Ada gasped in outrage. She had just lost everything—her family and her fortune—and had made a long and arduous journey across the country to build a new life. The very least she expected was for her aunt to meet her at the station.

"Something came up," the man replied. "Under the circumstances, she figured it might be better for me to bring you to her, anyway." He nodded, and two boys grasped her trunk, hefting it down the length of the station platform and into a handsome carriage with a pair of matched bays. After watching their progress, he tugged on his hat and lifted Ada's valise.

"Circumstances? What circumstances?" Ada stepped in front of him, blocking his path.

He moved around her quickly, striding down the length of the platform to the carriage, where the bays waited patiently. Ada scurried after him, trying to match his pace and failing miserably. He tossed a coin to the two boys, one of whom caught it in mid-air. When they dashed off, he stored her valise in the back of the carriage and stood patiently, waiting to hand her up.

"Just a moment," she panted, facing him squarely. "Why would it make more sense for you to pick me up at a train station? I don't even know you. My aunt should be here."

"My name is Jack Burnett." He looked at her steadily, from under the brim of his hat. "That name should mean something to you."

"Well, it does not." Ada's mouth went dry. *Calm down, you've been through much more frightening situations than this. Remember when you were egged in the last parade? This man is just obviously mad.*

"Mrs. Colgan said she wrote to you and explained everything." He took a step backward and tilted his hat brim up. "She said that we were all set."

"What are you talking about?" Ada was ready to stamp her foot in frustration. He must be deranged, and yet he looked perfectly sane. More to the point, the dawning comprehension on his handsome features showed that he knew more about this entire farce than she did. "Perhaps you would care to enlighten me, since apparently you know me better than I know you?"

"Sure." His expression darkened, as though he were unsure how to proceed. "You see, your aunt told me she had already arranged everything. We're getting married. You and I."

Jack Burnett waited, watching Miss Westmore with a wariness that served him well on the prairie. In height she stood only to the middle of his chest but gave the impression that she could lay him low if she got really riled up. She gazed up at him, her blue eyes darkening.

"That joke is in poor taste."

"It's not a joke." He didn't want to explain the whole thing out here, so close to the station platform. Too many people would see them, and this was not exactly the way he planned to start his married life. "Come on, I'll take you to Mrs. Colgan."

He handed her up into the buggy, then made his way to the driver's seat.

She sat, rigid on the bench, an expression of utter confusion on her face. He climbed beside her and started the horses. When they'd gotten far enough away that they could no longer be heard by people on the station platform, he glanced over at her, anxiety building in his chest. Why didn't she know about the arrangement? If she decided not to marry him, he would lose any hope of bringing his daughter home from boarding school.

He should explain, since it was pretty obvious that she'd never gotten her aunt's letter. On the other hand, when trouble brewed, sometimes it was better to just leave things simmering for a while. Whenever he and his first wife, Emily, had fought, he'd go for a long ride on the prairie. Eventually, when he came home, they'd pretend nothing had happened. This was the best way to handle it. In fact, it would be better for her to hear it from her aunt. That news was probably better told from one woman to another, anyway.

"Do you mind telling me what's going on?" She turned to look at him, her complexion drained of all color. "You are taking me to my aunt's home, aren't you? I warn you, I can kick hard, so don't try anything untoward with me, sir."

He wasn't sure if he should laugh or groan. "I was going to let your aunt have a talk with you." He would take himself out of the picture until things had settled down a bit. A man's place was nowhere near an angry woman.

"I would prefer not to wait," she replied crisply. "After all, you say we are betrothed. Why should I hear that only from you? Unless, of course, you are quite mad and this entire scenario is a figment of your imagination."

He slowed the horses. "I'm not crazy."

"Well, then." She settled herself against the back of the seat. "Tell me."

He sighed. This was not his strong suit. Confession didn't come easily to him; nor did asking for help. Telling Miss Westmore that he needed her in order to win his daughter back from his autocratic father-in-law was humiliating and humbling. There was no way to beg her assistance nicely, which was why he'd depended on Pearl to do it for him. Even when he had married for love, as he'd done with Emily, he was not the type to say flowery things to a lady. When he was a green young man, he would have at least tried to court a lady. But he was twenty-six and, thanks to his life experiences, jaded beyond his years. If only they could already be married, with him out working the ranch and Miss Westmore at home making things cozy. Laura would be there, his sweet little girl. She was the only reason he had agreed to this outlandish scheme.

"It's like this," he began, hesitantly. "I need a wife."

"Well, I don't need a husband," she shot back. "I can function quite well without one, thank you."

"I've known your aunt for many years," he went on, ignoring her. "When she got your letter, she came over and talked to me. I have the ranch next to hers. Anyway, she said that your family was pretty nigh desperate…" He trailed off. It was true that Mrs. Colgan had revealed that, but not, perhaps, the nicest thing to say aloud.

"So my aunt agreed to sell me into servitude, like a mail-order bride?" Miss Westmore's voice had grown dangerously high, and two bright spots of color appeared on her cheeks. He gazed at her. Mrs. Colgan had been right. She was a very pretty girl, even if she was a termagant. "I don't want to hear another word, Mr. Burnett."

"Well, all right, but you do deserve an explanation," he began. He'd be angry, too, come to think of it, if he came out to a new place and his whole life had been rearranged for him. "Sounds like Mrs. Colgan's letter never did reach you."

"Not another word," she breathed, her eyes snapping. "I need to speak to my aunt."

"I understand," he replied. "The justice of the peace is likely to be waiting there, anyway."

She shot him a look of pure loathing, and he was hard-pressed to keep from smiling. She certainly wasn't dull, and that was refreshing. Emily would have sweetly gone along with the plan and then gotten little digs in here and there. He preferred a woman who was direct. A man knew where he stood with someone like Miss Westmore.

He whipped up the horses with a click of his tongue and a flick of the reins. Anyone would have a hard time adjusting to life in Texas after a life of comfort back east. To come to Texas so quickly—and after such tough times—would be even more difficult. Miss Westmore had shown gumption, and that was a prized commodity out here. Besides which, she was very pretty. He had a marked weakness for large blue eyes ringed with long dark lashes.

As he adjusted in his seat, the letter in his pocket crackled. When he'd arrived at the station, a note from Laura had been waiting for him. She was now ten years old, and her handwriting had improved to the point that she had been allowed to write the address on the outside of the envelope. That was good. Her boarding school was all right for the time being, but soon enough he would bring her home and he'd have a family again, once he was married to Miss Westmore.

If she would agree to it.

Mrs. Colgan would surely help with that, wouldn't she?

He was so close to having his daughter home. What if Miss Westmore refused? She was really the perfect candidate for the job—wellborn, educated, cultured and refined. Without her help, everything would be just as it had been, with his wife's father controlling everything regarding his daughter from the St. Clair estate in Charleston. It didn't matter that Emily had died, or that the last few years of their marriage had been a sham. The St. Clairs were such an autocratic bunch. What a shame he'd married into them. At least he had gotten Laura out of the deal.

He clenched his jaw reflexively, as he always did when thinking about his daughter. He knew to the second when he'd last seen her. It was this past Christmas when he'd made the trip to St. Louis.

Miss Westmore was still stubbornly silent, staring fixedly at a point just in front of them. Pearl had said she would write to her niece and make the necessary arrangements. Either Pearl had failed to do so, which was unlikely, or her letter had somehow missed Miss Westmore. There was nothing to do now but wait until everything could be sorted out. It was a mighty strange ride, all told. At last, the large iron gates of the Colgan ranch loomed ahead. He let the horses bound through and then slowed them to a respectable pace as they neared the ranch house.

Sure enough, the justice of the peace's carriage was parked out front.

Miss Westmore gasped as they drew close enough that she could read the lettering on the carriage door.

"See? I told you." He couldn't resist reminding her. "They are probably ready to start the ceremony right now. Still think I've gone 'round the bend?"

She glowered at him and jumped down from the carriage, without waiting for help. Then she flounced inside the house, slamming the door shut behind her.

He stared after her. Maybe it would be better to leave her alone with her aunt for a while. He drove the horses around to Mrs. Colgan's stable, where they would be more sheltered from the wind and sun. He unhitched them and took a seat on a nearby bale of hay. Then he took Laura's letter out of his pocket.

"Thank you for the hair riben, Pa." It was written in her large, childish handwriting. Then *Pa* had been crossed out, and *Father* scribbled over it. For some strange reason, that hurt. Now, away from home, she was learning to call him Father, when all he could remember was her tiny, sweet voice saying "Pa." He had insisted that his daughter would call him Pa, which had made Emily roll her eyes. "I suppose she'll use suitable Western slang," she'd said, as soon as Laura's infant burbling had matured to recognizable speech. "But I prefer to be known as 'Mother' to her."

He folded the letter back up. No sense in going on until he knew whether or not he'd get to bring her home soon. It was painful to read, wondering if he would hear her call him anything again.

If he was a praying man, this would be a good time to raise his voice in prayer. But he had finished with the Lord a long time ago when his marriage had soured, and then his wife died and his only child was taken away.

There was nothing to do but wait a little longer and see if his betrothed would agree to be his bride.

Ada stared at Aunt Pearl. She had not seen her aunt since childhood, and those memories had long ago blurred to almost nothing. The tall, stern woman before her bore a strong resemblance to Father, especially in the way her every glance was a challenge. "So what Mr. Burnett said is true. You did sell me into servitude."

Aunt Pearl threw back her head and laughed, a hearty sound that made one feel utterly ridiculous. "I doubt Jack said that. Come, now. Have a little common sense. He needs a wife in order for his daughter to come home. You need a livelihood. The arrangement is simple. A marriage in name only, and you would be paid to make the kind of home that suits his in-laws. I'm sorry my letter didn't reach you in time, but there it is. Sometimes our best-laid plans get derailed."

Ada sank into a tufted velvet chair that had been recently—and hastily—vacated by the justice of the peace the moment she had hurtled into her aunt's parlor. Her head ached, pounding in her ears. Her breath came in short gasps. She was thousands of miles away from the only home she'd ever known and from her sisters. She had come out here specifically to raise the money needed to finance the rest of their education. Failing that, she would create a home for them, and they would come live with her.

Marriage to Jack Burnett, though distasteful, would solve both problems. She would earn money and create a home.

When her father died and his business affairs had collapsed, she had accepted her role as head of the family, even though she was just twenty years old. It was her duty to come out to Texas and create a life for herself and for her sisters so that they could all be together again someday. They were only a few years behind her, but she was miles ahead of them both in terms of maturity and a sense of duty. She had envisioned being her aunt's helpmate on her sprawling ranch. She had not planned on marrying and certainly never thought of marrying a stranger. Yet, by doing just that she could solve her problems immediately.

"I never considered getting married." She stated it slowly and firmly.

"Oh, you're just saying that because you're a suffragette," Aunt Pearl replied with a laugh. She settled into the chair opposite Ada and regarded her frankly.

"I prefer the term *suffragist.* Adding a diminutive suffix, such as-*ette*, to the noble cause of suffrage demeans our work, I feel." They were going off on a tangent, but at the same time, she had to take every opportunity, however untimely, to educate others about the cause. "But, no, that is not the reason, Aunt Pearl. I saw what happened in my parents' marriage. Father took Mother's fortune and ran through it like water. Mother was powerless to stop it. Once she married, all she had belonged to him." She shuddered. "That's why I campaign for the right to vote. Women should demand equality in all things. I refuse to suffer the same fate as my mother."

Aunt Pearl looked at her, silent for a moment. She resembled Father so closely. She had the same blue eyes and the same steel-gray hair. Even the way she folded her hands in her lap was a familiar gesture. It was strange, being around someone who looked so much like her parent and yet wasn't. The comparison between the two made a lump rise in her throat. Yes, she was angry at Father and had despaired of his wastefulness, but she did miss him all the same.

"I know Augustus was a poor businessman," Aunt Pearl finally admitted. "Even way out here, we heard of his goings-on. The big fancy house in New York, the debutante balls, the jewels…" She trailed off, shaking her head. "Then he started dabbling in politics. Gus always got in over his head with stuff like that. Did he really try to rig that election?"

Ada shrugged. "I don't know. I never had the chance to ask him. He died the day the scandal broke. I've been too busy trying to arrange things since then to even stop and wonder if he was guilty."

Aunt Pearl nodded. "Tell me, Ada, do you have faith?"

What a surprising question. Ada had never really considered the matter before. "Yes, of course. We go to church every Sunday."

"What I am talking about is faith, Ada, not worship. Living out here, you have to have a lot of trust in God. There isn't any other way to make it. Do you believe that God has a plan for you?"

"I suppose so." Uneasiness gripped Ada. "Are you saying that He wants me to marry Jack Burnett?"

Aunt Pearl laughed again. "Child, you are sharp. You don't need the suffrage movement, but I could see how it might need you. I am telling you that Jack Burnett is a fine young man, with a lot of land of his own and a pretty house up on the hill. He's handsome, to boot, but you've seen that for yourself. I've known him since he moved out here with his first wife, Emily. She was a bit hoity-toity for my tastes, and I think you'll be a better match for him than she was. You could do a lot worse."

"If I marry him, it would be in name only. You said so yourself." Ada stood her ground. She folded her arms across her chest.

"If you're worried that Jack Burnett will run through your money, like Gus did to your mother, just remember that you have not a cent to your name," her aunt warned her tartly. "Only through marriage will you gain anything. Now go upstairs and freshen up. I'll call the justice of the peace in."

Angry frustration rose in Ada's chest, but the solution was before her.

She hated being ordered around.

She left the parlor, shaking with anger, and made her way to the bedroom upstairs. She filled the basin with tepid water from the pitcher and scrubbed her face and hands with a bar of lavender-scented soap. The water ran down to the basin in muddy rivulets. She was filthy. There was nothing for it. She must empty the basin out and put in fresh water in order for her ablutions to have any benefit at all.

Ada heaved the basin up, dribbling some of the contents on her dress. How absolutely disgusting. She would not feel really refreshed until she'd taken a long bath in scented water and changed into a fresh dress. Until then, this would have to do.

Ada glanced over at the window. It was open, but a screen kept her from being able to fling the water from the second story. She struggled out of the room and down the stairs. It was going to be rather difficult to keep the water from sloshing over with each step, but if she took the stairs slowly, most of the water would be contained. When she reached the bottom stair, she hoisted the basin onto her hip. Where should she throw the water? Aunt Pearl was nowhere to be seen, and there seemed to be absolutely no servants anywhere. She paused, biting her lip. Well, she couldn't very well wander through the house with a bowl full of dirty water. She had already arrived looking ridiculous enough as it was.

She crossed the front entry and opened the screen door. Then, without pausing, she flung the water in the general direction of the yard.

A deep, decidedly male voice exclaimed, "Whoa, there."

Ada gasped, dropping the bowl in her surprise. It smashed, sending ceramic bits and pieces scattering over the length of the front porch. Horrified, she surveyed the damage and then raised her eyes to behold Jack Burnett, his face and the front of his shirt both dripping wet. If only the ground would open up and swallow her.

"I am so sorry, Mr. Burnett." She tugged inside her sleeve, pulling out her handkerchief. "Here. Take this."

He motioned the handkerchief away, his expression dark and unreadable. "No, thank you. I've got one of my own. I wouldn't want to ruin yours." He mopped his brow. "I suppose you and your aunt have had a chance to talk?"

"We have," she replied, with as much dignity as she could muster.

He tucked the bandanna back in his pocket, and a surge of some strange feeling grabbed hold of Ada. Surely she wasn't attracted to this man? He was no better than any other man of her acquaintance, arrogant and smug. No, she must be exhausted from the journey and from the emotional upheaval she had endured.

"Will you marry me?"

"For a price?" She couldn't keep her voice from trembling. She cleared her throat.

"Well, out here we would say we are killing two birds with one stone." His eyes gentled, and he gave her a smile. "You see, we need each other, and marriage would fix both of our problems. If you make me a nice home, then I get my daughter. I pay you for your trouble, and you can keep your sisters in school. What do you think?"

"Aunt Pearl makes it sound as though I have no choice in the matter." She admitted it grudgingly. Life had been constant humiliation for months now, and everywhere she turned, doors had closed in her face.

"Of course, you have a choice." He leaned up against the porch column, eyeing her squarely. "The only reason I acted the way I did is because, well, I thought you had come to an understanding already with your aunt. I thought you two had corresponded and she had explained matters. But maybe that was the wrong way to handle things. You see, there's a reason why I want to marry you. As I said before, I need a wife."

"Surely there's someone around here you know better than me." For the first time since their meeting, a real curiosity seized her. Why on earth did this man want to marry her, after all? It didn't really make sense.

"It's not that simple." He glanced down at his boots, his jaw tightening. "My first wife died eight years ago, and her father thinks that Winchester Falls is no place for his granddaughter to grow up. He placed Laura in a boarding school a few years back. I visit her during the holidays. It's not worth bringing her to Texas for visits. My father-in-law raises such a fuss that bringing her here causes a lot of trouble. In fact, he was threatening to take Laura away for good. I can't let that happen. She's only ten years old, and she needs a real family. Your aunt Pearl was kind enough to offer a compromise."

"Why would Aunt Pearl even get involved?" None of this made much sense.

"Your aunt has been a friend of my family since we moved out here. She became acquainted with my father-in-law and, well, people have a tendency to listen to Pearl Colgan when she speaks. So she was a good person to step in and settle matters before it got too ugly." He gave a wry smile, but the expression in his green eyes was still dark.

"One of the conditions my father-in-law agreed to was that if I could marry a girl from a fine family, and set up housekeeping here in Winchester Falls— proper housekeeping, not frontier living like I've been doing—then he will allow Laura to come live with me." He gave her a searching glance. "You're from an excellent family back east. My father-in-law would approve of you. Besides which, you're related to Pearl Colgan, which makes you okay in my book." He lifted one shoulder laconically. "If you agree to the bargain, my daughter gets to come home. I don't even want to wait for the end of the school year—we'd go get her as soon as possible. You'll have a nice place to call your own. I'll pay you wages, so that you can keep your sisters in school. I'm a good provider, and I even know how to make a decent cup of coffee. What do you say? Will you marry me?"

Ada hesitated. "I've never thought of marrying anyone, to be honest. My work in the women's suffrage movement means a lot to me." She lifted her chin. "I believe that women should have the same rights as men."

He grinned, a boyish smile that made her heart flutter ridiculously in her chest. "Fine with me. If you think you're the equal of any man, I'll take your word for it. In fact, I challenge you to prove it. Show everyone out here that you are made of sterner stuff than your average New York belle."

She eyed him warily. "You'll get to have the family situation your father-in-law demands of you."

He shrugged. "Sure. I'm aiming for an agreement that's acceptable to both parties."

Ada swallowed, nervousness gripping her tight. There was no reasonable way to decline. She had no place to go, after all. Aunt Pearl had made that quite clear. If she married Jack, she would help him to bring his daughter home. It was sweet that he cared so much. Her father couldn't have been bothered to bring any of his daughters home. No, in fact, the arranging of schooling and vacations, trips and homes had been done by Mother. After Mother died, Ada had assumed that role for the family.

Her sisters had come to rely on her for strength and security. This arrangement would allow her to continue to provide both. If they wanted to remain in school, she would have the funds to make that possible. If they preferred to come to Texas, she would have created a suitable home, not just for Laura but also for her sisters.

On the other hand, she had never intended to marry. Marriage made her suspicious. It seemed that men used matrimony as a kind of weapon to get what they wanted, as Jack was doing now. "If I agree to it, I have one condition."

"Name it." He had grown suddenly still, watching her with those disconcertingly green eyes.

"If we marry, I'm an equal partner in this venture," she replied, slowly forming the words that had entered her mind. "I must have my rights. I need to be able to continue my work as a suffragist. I must maintain my own funds, which cannot be touched by anyone. The lack of equality in the wedded state that I have been witness to has made me hostile to the institution of marriage for many years."

He stared at her, as though taking a few moments to process all that she had just said. His expression was shuttered a little, as though he were distrustful of her intentions, as well. Her heart continued its heavy pounding against her rib cage, and she surreptitiously wiped her palms on the front of her dusty black skirt. What if he said no to her conditions? What then?

After a small eternity, he stuck out his hand. "Miss Westmore, you have yourself a deal."

Chapter Two

As soon as Jack grasped Miss Westmore's hand in a firm shake, a sense of loss tugged at him. Another marriage that didn't mean anything, at least in the traditional sense. That seemed to be his lot in life. Well, there was no use in getting upset. Miss Westmore was everything his father-in-law wanted in a stepmother for Laura. She was educated, cultured and pretty. So, just as with his first marriage, he'd at least get Laura out of the deal.

"I suppose we should go into the parlor," he remarked, releasing her hand."

Miss Westmore nodded and peeked around the corner of the veranda. "Tell me, why aren't we being married in a church? It seems strange for so solemn a ceremony to take place in front of a judge."

"There's no church in Winchester Falls." He never even missed it, to be honest. "I guess there aren't enough people."

"Hmm." Miss Westmore's eyebrows drew together. "I've never lived anywhere that didn't have a church of some kind."

"Winchester Falls is still pretty new." He shrugged. "We're building this town from scratch." He offered her his arm, a bit rustily. He'd have to get used to squiring a lady around again. "Should we go?"

She nodded, taking his arm. All the color had drained from her face. She must be nervous. Who could blame her? This was a lot to take in all at once, and even more to handle gracefully. She didn't seem the type of woman to appreciate much coddling, though.

He led her around the veranda and into the front vestibule. "Don't be chicken," he whispered. Maybe teasing her would brace her a little.

"I beg your pardon?" She halted, looking up at him with a sharp, startled expression.

Maybe teasing wasn't the right road to take, either. "I just meant—don't be scared."

She squared her jaw, looking at him frankly. "I've never been afraid of any man in my life." Then she squeezed his elbow, propelling him into the parlor. Sure enough, Pearl and Frank Lowe, the judge, stood waiting before the fireplace mantel.

"So you were able to talk some sense into her." Pearl laughed. "You have succeeded where I failed, Jack. Of course, a handsome fellow like you is more persuasive than an old farm woman like me."

"I am an entirely sensible creature," Miss Westmore said, breaking away from him. "We've come to an agreement that is acceptable to all parties. There's no need to be so ridiculous, Aunt Pearl."

Frank shot Jack an amused look that said, plainer than spoken words, *Are you sure you want to get hitched to that?*

For his part, a grudging respect surged through Jack as he stood beside her, waiting for the ceremony to begin. She was small of stature but stout of heart. It would be hard to picture anyone coercing her into doing anything she didn't want to do. His first wife had simply gone along with whatever the St. Clair family wanted. Even miles away, they had controlled every movement of the Burnetts. Which, incidentally, his father-in-law still was capable of doing. After all, here he was, marrying a woman he barely knew just to please the man.

The ceremony was over as soon as it started. Miss Westmore gave him a startled glance as he slipped a ring on her finger. He kissed her briefly on the cheek, and they were married. It was as simple as that.

Pearl came forward to embrace them both, and Frank shook Jack's hand as he passed through the parlor and out the front door.

"I suppose you want some supper." Pearl smiled at her niece. "You must be starving."

"Actually, I prefer to go home," Miss Westmore replied, her voice sounding tired. But she wasn't Miss Westmore any longer. Now she was Mrs. Burnett. That would take some getting used to.

Pearl looked as though she'd been slapped but gave a strained smile.

"Sure." Jack stepped in between the two women. "I know you're probably worn-out."

Miss Westmore nodded. No, she was no longer Miss Westmore. She was Mrs. Burnett now, but that seemed too strange to accept just yet. He'd just call her Ada. That seemed less formal. "Is my trunk still in your carriage?"

"It is. I just need to go hitch up the horses and bring them around front." He hesitated, glancing from one woman to the other. The air had become distinctly frosty despite the balmy early-spring weather.

"I'd prefer to go with you to do that," Ada replied. "Goodbye, Aunt Pearl." She gave her aunt a curt nod and then flounced out of the room.

"She's mad at me," Pearl fretted, turning to Jack. "Hopefully she'll come around. I do think this is for the best. I wouldn't have suggested it, otherwise. You know me—I am always looking for the sensible solution."

Jack nodded. It was better not to get involved in a family argument. He'd learned that one the hard way. "We'll be seeing you, Pearl. Give her a few days to get used to things. I'll bring her by once she's settled in."

Tears filled Pearl's eyes, but she said nothing. She merely nodded and patted his shoulder. A prickle of unease worked its way down Jack's spine. This didn't feel right—the rushed wedding to a stranger, the tense surroundings. Even Pearl's tears were unusual and made a fellow feel off balance. He hadn't seen her cry since the day her husband, R. H. Colgan, had died. She was as tough and salt of the earth as they came. That she was crying now over her niece's situation was downright odd.

The sooner they were home, the better.

He left the parlor and joined Ada on the porch. "Have you ever hitched up a carriage before?"

She shook her head. "I had my own curricle at home, but the groom always readied it for me."

"Well, if you're going to be as equal as me out here,

you might as well start with hitching up your own horses," he replied. He wasn't trying to be fresh with her, but, on the other hand, it really was time for her to learn how to handle a few things herself.

He showed her how to hitch the horses to the harness, and she stroked their necks with a gentle hand. "Such beautiful bays. I've missed being around horses. Mine were sold before I left New York."

He glanced over at her in startled surprise. "You know about horses?"

"Of course." She heaved herself up into the wagon, disdaining his outstretched hand. "I've ridden every single day since I was six years old. I've been on several fox hunts, of course, and even tried my hand at a steeplechase once." She leaned forward, her eyes glowing at the memory. "Father never knew about that. He would have been appalled."

Fox hunting was a St. Clair pastime, a ridiculous waste of horseflesh and energy. He pulled himself up beside her and flicked the reins. The bays moved forward as he pointed them toward home. He could tell her, on no uncertain terms, just what he thought of the kind of people who went fox hunting in Virginia. That, of course, would mean starting a fight. He'd like to at least get her home before they had another row.

He lapsed into silence as they rolled over the hilly road that stretched between his property and Pearl Colgan's. If Ada could ride well enough to keep her seat during a steeplechase, then she might be of help around the ranch. He'd never really had help unless it was his hired hands. Emily had been afraid of horses—the only St. Clair to be terrified of the animal.

So it took everything he had to try to get her to drive a gig alone. After all, he couldn't be at her beck and call to drive her to every social function in the county.

Ada was quiet, too, but not in an uncomfortable way. He looked over at her once more. Dust still covered her traveling dress and dark circles ringed her eyes.

"Only one more turn and we're there," he said in a hearty tone of voice. "Hope you'll like it."

"I am sure I will," she replied, so promptly that it was obvious this was her training as a well-bred young woman talking and not any special enthusiasm.

He guided the horses around the bend in the road, but they were so used to taking this route that he hardly needed to twitch the reins at all. They passed through the front gate and wound their way up the drive to the house.

They traced the semicircle around the front and drew to a halt before the front porch. He paused a moment, savoring the feeling of the wind. His ranch had the advantage of being on a bit of a hill, the only raised part of earth for miles around on the prairie. This location gave a great view of the patchwork fields down below, some green and others brown, depending on what was growing and what had been harvested.

He jumped down from the seat and walked around to her side of the carriage. He extended his hand to help her down. "Well, what do you think?"

Ada took his hand, gathering her skirts as best she could in her other hand, and then leaped down from the carriage. As soon as she gained purchase, she dropped his hand quickly. She might be his wife in theory, but too much physical contact was unsavory, given the reality of their situation. She glanced up at the house, shading her eyes from the sun.

"It's very pretty," she said mechanically. Although, to be honest, *pretty* was an inadequate word. How best to describe this house? She was used to imposing, majestic brick facades, usually with tendrils of ivy clinging to the walls. Jack's house was very large, too, but airier. It was a two-story structure, painted white, with bottle-green shutters framing each window. A large, curving veranda wrapped around the front of the house, supported by tall columns. Wooden lacework, also painted that same snowy shade, peeked around the columns and was tucked underneath the eaves of the roof. The comparative elegance of the house contrasted sharply with the rough-and-ready Texas terrain. "I don't understand why your father-in-law finds it inadequate for your daughter."

"The St. Clairs are snobs," he replied tersely. "I'll bring your trunk in. You'll be staying in the spare bedroom."

"Thank you." She meant it, too. What a relief to finally be in her own room after what seemed an eternity of travel.

He nodded and retrieved her trunk and her valise from the bed of the carriage, and she hastened to open the front door for him. He brushed past her, carrying her trunk as easily as if it were no heavier than a small sack of cotton. As she followed, she clutched the banister for support. A heavy layer of dust stained her gloves.

The stairs creaked as they ascended. At the top of the stairs, Jack made a right turn and opened a door off the hallway. "It's a little unkempt," he admitted, tossing her trunk at the foot of an iron bedpost. "But it's got a nice view of the fields."

Ada glanced around, taking off her gloves. She schooled her features into blank politeness, but inwardly she was shocked. How on earth did a room get so dirty? Cobwebs hung in the corners of the ceiling, and dust had settled over all of the surfaces. The window was gray, lending a kind of grubby filter to the view of the fields outside.

"Do you have a maid?" She kept her voice as even as she could under the circumstances.

"Yes, two of them," he responded. If the soiled state of the house appalled him, he was good at hiding his dismay.

"Do they have other duties besides taking care of the house? Do you share their services with anyone else?" That would be the only way such slipshod cleaning could possibly happen.

"No, they're both employed to take care of the house and make meals," he replied. "Speaking of which, I think you must be pretty tired and hungry by now. I can find Mrs. H. and have her make us something."

"Aren't meals served at regular times?" At this point, it was no longer possible to avoid arching her eyebrows. Two servants, a filthy house, meals served haphazardly—this place was in need of serious management.

"Naw, just whenever I am starving enough to ask them to rustle up some grub," he replied, flashing a bewildered grin. "After all, it's just me here. No need for them to go to any kind of trouble for a widower."

Why employ anyone, then? What exactly did two maids do all day? They obviously didn't keep themselves busy by cleaning the house. Should she throttle him for expecting so little out of life or feel sorry for him for his lonely bachelor existence? Ada forced a smile. "Well, that's going to change. No wonder your father-in-law doesn't want Laura to stay here. This place is ridiculously filthy."

The grin faded from his face. "When my wife was alive, the house was spotless, and the only time he came here was when Emily was still living. So you can't hang this one on my poor housekeeping skills."

Ada tossed her gloves onto the dresser, raising a small cloud of dust. "You married me for one purpose—to be a wife, which means running your household. I need a home, too, and I want it to be nice. So, if you have no objection, I shall get started without delay."

His square jaw tightened. "Be my guest," he replied curtly. "I need to see to the horses." He brushed past her and closed the door with a snap.

Ada sat on the bed, removing her hat pins with hands that trembled. Her life had taken such an odd turn the moment she'd stepped onto the train platform that morning. She opened her valise, removing her silver-backed hairbrush-and-mirror set. She unwound her hair and began brushing it with long, smooth strokes to remove the travel dust.

If Jack had known they were going to be married when he came to fetch her that morning, then this house was in the kind of condition he expected her to appreciate when he brought her home as his bride. That was absurd, for no woman would delight in a wretchedly ill-kept house. On the other hand, he seemed genuinely startled and then offended when she pointed out that regular meals and a clean environment must be maintained in a home when raising a child.

She wound her hair back up in its coil, pinning it into place, and changed from her traveling dress into a clean housedress. She removed her boots, which had started pinching her toes, and reveled in the feel of her slippers, so soft and accommodating for tired, achy feet.

Well, there was nothing for it. She would have to seek out the maids and put them to work. Otherwise, she would find her newfound life too tinted with squalor. She made her way downstairs, avoiding the banister, and crossed the front vestibule.

The entryway was covered in dust, as was the parlor and the dining room. There was no sign of anyone else in the house. Her slippers didn't make any sound as she drifted from room to room. It was almost as though she had imagined this whole scenario and would soon find herself in New York again.

The house was larger than it had looked from the outside, with high ceilings and arched hallways. The furniture was—all of it—mahogany. Painted glass ceiling fixtures, with prisms dangling, were covered in filth. This could be a very fine home. Why, it was prettier than Aunt Pearl's—at least what she'd glimpsed of Aunt Pearl's house. If only it were cleaned up and made to look as gracious as it truly was.

She passed through the dining room and onto the back veranda. A small outbuilding caught her eye, as it had a very large chimney. Perhaps the kitchen was separate from the house. That would make sense.

After all, in this heat, having a kitchen inside would make the living areas almost unbearable.

She ventured across the yard, holding her skirts above the grass. An older woman and a young woman stepped out of the building, eyeing her warily as she approached.

As soon as she came close enough to speak without shouting, she said, "Hello."

The two women mumbled their greetings. The older woman had keen brown eyes and gray hair scraped back into a serviceable bun. The younger woman had two long braids of blond hair, one over each shoulder, but the same brown eyes as her older counterpart. Mother and daughter, perhaps?

"I am Miss W— I beg your pardon, I meant to say Mrs. Burnett." She gave them each a polite smile in turn. "I believe you work for Mr. Burnett?"

"Yes." The older woman crossed her arms over her chest. "We do."

"Is it just you two?" Although Jack had assured her he only employed two maids, she had no inkling of just how to open the conversation. How should one approach upbraiding the women for the deplorable condition of the house? An idea began to form in the back of her mind. "That's not very many servants for such a large house. Are you, perhaps, overworked?"

The older woman eyed her with skepticism. "No, ma'am. We can handle anything."

The younger woman nodded, keeping her gaze turned toward the ground.

"Well, I have half a mind to tell my new husband off." She shook her head with mock indignation. "Men! The idea that two women would be adequate staff for cleaning such a large house, not to mention providing meals in a timely manner, is preposterous." She gave them both encouraging smiles. "Thank you for all you have done. I suppose I should begin hiring more staff tomorrow. Do you know of anyone who would be willing to help?"

The younger woman spoke up. "Yes, ma'am. One of my friends, Cathy Chalmers, was let go from the Hudson place when they packed up and moved back east. She's a good maid and a deft hand with laundry."

"Excellent. Can you get word to her? I'd like for Cathy to start this week."

The younger woman nodded. She wasn't smiling, but she did seem somewhat less abashed.

Ada pressed on. "Both of you have me at a bit of a disadvantage. Would you please tell me your names, and how long you've been in service to the Burnett family?"

"I'm Loretta Holcomb, but you can call me Mrs. H. or Betty. My daughter here is Maggie. We've been working for the Burnetts since the first Mrs. Burnett passed. All her servants went back to Charleston."

"I see." So both women had come on board when Jack's life had been utter chaos and confusion—dealing with his wife's death, losing his child, having to placate his father-in-law. No small wonder, then, that they had been allowed to do such a poor job. Perhaps they even thought they were doing credible work. After all, Jack was a widower and spent most of his time, in all likelihood, outdoors.

That was going to change.

"It's very nice to meet you both. I am not from Texas, so I am sure I shall rely on you to help me as I learn what life is like out here." Now that she had in-troduced herself and found out more about the women, it was time to get to work. "Mrs. H., are you the cook, primarily?"

"Yes." Her posture relaxed somewhat, though her arms remained crossed over her chest.

"Very good. Well, I need you to make a good din-ner for us tonight, to be served in the dining room." She turned to Maggie. "And I will require your help on cleaning the dining room. Bachelor living, you know." It was as close as she could reasonably come to pointing out the disastrous condition of the house. She needed these women to stay, and she needed the assistance of even more servants. She would accom-plish nothing by using heavy-handed tactics.

"Mr. Burnett usually takes a plate and goes to the barn," Mrs. H. replied, looking distinctly mulish.

"How appalling." The words slipped out before she could check herself. She must not offend the two women who could help her in this bizarre arrange-ment. "Dining in that fashion certainly does your cooking no credit, Mrs. H. We shall rectify that. What are we having for supper?"

The older woman hesitated a moment. "I was just going to make him a sandwich." She shifted uncom-fortably. "Seeing as how you're here, though—"

"Actually, a sandwich platter sounds delightful. Nice and cool on such a hot day. Do we have any vegetables to go with?"

Mrs. H. nodded slowly. "Yes. Early cucumbers and green tomatoes. I picked some in the garden this morning."

"Perfect." Ada gave her an encouraging smile.

"Let's go with that for tonight. Perhaps tomorrow we can begin making up a menu for the week. Come, Maggie, let's see what we can do with the dining room."

Ada strode back toward the house, with Maggie trotting along behind her.

No one could say she wasn't holding up her end of the bargain. Jack Burnett was going to eat dinner at a proper table instead of in a barn.

Jack sat in his chair in the dining room. It was hard not to feel rusty and stiff, at least when surrounded by such grandeur. Mrs. H. came bustling in, bearing a large china tray of small sandwiches, cut into triangles. Behind her, Maggie trailed along, carrying a large bowl of some kind.

Ada thanked both women, who bowed awkwardly.

"We'll come check on you in a few minutes," Mrs. H. remarked.

"Just a moment. Mrs. H., have you had your supper yet? Has Maggie?" Ada looked over at both women, her eyebrows drawing together.

"No, ma'am. We were getting yours ready." Mrs. H. sounded a little self-righteous about that. Jack stifled a grin. How would Ada handle that kind of tone?

"Do go ahead and eat. I'll ring the bell when the dishes are ready to be cleared." Ada waved to indicate a small silver bell sitting on a nearby table. As she moved, Jack caught a glimpse of a bandage wound tightly around her hand. "There's no need for you two to have to wait on your meal just because of us."

"Thank you, Mrs. Burnett." Mrs. H. curtsied awkwardly and then prodded Maggie's shoulder, forcing her to follow suit. They left the dining room, closing the door behind them.

He was impressed. Ada didn't allow herself to be needled into an argument, and she showed concern for others. Both of those were good qualities in a woman.

Ada picked up the bowl. "Would you care for cucumber and tomato salad?"

"Sure." He brushed against her as he reached for the bowl, and a shock went through his arm at the unexpected contact. He drew back sharply. It was not acceptable to have any kind of attraction to Miss Westmore—nope, she was Mrs. Burnett now—for she was here for one purpose only. If she felt the same way, she kept her composure, merely leaning forward to help him. He caught a glimpse of her bandaged hand again as she spooned the salad onto his plate. "What happened there?"

She snatched her hand back, the color rising in her cheeks. "I had a bit of a run-in with a glass candy dish."

He expected her, if injured, to cry and carry on or, at the very least, grow faint. Instead, she seemed downright embarrassed by the situation. "You going to be all right?"

"Of course, Mr. Burnett." She gave him a crisp smile. "Sandwiches?"

"You can call me Jack," he reminded her as he piled several sandwiches on his plate. "I've already been calling you Ada. At least, in my mind I have."

"Oh, yes." The flush in her cheeks deepened. "I am so sorry. I am tired, and I keep making foolish mistakes."

"That's understandable." He took a bite of the sandwich. "This is pretty nice, I've got to say."

Ada cleared her throat. "Jack, we haven't said grace yet."

He stopped chewing for a moment. "Grace?"

"Yes. Of course. Will you do the honors? I'd rather not." He tried to speak casually, like tossing a horseshoe. But, as with a horseshoe, his words landed with a thunk.

Ada shrugged. "Very well. Then I shall do so." She nodded at him.

"For what we are about to receive, may the Lord make us truly thankful," Ada intoned. "Amen."

He muttered his "amen," even though he was every inch the hypocrite to do so. Men who didn't believe in God shouldn't pray as though they did.

Ada helped herself to sandwiches and then began eating. He ate, too, gazing around the room in wonder. It looked different. Brighter, somehow. It smelled like lemons, too.

"Looks good in here," he said. "I guess you've been putting those gals to work."

Ada tilted her head to one side, as though thinking things over. "I don't know. I don't think they're lazy. I think they just have no direction. Plus, if you've been eating in a barn, they don't have much motivation to make the house look pretty."

The chicken sandwiches were tasty, and so was this cucumber-tomato concoction. It was a good thing, too, because it put him in a better mood. He could go toe-to-toe with Ada Burnett if he was well fed and in a nice kind of environment. "Look, a cowboy has to take care of his horses. I learned this way of life when

I was a kid. It's a hard habit to break. Besides which, it would be silly to sit in here and eat alone." It was lonely, too. He'd tried it once and felt miserable for days afterward.

Ada ate a bite of the cucumber salad. "I suppose I could understand that."

He nodded, satisfied. It was pleasant here, with the breeze blowing in through the open windows. Ada looked nice, too. She had changed at some point and was wearing a dress that was less stiff and severe. Her hair had been redone, too. She was very pretty, sitting there, and her presence and the cleanliness of the house made him feel better. Not that it mattered what she looked like, since she was here to serve one purpose: bringing Laura home.

Still and all, it was mighty enjoyable to be dining in the company of a good-looking girl again, and in such a fresh, sparkling room. The food was better than Mrs. H.'s usual fare, too.

Maybe this plan would work out, after all.

Ada passed him the sandwich platter once more, and he caught a glimpse of an ugly red mark across her wrist. "What happened there?"

"Oh, that." She gave an embarrassed laugh. "I tried to help lift a pot of boiling water and ended up scalding myself a little."

He shook his head and rose. A little aloe-vera juice would keep that burn from turning worse. He went out onto the front veranda and cut off a spike of the ugly little plant. Then he brought it back inside and knelt beside Ada's chair. She looked down at him in startled wonder, her blue eyes growing wide.

"Let's see it." He took her wrist in his hand and

pushed back her sleeve. Her skin was as pale as moon-light, with the scald mark glaring angrily across the smooth surface. When was the last time he'd been this close to a lady? Her skin was so soft under his callused fingers.

He was acting like a fool. He forced himself back to the problem at hand.

The burn was bad but not the worst he'd laid eyes on. He squeezed some of the juice from the plant onto the wound.

"What on earth is that?" Ada demanded. "It looks like nothing I've ever seen."

"It's aloe vera. It's a desert plant. It grows wild out in west Texas," he replied, gently rubbing the juice onto the wound. She flinched and held her breath. He took care to be gentle, given that her skin was raw and her wrist delicate. "I took a cutting years ago, when I was bringing some cattle through Odessa. Folks out West use it to help heal burns." He paused, survey-ing his work while trying to maintain calm. Ada was now a permanent member of the household, and he needed to get used to being around her without think-ing of her as a woman—if that made any sense. "Does that feel better?"

"Yes, surprisingly." Ada stared at her wound. "It doesn't sting nearly as much."

"Good." He released her hand and tossed the aloe onto the table. She looked at it pointedly, but he re-fused to pick it up. He would eat at a table and even eat vegetables, but he would not tidy up in the midst of a meal.

Was now a good time to bring up the trip they'd have to make? Probably not, but then, there might not ever be a perfect time. He took a bite of his chicken sandwich to fortify him for the task ahead.

"So," he began in what he hoped was a conversational tone, "are you up for a honeymoon?"

Chapter Three

Ada stood on the train platform, waiting for her husband's private train cars to be hitched to the train itself. Just a few short days ago, she had occupied this same spot, waiting for Aunt Pearl and an unknown future. Now she was waiting to go to St. Louis, to collect the stepdaughter she'd never met. An unlikely honeymoon, but one completely in keeping with their arrangement.

She glanced down at the pocket watch on her lavender lace lapel. She had changed to half-mourning after her first day in the Burnett home and not just because her sudden matrimony should, at least to outsiders, seem like a cause for celebration. No, it was merely that her frocks in shades of purple and gray were made of lighter fabrics for summer wear and thus more practical for life out on the prairie.

"Well, don't you look pretty as a picture," a female voice crowed behind her.

Ada jumped and whirled around. "Aunt Pearl," she gasped. She was not really ready to see her aunt yet. A large part of her was still angry at being traded as casually as a mule, even though she admitted it was a practical solution to her problems.

Some of her hesitation must have shown on her face, for Aunt Pearl held up her gloved hands in protest. "Now, now, I'm not here for a lecture, Ada. I just wanted to say goodbye and God be with you. Lord knows that poor child has been through enough already. It will be such a wonderful thing for her to be home with her daddy."

Sudden nervousness flooded Ada's being. She wasn't ready for this. She was not prepared to be this great a part of a stranger's life. What if she couldn't measure up? She glanced down at her burned wrist and bandaged hand, recalling accident after accident she'd had in the past few days. Sugar in the saltshaker. Baking soda in the bread instead of baking powder. So much starch in Jack's shirts that they stood up by themselves. One broken item after another. True, there were two maids to do the work, but she insisted on helping. The only problem was, her attempts to assist met with constant catastrophes. If she was this big a failure at being a wife, how much more of one could she possibly be as a mother?

"Aunt Pearl, I can't do this," she cried. It was a relief to voice her fears aloud. "I know it's part of the bargain that I make sure the house is clean and presentable, but it isn't ready for a child. I've been working with his maids, but they are used to slacking because Jack won't raise a fuss. It's been his bachelor headquarters for years. I don't know how to take on this role. I'm not ready to be anyone's mother." She held up her hand. "I can't even take care of myself." She was angry at

Pearl, to be sure, but Pearl was family. She could show a little weakness to her own flesh and blood.

"Don't take on so, child. You've done more in a few days than most women could do in a year. Besides, remember what I told you. It's time for you to grow in faith. This is a good chance to see the hand of God in your life." Her aunt gave her a hearty slap on the back. "Now, I heard you hired Cathy. Do you need more servants than that? Has Cathy started yet?"

"Yes, and yes." Ada gazed at her aunt in wonder. "How did you know I had hired anyone?"

Pearl laughed, and the ruby earrings she wore bobbed against her cheeks. "Ada, you need to know something about life in Winchester Falls. It's not like living in New York, where all you need to worry about is Mrs. Astor's Four Hundred. Here, you have four hundred people in all, including every single family and every single servant. Word gets around. We've got no one else to gossip about."

Ada was no stranger to tittle-tattle. The Four Hundred her aunt spoke of so lightly had begun cutting her out as soon as her father's scandal had broken. After enduring the petty slights of her former friends for weeks, a complete change had seemed in order. That was, after all, how she'd decided that making a clean break and starting life anew in Texas was the only sensible course of action open to her.

Yet here she was, failing already.

"Listen, Aunt Pearl," she added hastily, "I need your assistance. The house is improving, but I'm afraid, now that I'm leaving, it will fall right back into chaos. I can't bring Laura home to a dusty, musty house. Would you help me to make sure the servants are doing the work? I can send telegrams at every stop."

"Why sure," Aunt Pearl replied. She gave Ada a searching look. "Are you so desperate for help that you would ask anyone right now? Or am I forgiven?"

Ada stiffened. Blood had to be thicker than all the problems in the world. "I don't know what to say, Aunt Pearl. I mean, I'm angry still that I was pressured into marrying Jack Burnett, but I don't hate you. I could never hate you."

"That's good enough for me." The older woman wrapped Ada in a tight hug.

"Hey, Pearl," Jack called, making his way up the station platform. "Did you come to see us off?"

"I sure did." Pearl broke free from Ada and gave Jack the same tight embrace she had given Ada. They really must think of each other as family. How very odd. "Take care of my gal, there, Jack. And bring Laura home to me safely. I don't think I've seen her since she was knee-high to a june bug."

Ada stood slightly apart from them, watching her aunt. Funny, Aunt Pearl had been raised in the same family as Father. She went to an elite boarding school and women's college. She had made her debut at the age of sixteen. But when she married R. H. Colgan, it was as though all those years of polish and breeding fell away. Here she was, using outlandish phrases and hugging them all like children. Father never embraced his daughters and certainly never used hyperbole or exaggeration.

Was Texas responsible for Aunt Pearl's roughened character?

Would Ada be the same way in twenty years?

What an appalling thought.

Jack offered Ada his arm and, with a final wave to Aunt Pearl, Ada followed him down the platform and to their waiting car. Then he helped her make her way up the steps. The pressure of his arm was both familiar and strangely exhilarating. She must be more nervous than she thought. She certainly wasn't developing any kind of silly, girlish feelings for Jack Burnett, for that would never do. She was a strong and sensible suffragist.

As she entered the car, Ada looked around in awe. Not that she hadn't seen grand living spaces before, but a private train car so luxuriously appointed rather took her breath away. The ceiling was padded with sky-blue satin, and heavy velvet draperies shut out the blazing morning sun. Brass and crystal lamps glowed invitingly on graceful mahogany tables.

She sank onto a leather armchair and placed her feet up on a deep blue hassock. "This is lovely. I had no idea you owned such a fine thing. When you said private cars, I thought for sure you meant something in which you hauled cattle at one time or another." Teasing Jack seemed to be the only way to get along with him. In the brief time she had known him, she realized one thing about Jack Burnett. If things got too serious, he would simply leave for hours at a time.

He took off his hat and cast it into a nearby chair. "Nope. When I was first married, I commissioned this. We've got a separate sleeper car, too, with bedrooms for each member of the family. I wanted for us all to travel in comfort. We didn't use it much, though." He frowned deeply, as he usually did when speaking about his first wife.

She didn't know what to say. When he went silent like that, he would usually stalk off. There was no way he could do that on board a train. So they had to find a way to be polite in each other's company for the duration of the journey. How long would she have to strain at being civil?

"When will we reach St. Louis?" she asked, stripping off her gloves and laying them beside her on the table. She had been living with him now for days, but she had her own room and he rarely stayed for long in the house. The close proximity forced upon them by the car made even small gestures like removing her gloves seem somehow more intimate. Perhaps the sudden rush of heat to her cheeks could be blamed on Texas weather.

"In about a day and a half." His handsome face had settled into a brooding expression. "But we won't see Laura right away."

"Why not? Won't her school allow it?" Ada withdrew her hat pins. If she stayed busy and kept peppering Jack with questions, perhaps her ridiculous blushing would pass by unnoticed. It was absolutely appalling for a young, serious suffragist to be simpering like a debutante at her first ball. She was stronger than that…wasn't she? She laid her heavy hat to one side.

"The school will." Jack rubbed his thumb meditatively over his lower lip. "But my father-in-law might not."

Jack strode around the perimeter of the Grand Hall of Union Station, jostled along by hundreds of fellow travelers. The sunlight streaming in from the stained glass windows cast a kaleidoscope of colors onto the faces of the passersby. His mouth was dry and his brain feverish. If only Ada would hurry up. But she had insisted on taking time to change and arrange her hair in one of the station dressing rooms.

"Well, why can't you dress here?" he had demanded, waving his arm at the ridiculously luxurious private car.

"I want to look my best, and there is no full-length mirror here," she had stated flatly. "I need to see the overall effect of my costume. After all, we have one opportunity to impress your father-in-law."

So here he was, pacing the crowded station, as Ada primped and preened. He should be happy that she was working so hard to be presentable to his father-in-law. As it was, his anger at having to dine with the old man and meet with his approval yet again was galling.

He took out the souvenir he had purchased for Laura from one of the peddlers in the station. It was a little doll, dressed in silk and lace. A banner wrapped diagonally across her middle read "St. Louis."

A ten-year-old would still play with dolls, wouldn't she? He stuffed it back in his pocket.

The clock tower, a massive structure that rose majestically to the ceiling, tolled the hour. Out of habit, he checked his pocket watch to make sure it was keeping accurate time. It was. Both clocks showed that unless Ada hurried up, they would be late to meet Edmund St. Clair.

He circled back around to the ladies' waiting area and dressing rooms, and as he grew closer, Ada stepped out. She was swaying against the press of humanity swirling around her, but in the midst of utter pandemonium, she was an oasis of calm. He caught his breath a little, looking at her. She was stunning, as pretty as the society debutante she had been raised to be. She had changed into a violet dress trimmed with black ribbons, the dark colors setting off her pale complexion and vivid blue eyes. A wide black hat trimmed with purple feathers was settled atop the waves of her black hair.

He'd grown so used to seeing her in simple housedresses that he didn't realize how lovely she could be.

He'd have to guard his heart carefully with this one. He had been turned by a beautiful face before, and it had ended in disaster. There was no sense in repeating the process.

"Jack," she called, raising her voice over the din.

He held up his hand in greeting and made his way over to her side.

"I declare, I'm not used to crowds any longer," she gasped with a little laugh. "Though I've only been in Winchester Falls a short time, it seems to have rubbed off on me already. This seems quite daunting."

"It'll be fine. We only have a little ways to go. St. Clair is meeting us at the train-station restaurant." He tucked her arm into his elbow and ventured out into the milling throngs of travelers. Somehow, he felt calmer now that Ada was with him. So many times he had argued with his in-laws alone. Now he had someone on his side. True, she was somewhat forced to be on his side, but it was comforting, anyway.

He steered them over to the restaurant. St. Clair stood at the entrance, leaning on an ebony walking stick. The old man was as immaculate as always in his Savile Row suit, with a carnation in his buttonhole and his gray hair brushed sleekly back from his head. The old man took in Ada, surveying her from the crown of her hat to the tips of her boots peeking out from beneath her skirt.

"My dear," he enthused, his thick Southern accent making it sound as though he said *mah deah*. He came closer and held his hand out to Ada. "You must be Miss Westmore."

"Mrs. Burnett," she corrected him, giving him a graceful smile. "Mr. St. Clair, I believe?"

"You believe correctly," he replied, kissing the back of her gloved hand. Then he turned his gaze to Jack. "Burnett," he barked.

"Sir," Jack replied. There was no shaking of hands, and no politeness in their meeting. There had been too much ugliness between them over the years.

St. Clair turned his attention back to Ada. "Come, my dear. I've reserved a table for our party." He offered her his elbow.

With a puzzled glance at Jack, Ada broke free of his hold and took St. Clair's elbow. Jack followed behind them into the restaurant, already beginning to seethe. The old man knew exactly what it took to enrage him, and already he was making progress.

St. Clair held Ada's chair for her. Once she was settled, the two men sat. The glasses on the table were filled with water and lemonade, and no menus awaited their perusal.

"I hope it's all right, Mrs. Burnett, but I presumed to order our meal," the old man drawled. He cast a malicious glance in Jack's direction. "If I let your husband order, he might make us eat a bowl of chili con carne with cornbread muffins." He chuckled in appreciation of his dig at Jack.

Jack would not be riled. Too much was at stake. "Yup," he responded, keeping his tone light. "There's nothing like a good bowl of chili and corn bread."

Ada was smiling, but it was a smile he had come to know as being one of tremendous strain and not of genuine good feeling. She took a sip of her lemonade. "I'm sure that any meal will be quite fine, Mr. St. Clair. In fact, I relish this opportunity to know you better. I understand that your daughter was married to Mr. Burnett."

"Yes, my only daughter, Emily. She was a rare creature, Mrs. Burnett, as blond as you are brunette. I have no idea what such a gentle, sweet child saw in Jack Burnett, I can tell you that." St. Clair flicked an appraising glance at Jack. "He came out to our home in Charleston to buy a few of my horses, and they fell in love, I suppose. They eloped and he carried her back to Texas. Emily died only a few years later."

"I am sorry to hear it." Ada looked at a loss for words. She glanced at Jack, as though appealing to him to help carry the conversational load.

Although he'd like to rebut the older man's story—and many detestable remarks hung on Jack's tongue—he wouldn't do it. Instead, he fisted his hands on his lap and gritted his teeth to keep his thoughts from spilling forth. Anything he said would make St. Clair angrier and more stubborn. Ada had a job to do. It was up to her charm and wit to bring Laura home. He had tried too many times in the past and failed.

St. Clair nodded as the waitress approached their table, bearing a tray of toast rounds and caviar. Jack despised caviar. He had never understood why such a disgusting thing was considered a delicacy. But if he refused, St. Clair would start ribbing him about being a backward cowboy, and he could only take so much of that before he snapped. So he helped himself to two, ready to choke them down.

"So, Mrs. Burnett, you are of the Westmore family in New York. I knew of your father, Augustus. I never met him personally, but one hears of such a powerful man, you know." St. Clair took a careful bite of his caviar. "Tell me, did the scandal surrounding his memory have a basis in truth? The word is, he was trying to fix a local election."

Ada grew pale and pushed her toast round away. "I never had a chance to ask him, Mr. St. Clair. He died before I could learn what really happened. Of course, I don't believe it has basis in fact."

"Pardon my asking, my dear." St. Clair leaned across the table, his gray hair glinting in the sunlight. "It's just that I have to make certain that Laura is going to a good home. I want her to be raised in a proper manner, in genteel surroundings. Now, as you have seen yourself, Winchester Falls is a rather rough-and-ready town."

Ada inclined her head a trifle. "Yes, it is." She fixed St. Clair with an understanding look. "On the other hand, I must say that Jack's deep love for his daughter is abundantly clear to me. I think that having a loving parent—two loving parents, that is—accounts for as much or even more than a polished atmosphere."

Jack glanced over at Ada. No one except Pearl Colgan had defended him to the St. Clair family. She gave him a warm smile, her blue eyes twinkling.

All talk lapsed as the waitress took away the caviar and replaced it with bowls of clear chicken broth. This was better than the previous course but, still, hardly filling.

St. Clair sipped at his soup. "You are active in the suffragette movement, are you not?" He spoke so abruptly that Ada choked on her broth. The old man waited until she had taken a sip of water and then pressed on. "I'm not certain that I want Laura exposed to progressive ideals."

Ada, red faced from swallowing wrong or from the line of questioning—or possibly both—turned to Jack, the light of appeal in her blue eyes.

He gave in to pity. She was doing the best she could, and he needed to step up, too. He turned to the old man. "Laura's my daughter, St. Clair," he responded. "If I don't mind Ada as her mother, then neither should you."

These were fighting words, and he knew it. On the other hand, he wasn't going to permit St. Clair attacking Ada. She was trying to help. Because of her, he might get Laura back. If the old man wanted to mock him for being a rube, he could have at it. These insults were nothing new. Insulting Ada was an entirely different matter.

St. Clair glared at him. "You know full well that my daughter's will gave me authority over certain aspects of Laura's life. She didn't trust you to do much of anything with Laura in the event of her death."

Jack fixed his father-in-law with a defiant stare, all the rage he had initially felt over Emily's will rushing back, filling him with anger so potent that he clenched his fists.

The waitress chose that opportune moment to clear the soup bowls away and brought the main course.

"Chicken à la King," Ada murmured appreciatively. "I haven't had this since leaving New York. It's one of my favorites. Our cook had just learned the recipe."

Jack shifted his attention to her. How could she even have an appetite now? Was the woman made of stone? Yet, as he glowered at her, her hands trembled when she took up her fork. Her face was now drained of all color.

Her enthusiasm was a ruse to break the tension. She took an unsteady bite of her dinner, and as she chewed, her jaw squared. She was girding herself, in the same way he had done, for battle. Ada was nobody's fool. By this time she had surely learned his father-in-law's manner. First, flattery. Later, he would go for the kill.

"I understand your hesitation, Mr. St. Clair," she continued, as though the fracas between the two men had never happened. "After all, you are Laura's grandfather. She is your treasure, too. I assure you that my intention is to help bring her up as a young woman should be raised."

St. Clair nodded, looking at Ada, and his keen brown eyes narrowed. "I worry that if I release her to your care, I'll never see her again. St. Louis is neutral territory. If she goes with you to Winchester Falls, then I would probably have to journey to that rustic community just to see her."

Ada shot Jack a pleading glance. "I'm sure my husband would have no objection if Laura came to visit."

"I want her to come to Evermore, our family home, for two weeks every year. The rest of her family—cousins, aunts, uncles—wish to see her as much as I do." St. Clair's voice took on a clipped tone. He was in full bargaining mode now.

"One week," Jack countered. He was feeling reckless. St. Clair had managed to rile him up enough that he was beginning to enjoy the thought of needling the old man.

"It will take at least a few days for her to journey there and back," Ada spoke up. "Two weeks must include her traveling."

"Two weeks if Ada goes along as her chaperone," Jack snapped. Ada had no business lengthening the visit without his consent.

"Don't you want to go?" Ada asked, her eyes widening.

"I'm never setting foot on Evermore soil again." He leaned across the table, staring down his father-in-law.

"That, young man, is certainly fine with me," St. Clair retorted.

Ada gasped. "Gentlemen." It was the first time she had intervened without merely trying to change the subject.

Things must be too far gone if she was stepping in like this. A hollow feeling filled the pit of Jack's stomach. Had he allowed himself to be goaded to the point that there was no way Laura could come home?

"Perhaps it would be best if I laid out a few plans," Ada continued, giving each man a glare that easily said, clearer than words, *Behave yourselves.* "After all, each of you feels passionately about Laura's welfare. That speaks highly of both your characters. Let us, then, come to an arrangement that will benefit the child, and not one borne of a grudge."

St. Clair opened his mouth, probably to protest, but Ada quieted him with a wave of her hand.

"Your first concern was of my pedigree, Mr. St. Clair. As you have demonstrated, you know as much about my family as most people do. If my family background is repugnant to you, I beg you would say so now. It is still difficult for me to speak of my father's passing. As much as he was flawed, I loved him in my way and I miss him."

St. Clair flushed. He shook his head. "No, my dear. I have no objection to your family. Quite the contrary, in fact. The Westmores have been known in social circles for generations."

Ada turned to Jack. "Your father-in-law is worried that he will not get to see Laura if she is removed from school. No matter how you feel about the man, he is Laura's grandfather. A few visits to Charleston for her to know her mother's family is not too much for him to ask." Though her voice was sharp, her eyes held a beseeching look.

"I would like, in addition to a summer visit, to have regular reports on her progress," St. Clair continued. "If at any time I feel Laura is not receiving adequate care, I will bring her back to boarding school."

Jack's anger, which had begun to cool, hit the boiling point once again. He opened his mouth to tell the old man to jump in a river, but Ada touched his arm under the tablecloth. He glanced over at her. She gave him a barely perceptible shake of her head.

Her touch was calming. He took a deep breath, willing his fury to ebb.

"I can send weekly letters, if you wish," Ada replied. She started to withdraw her hand from his arm, but he grabbed it and held on tightly. He needed her. She was the only thing standing between him and disaster.

St. Clair looked skeptical, as though he didn't expect Ada to be entirely honest when writing. She returned his stare evenly. Jack glared at the old man, too. If he spoke just one word against his wife— He was already thinking of Ada as his wife. That was an odd sensation. Even after he had been married to Emily for a year, he didn't feel as close to her as he did to Ada.

"I suppose that will be sufficient, although I might have my man of affairs stop in now and then, when he can be spared," St. Clair retorted. "And the summer visit?"

"Laura can go if Ada accompanies her," Jack repeated shortly. It was all he could promise. He looked over at Ada, and she gave him an encouraging smile. It felt good and right to receive her support in all this. She had done so much more for him than he expected. In times past, a meeting like this would have drawn to an unsuccessful close much, much sooner.

Ada turned back to St. Clair. "Is that agreeable to you, sir?"

"I should be happy to have you as my guest," St. Clair replied with a courtly little bow.

Ada took a sip of water. Her hand, still clutched in his, trembled.

Jack squeezed her hand gently and glanced coolly over at his father-in-law. She deserved the same sort of backup that she had bestowed on him. It was going to be all right if St. Clair stopped being stubborn. Would the old man relent? Ada had promised more than Jack had ever consented to before. Was this enough? Or would the autocrat continue pulling all the strings in Jack's life?

"So?" Jack snarled.

St. Clair ignored him completely and focused his attention on Ada. "I would never give my approval without you here, my dear. I think, though, that aside from some troubling progressive tendencies, you would make a good stepmother for Laura."

Ada gave an uncertain laugh. Jack's gut wrenched. How could they continue bantering when so much was at stake?

"Does that mean we can take her home?" Ada's voice was high and tremulous.

"Yes." St. Clair beckoned the waitress over. "Now, let's have some chocolate cake, shall we? Negotiations of this magnitude are deserving of a little reward."

Ada's knees still trembled, even though she sat in a carriage and the restaurant and train station were far behind them. She could still feel Jack's touch burning through her glove despite the fact that he'd stopped holding her hand the moment dessert had been ordered. If only Jack would say something soon. His continued silence, since they had left the restaurant, was troubling. Part of her wanted to commiserate with him on their harrowing negotiations, and another part of her wondered if his silence was, in actuality, a reaction to finally getting what he wanted. The entire luncheon had been a sort of battle, and she craved the opportunity to decompress with her fellow soldier.

The driver negotiated the heavy afternoon traffic as they rolled through the streets on the way to Mrs. Erskine's Seminary. She had to stop thinking of Jack

and focus instead on her role. In just a few short minutes, she would meet Laura—her daughter. She was
Laura's stepmother now and would be charged with
her care. Make no mistake about it, St. Clair would
follow the progress of the entire family. If her guardianship failed to meet with his approval, Laura would
likely be shipped right back to St. Louis. No, despite
what he said about boarding school, he would probably insist on her coming home to Charleston.

She would have to send a few more telegrams to
Aunt Pearl, making certain the house looked absolutely spotless.

Ada glanced over at her husband, who was still
brooding out the window. Silhouetted against the curtains, he cut a very handsome figure. Even sitting, it
was obvious that he was quite tall and powerful. A
sudden burst of loneliness struck her as she looked
over at him. What was the use of being a wife—or a
paid mother, or whatever you could call her place in
his family—if she had no one to confide in? It could
be nice to talk to Jack.

Well, Jack wasn't going to say anything. It was up
to her to break the tension, just as she had when their
argument had heated up in the restaurant.

"In a few moments, you'll get to see her again," she
said with a smile. "Are you ready?"

"No," he admitted, his voice on edge. He settled back against the cushions and then straightened
abruptly. "I wish he'd hurry up."

"Traffic makes for slow going," she responded. He
was nervous. Well, that was understandable. She was,
too.

"Why'd you say you'd let Laura go there in the

summer?" It wasn't a mere question. He was demanding an answer.

"Because the situation was quickly unraveling." She was not going to get a thank-you from him, not from the sound of it. "Moreover, it really isn't too much for him to ask. Laura should know her mother's people."

"I don't like the St. Clairs," he responded. A muscle in his jaw twitched.

"You made that abundantly clear," she retorted. If only they could get back to the teasing manner to which she had grown accustomed. "I wasn't overly fond of him myself. He was rather rude about my family and about my work in the suffrage movement."

Jack turned to face her. Ada struggled to maintain her composure. When he focused his full attention on her like that, it made her feel as shaky as that first day at the train depot when she met him. "I'm sorry for his behavior," he said. "He is just that way. They all are. Emily was, too. I guess I was charmed by her at first. I soon regretted it, I can tell you."

Mixed feelings swirled within Ada. On the one hand, it would be good to learn more about Emily and how happy her relationship with Jack had been. Knowing these things might help Ada to understand Laura better. On the other hand, it was somehow distasteful to her to learn more about his first wife. How did Ada measure up to Emily? Was she sweeter and prettier? Mr. St. Clair had said she was blond. Ada caught a glimpse of a straggling dark lock of her own hair and sighed.

Here she was, falling into unhelpful comparisons. To compare herself to any other woman, in how they might be pleasing to men, was a betrayal of sorts to the sisterhood. It reduced all women to one common denominator: how they suited the men in their lives.

Besides, it didn't matter how Jack felt about her or how she looked to him. Their marriage was forged for only two purposes: to help Ada provide for her sisters and to bring Laura home to her father.

The carriage swung onto a gravel driveway. A sign flashed past that read Mrs. Erskine's Seminary for Young Ladies. They had arrived. One of the purposes for which they had wed was about to be fulfilled.

In a voice rough with emotion, Jack said, "Let's get Laura and take her home."

Chapter Four

Jack stood in the school's parlor, his hat in his hands, distinctly ill at ease. This stuffy school always put him on his guard, for it was nothing like home and everything he was used to. He was also facing it alone, as Mrs. Erskine had requested to speak to Ada privately about Laura's progress. In some ways, he was annoyed that he wasn't receiving that information. After all, he was Laura's father, but since Ada would be in charge of Laura's education, it was likely for the best. Besides, it might be nice to meet with Laura alone and explain everything to her before she met Ada.

The parlor door opened, and a maid ushered Laura into the room.

Jack drew in his breath sharply. She looked more like her mother than ever, more so than when he had seen her at Christmas. Emily had been a regular china doll, with pale skin, golden-blond curls and wide blue eyes. Like her mother, Laura possessed all these features. Also, just like her mother, she wore a fixed expression of angry disapproval. Maybe that's why she favored Emily so much at this moment. Why was his little girl upset?

"Father." She stood in the doorway until the maid ushered her in. Then the door closed behind Laura, and they were alone in the room.

"Hey there, my chickadee," he said heartily, reverting to his pet name for her. He came forward to gather her into a hug, but she put her cheek up, coolly awaiting a kiss. He paused, disconcerted. "How's my sunshine gal? Don't I get a hug?"

She drew away from him, gazing up with a grave expression on her face. "Mrs. Erskine told me you married someone."

"Yes." He didn't know what to do with his hands. He'd expected to get the chance to squeeze her and then sit down with her talking excitedly as she always did, but she didn't seem to be in a happy mood. "I went out and got my little girl a new mama. Now we can all live together as a family."

Her eyes filled with tears. "I have a mama. She's in heaven."

"Well, now." He cleared his throat. This wasn't going at all as he'd expected. "That's true. Mrs. Ada is just going to take care of you so we can all live in Winchester Falls together." A terrible pain stabbed him. "You do want to come live with me, don't you?"

"I don't know." She shook her head. "This is my home, you see, Father. I know where everything is. I know what to do. I like it here."

He stared at his daughter, unsure he even understood what she was saying. "Your home is with me. This is just your school."

"I don't want to go." She said it firmly and clearly, a mulish expression stealing over her face.

He had never seen her in such a temper before. After recent events, especially the bout with his father-in-law, he wasn't about to stand for this. "You're going." He stated the truth firmly and flatly. "Is your trunk packed?"

"Yes, but I can unpack it." She scowled at him, lowering her brows in the same way Emily used to when she was in a fighting mood.

"No, you can't. I'll make sure they go ahead and load it in the carriage." He crossed the room and grasped the bellpull, preparing to give it a good hard yank.

"I am not going with *her*." Laura stamped her foot. "She is not my mother."

"What does that matter?" Jack was incredulous. Was he really going to have a fight with Laura after all he had done to make them a family? Did she have any idea what he had been through to make this happen? So many lives had been turned upside down just to bring them together again. "If your trunk is packed, then we'll get going. I am sure Ada is done with Mrs. Erskine by now."

"I'm not leaving here." Laura folded her skinny arms across her chest and glared at him.

He looked at his daughter, still unsure if this was some sort of bad joke or a nightmare. She stood before him in her gray cotton uniform, with her long hair in a tangle of blond ringlets and her black tights bagging at the knees. Her black hair ribbon tilted crazily over one ear, giving her the look of someone who had been scuffling with an unseen enemy.

Laura had always been an easy child, his "little chickadee," his "sunshine baby." This new behavior was likely the result of life in a highfalutin boarding school and not enough time out on the prairie. The sooner he brought her home, the better. She would get over this sulk and go back to being the sweet-tempered child she had always been.

"Stop this nonsense and come on," he ordered. If he gave in to this kind of behavior, she'd end up as spoiled and entitled as Emily.

"I. Will. Not." She punctuated each word with a stamp of her foot.

Anger and helplessness boiled within Jack. He had no idea what to do. Unless he threw her over his shoulder like a bag of potatoes, kicking and screaming, there was no way to get her out of this parlor and down to the waiting carriage.

Without another word, he turned and left the room, slamming the parlor door behind him. A walk would cool him off. A walk would enable him to think. He'd been through plenty the past few days, living with a strange woman in his home and then meeting with Edmund St. Clair. A man had his limits.

As he dashed down the stairs, Ada and Mrs. Erskine stepped out of an office on the first floor. "Mr. Burnett," Mrs. Erskine effused, holding out her hand. "How nice to see you again. I'm so sorry we will be bidding farewell to Laura. She has always been one of my favorites."

"Well, you might be keeping her, after all," he snapped. "Seems she likes it so much here that she doesn't want to leave."

"Oh, dear," Mrs. Erskine replied with a polite little laugh. "How nice to know our school is so beloved."

Ada put her hand on his arm, her complexion draining of all color. "You look…rather upset."

"Going for a walk," he announced coldly. "Be back in a while. Then we will see if we're taking her home or not."

He slammed out of the front door and ran down the steps. The long, curving driveway gave him enough room to walk without having to worry about being knocked down by cars. He tugged on his hat and strode off, walking the same way he did at the ranch, with long and easy strides.

This was what came of allowing a St. Clair to dictate your child's life. She had gone from being a sweet and simple child to a terror under their tutelage. How was he ever going to turn this around? If he could only get her home, where she would be immersed in prairie life again, she would learn to forget this nonsense. Hard work, clean living and no ridiculous nonsense— that's what made a strong and sensible person.

He paused at the end of the driveway, before it joined the busy, bustling St. Louis thoroughfare. He was no part of the crowd. In fact, anyone looking upon the scene would recognize him as the piece that was out of place. Tilting his straw cowboy hat back, he gazed up at the blue sky. He wasn't a praying man, so he couldn't pray. He wasn't a drinking man, so he couldn't drink. There was nothing he could do but walk around until he had calmed himself down and pushed his emotions back so hard they would no longer interfere in his daily existence.

He tugged his hat down and turned the corner into

the busy street. Milling around with dozens of other people would help calm him or at least put his trouble in perspective. He made his way past a woman with a baby carriage. Emily had owned a pram that looked almost exactly like that one. She would wheel Laura out into the garden in it when the wind wasn't too strong, pulling the cover up for shade, draping her shawl over the top so that Laura wouldn't get sunburned. Then, once their daughter was settled, she would turn to him and say, "You dragged me out here. My poor baby, she's stifling in this heat. Take us home. I want to live in Charleston." He would never forget the accusing glare in Emily's eyes as she turned on him, her hands on her hips.

Our place is here. This is our home. He would try wheedling and cajoling, but it was no good. When he saw his efforts were being wasted, he would leave for hours, giving Emily the time she needed to cool her temper.

He continued his path down the street, winding in and out of people milling around. Their mouths opened and shut, but no sound came out. All he could hear was the pounding of his own heart. What if he couldn't make Laura see reason? What if she refused to come back to Texas with them? His father-in-law would certainly be pleased.

He paused at the street corner, unsure of what to do. Should he round the corner and keep walking or turn back and return to Mrs. Erskine's? He hadn't solved anything by walking away. His anger still boiled near the surface and, with it, an underlying despair.

A girl should be with her father.

She should never prefer boarding school to life on the prairie.

He had failed as a husband. Was he failing as a father, too?

Ada stared after Jack as he slammed the door of the school. A quick glance showed that, per his usual routine in times of stress, he was off taking a walk. What on earth had happened to cause him to grow so angry in such a short period of time?

She turned to Mrs. Erskine, a polite smile stretching across her face. "I'm sure he's gone to see to the horses," she said quietly, by way of trying to explain away this sudden mess.

The fact that it was a hired gig and would be amply cared for by the driver did not seem to escape Mrs. Erskine, who gave an equally well-mannered but strained smile. "Of course," she replied with a gracious incline of her chin. "Now, Mrs. Burnett, as I was saying, Laura has been an excellent pupil. With proper study and application, she will do well in school, no matter where she is. You do have a school in Winchester Falls, do you not?"

Ada paused. Did they have a school? Well, they did not have a church. It was likely that there were some children in the area and that they needed a way to learn. Why hadn't she asked Jack about that? More to the point, why hadn't he told her? His plan was so simple: bring Laura home. He didn't seem to have gotten beyond that initial goal.

"Yes." If they didn't have a school, she would tutor Laura until one could be established.

She followed Mrs. Erskine up the stairs into the

second-floor parlor. The school was nice, not overly lavish, but with tasteful ornamentation. The doors to the parlor had been closed, and, through the lace curtains lining the leaded-glass panes, she could just discern the figure of a young girl.

Her new daughter.

Mrs. Erskine opened the door and ushered Ada in. "Laura, this is your new mother, Mrs. Burnett. Mrs. Burnett, may I present Laura Burnett."

It was a ridiculously formal greeting, and somewhat out of place, too. It was really the kind of thing that should have been handled by Jack. Of course, he had gone to cool his anger.

"Hello, dear Laura," she effused, coming forward. Her stepdaughter rose from her position on the settee. She was a slight, pretty child, her uniform almost too large for her frame. A strangely protective rush surged through Ada as she took Laura's hand.

"Good afternoon," Laura replied stiffly. Her handshake was cold, and she shook off Ada's touch as quickly as was permissible.

"I'm sure you two have much to discuss," Mrs. Erskine said from the doorway. "I shall see to having your trunk moved down to the carriage, Laura."

The girl opened her mouth as if to protest, but Mrs. Erskine cast a frosty look her way. Laura shut her mouth with a snap and, after her school mistress had closed the door, flung herself back onto the settee.

"I wish your father had introduced us," Ada began tentatively, after an awkward pause. "It might have been nicer if he had done the honors."

Laura shrugged, her uniform sagging against her thin shoulders. "I doubt it."

Ada recoiled as though she had been slapped. From the defiant tilt of her chin to her sullen tone of voice, Laura was making one thing abundantly clear: she was not happy to see Ada. A cold rush of nervousness gripped Ada. She had never thought of this as being a potential outcome of all of Jack's planning. The main thought on everyone's mind had been for Jack and Ada to marry and bring Laura home. No one had accounted for Laura disliking her father's new bride.

What should she say to diffuse the tense atmosphere? Was there any way to make someone like you? She had endured having rotten tomatoes thrown at her during a suffrage rights parade. Women had jeered and mocked from the sidelines while men made catcalls and shouted rudely. Somehow, she would go through all of that a dozen times rather than have Laura stare at her so coolly.

She took a deep breath and, to cover the fact that she was still scrambling for a response, made an elaborate show of taking a seat on one of the velvet chairs nearby. There must be some common ground they could meet upon. After all, Laura was having her entire life uprooted. Rather like how Ada's own world had tilted crazily, dumping her into Jack Burnett's arms. Well, not his arms, per se. Even though his arms were quite nice and strong.

Ada gave herself a brisk mental shake. What on earth was happening to her?

"Laura," she rushed on, because lingering in her own thoughts was proving to be no help at all. "I imagine it is difficult for you to have me here. After all, this is a great deal to take in at once." A sudden thought piqued her curiosity. "How were you told that your father had married me?"

"Mrs. Erskine told me." Laura's voice still held a sulky note, and her eyes were fixed stubbornly on the floor.

"What did she say?"

"That I had a new mother, and now I must go home." Laura punctuated the end of the sentence by digging the toe of her boot into the pile of the Oriental carpet on the floor.

"And what did your father say?" Ada watched her stepdaughter carefully.

"He said the same thing." Laura's toe stopped digging.

"Well, in some ways, what they say is true, but there is an important distinction we must make, from the very beginning," Ada replied, straightening her spine and placing her hands in her lap. She must compose herself and make certain she said this well, for it could either help her with Laura or make it even harder for them to bring her home. "I married your father, it is true. But I have no desire to replace your mother. You see, I met with your grandfather just a little bit ago, and he told me about her. She seemed like a lovely person. From what I understand, you even look a lot like her. So you see, Emily Burnett was a special woman. She will always be your mother."

Laura's features softened. "You met Grandfather?"

Ada forced herself to give a gentle smile, for it had not been an easy meeting. But Laura didn't need to know that. "Of course. After all, I had to get his blessing."

"Grandfather knows I'm going back to Winchester

Falls?" Laura sat forward on the settee, her eyebrows raised. "And he didn't say no?"

That was the first indication she'd had that Laura was willing to return to Texas. It must be a good sign. Evidently, Laura loved her grandfather and took his judgment to heart. "Yes, he knows. He did seem concerned at first, for he wants what is best for you. But I convinced him that a life with your father is the best thing for you, for no school can replace a family." As she spoke the words, her voice caught in her throat. Her own sisters were finishing out the term in a boarding school. Of course, that was what everyone in her family had grown accustomed to—not being particularly close.

Obviously, the Burnetts were both similar and different from the Westmores.

"I don't think I want to go back to Texas," Laura said, her voice quiet. "Grandfather hates Texas."

"I'm new to Texas, myself." Ada nodded. "I could see how it would take some getting used to, if you were accustomed to living someplace as civilized as Charleston. I'm from New York. I must say, the first time I stepped on the train platform in Texas, I nearly lost my hat."

Laura laughed, and then just as suddenly as it had started, her laughter died away. Her expression grew ashamed, as though she were embarrassed for her outburst. "That must have been funny," she said, her voice growing gloomy again.

"Indeed, it was not!" Ada tilted her chin haughtily in the air, putting her hand up to touch the brim of her ostrich-plumed chapeau. "This confection is far too grand to be tossed around on the prairie wind like a tumbleweed."

For a moment, Laura stared at Ada, her eyes narrowed.

Was she going to laugh? For good measure, Ada rolled her eyes and touched the tip of one ostrich plume.

Laura smiled a genuine though tentative smile that made Ada's heart grow warmer. Oh, good. Her play-acting had been appreciated, and perhaps Laura had thawed just a trifle.

"I'll write to your grandfather every week to let him know how you are coming along," Ada went on, deciding against pressing on with the hat joke. It was better, while Laura was feeling friendlier, to delve further into moving back to Texas. "You can write to him, too. Then, later in the year, we have been invited to pay him a visit."

Laura's blue eyes lit up. "A visit to Evermore? Oh, I love it there. Would Father come, too?"

"We'll see if we can convince him to leave his beloved Texas," Ada replied, giving an exaggerated shrug of her shoulders. "You know how these cowboys are." Better to play the tense situation between the Burnetts and the St. Clairs as a joke rather than tell Laura plainly that her father had no intention of ever visiting Charleston. She didn't need to make Laura aware of any animosity among family members.

She rose and walked over to the curtained windows across the room, twitching the lace panels aside so she had a clearer view of the waiting carriage below. As she glanced down, a familiar figure came striding up the driveway, his hat tugged down on his head and his shoulders hunched.

"Your father is waiting for us." She turned to face Laura, holding out her hand. "Shall we go down and join him at the carriage? I believe we still have time to make our evening train."

Laura paused for a moment. In that time, Ada's heart sank. How much more would she have to fight today to make this child rejoin her father?

Perhaps if she made it into a game or a challenge? "He's just coming back from wherever he walked off to," she said, giving Laura an encouraging smile. "Shall we surprise him by hurrying down and beating him to the carriage? Then we can complain about how long he kept us waiting while he perambulated about the grounds."

A hesitant smile broke across Laura's face, completely transforming her. She was no longer a morose child on the verge of a tantrum. She was a pretty young lady. Laura reached out, pulling on Ada's hands.

"Yes. Let's run!"

Chapter Five

Ada Westmore Burnett had accomplished the impossible. That was the simple truth. Jack glanced across the train car at his daughter, who was tucked up on a settee reading a book. Since the moment he had returned from his anguished walk around St. Louis, he had expected another fight. But what he found instead was Ada and Laura waiting for him in the carriage, packed and ready to get back to the train station. Laura was no longer sullen. She was quiet and perhaps a little melancholy, but her temper was not getting the better of her anymore.

Jack turned his attention to Ada. She sat at a small writing desk in the corner of the car, scribbling on a piece of paper with her pen. He got up and crossed the room, settling next to her. She did not pause in her writing as he sat down.

"What are you up to?" He darted a quick glance at Laura, but she was engrossed in her book. For some reason, he was self-conscious about being too close to Ada in his daughter's presence. He was a fool to feel that way, but he couldn't help it. He wanted to keep the peace, and if he showed too much interest in his wife, it might upset his daughter.

Ada looked over at him, her expression distracted. "I am writing down my thoughts for Laura's school and upbringing. Will she be attending school locally, or shall I hire a governess to teach her?"

Governess—the word had a distinct whiff of St. Clair about it. So no, that wouldn't do. "She can go to school with the other children in the area. There's a schoolhouse about a mile down the road from our place."

"Very good." Ada turned her attention back to her paper. "I shall make a note of that."

He drummed his fingers on the arm of his chair. It was a good thing that this was the last leg of their journey home. He was tired of being cooped up in the train car, forced to be on his best behavior for the past few days. Once they got home, the first thing he'd do was take a long ride out onto the prairie.

"Do you need something to do?" Ada's voice was unexpectedly sharp, and she gave him a pointed glare from her position at the desk. Being regarded so piercingly by those large blue eyes of hers was like being doused with a bucket of ice-cold water. It brought you to your senses, that was for sure. "I can certainly give you a job if you are bored."

"Not bored. Just restless. Ready to be home." He forced his fingers to be still.

"Well, then I shall distract you by asking you more details," she replied primly.

He stifled a grin, along with the urge to tease her. Ada was always so proper and so serious. Of course, she was doing all of this for his benefit, so he should just be still and let her ramble on about houses and maids and schools. But something about her just begged for silliness. If only he could reach over and find out if she was ticklish, just to see her reaction. He leaned forward slightly, and as he did so, Laura drifted back into his view. He sat back abruptly. He couldn't tease Ada in front of Laura. Everyone's peace seemed so precariously balanced that there was no telling what could make it topple.

"You have the strangest look on your face just now," Ada spoke up, shaking her head. "Oh well. I suppose the rigors of travel get to the best of us. How much longer until we reach home?"

It was gratifying to hear Ada speak of Winchester Falls as home. Did she really feel that way, or was she merely saying it for Laura's benefit? Well, he would take what he could get. Amazing how lonely he'd been after Emily died. Not that she was very good company in life, at least not in those last years. She was, though, another presence around the house. Then, of course, they had Laura together. When they were both gone, it was very quiet.

"We just passed the turnoff for the Falls," he replied. "Just a few more minutes."

"Good." Ada turned to Laura. "My dear, you should put away your book and anything else you brought from the sleeping car. Time to tidy up. We will be pulling into the station soon."

Laura shot her stepmother a slightly sour look over the edges of her book, but she did as she was told. Ada bustled around, gathering her scattered pieces of paper.

"Oh, do help out, Jack. We have so much to do to

get ready." Ada brushed past him, her skirt catching on his bent knees as she flounced by.

He resisted the urge to tug at the fabric, forcing her to slow down and pay attention to him, and instead carefully unwound her skirts from around his leg. Ada didn't even notice that she had gotten caught, so intent was she on getting all her trifles picked up before they reached Winchester Falls.

What was wrong with him? He was spending entirely too much time thinking about Ada and about her reactions to every little thing. This was what came of being too long inside and too long away from home. It was time for him to stop watching her every move and, instead, to focus on important things. He was, after all, a husband in name only. But he was a father in fact.

He shifted around and, as he did so, his hand brushed against his jacket pocket. Absentmindedly he stuffed his hand down inside, and his fingers clasped a doll. The toy he had purchased for his daughter in St. Louis had been riding around inside his jacket for days now. He withdrew it from his pocket and disentangled the doll from his handkerchief he had used to wrap it up and protect it. The doll looked none the worse for wear, fortunately.

"Here." He handed the doll to Laura, who was putting her book away in a satchel. "I bought this for you in St. Louis." He waited, his breath catching a little in his throat, as Laura took it from his grasp.

She smoothed the doll's skirts and then carefully traced her finger down the banner that read St. Louis.

"What a lovely doll," Ada spoke up from her end of the car.

Laura glanced up, frowning. "Thank you, Father,"

she said, her voice prim. She tucked the doll inside the satchel with her book and then busied herself fluffing up the pillows she had lain upon.

His heart dropped a little. She just wasn't willing to be natural with him. What would happen if he started teasing her, calling her his sunshine baby just as he had when she was little? Likely she would fix him with that glare, the one that made her look like the spitting image of her mother.

Well, glare or no glare, they would have to set one thing straight. It had been bothering him since before he brought her home from boarding school.

"Now that we're in Winchester Falls, I expect you to call me Pa." His voice was harsher than he meant it to be. He'd better take things easy. "We aren't very formal out here."

"I was told that Pa was what uneducated yokels called their fathers." She kept her back to him, fussing with the ties on her satchel.

Ada took a step forward as though to physically stand between them, but he held up a warning hand. She paused, her eyes widening.

"Told by whom? Those uppity boarding-school teachers or your snob of a grandfather?" He should not have put it that way. He should have kept the peace. The moment the words left his mouth, he knew he had started yet another battle.

Ada gasped. "Jack, really."

Laura spun around, her eyes blazing. "Grandfather wants what is best for me," she cried. "I was being raised to be a lady, not some old ranch woman. I want to go back to St. Louis." The last words were choked out on a sob.

Jack pointed at Ada. "She's not lady enough for you, then?"

"That's quite enough." Ada stepped around them, crossing her arms over her chest. "Jack, you simply must work on that temper of yours. Laura's had a difficult journey. Her world has been turned upside down. It's quite natural for her to be feeling overwhelmed."

Laura sniffed and gulped, still looking daggers at her father.

Ada turned to her stepdaughter. "Laura, your father has requested that you refer to him as Pa, and as a dutiful daughter, you must do so."

Laura stared down at the carpet but gave a brief shrug.

The train began to slow, its wheels grinding and the brakes squealing. They must finally be at Winchester Falls. At last, he would be home, where he was king of his dominion. No more fancy restaurants, no more St. Clairs, no more train travel in close proximity to Ada Burnett. He would be back on the range, where a man could be free.

Without waiting for his wife or daughter, he clamped his hat on his head and swung down the steps to the station platform while the train crept into the station.

As soon as his boots touched the wooden planks, a familiar voice crowed, "Well, howdy, Jack! Are you just champing at the bit to be home?"

He turned, smiling at Pearl Colgan. "Good to see you, Pearl."

She embraced him, giving his back a hearty whack. "So where's that little scamp Laura? Don't tell me you came back alone. Did you leave Ada in St. Louis?"

"They're still on the train, getting their things. A man needs to breathe after being cooped up with two females for so long," he replied, trying to make his response sound breezy.

Pearl nodded, assessing him as carefully as she would another trader before making a deal. "So Ada was successful in convincing Edmund?"

"Ada," he replied, sudden heat flooding his face, "was incredible."

Pearl fixed him with a stare, raising one gray eyebrow. "Was she?"

He didn't usually get enthusiastic about anything, but as he remembered their dinner with St. Clair, he felt the same tug of gratitude and solidarity he had experienced that day. "Without her intervention, I don't think the old man would have let me have my Laura."

"And how has Laura been?" She was still looking at him carefully, trying to pry the truth out without having to use any words. It was her way. He was used to it by now.

"Without Ada, I'm not sure Laura would be here," he replied. "Somehow, she convinced my daughter to come down to the carriage so we could leave. The little runt was stalling, saying she didn't want me to be remarried."

"Well, you got to understand where she's coming from." Pearl patted his shoulder. "Laura was only two when her mother died. Though she probably doesn't remember her, I am sure she doesn't want anyone to take her place. It's family loyalty. She doesn't know that Ada is your wife in name only. She doesn't understand that Ada has a paid position to help you out.

She thinks you fell in love again, and that's bound to rankle."

He shrugged. "I guess that's true. Don't know what I'm supposed to do about it."

"Give it time. If you were a praying man, I would tell you to pray on it. As it is, I'll pray for you." Pearl issued him a challenging smile.

Somehow, it felt good to know that Pearl would be praying for him. It meant a lot to have another friend helping him out.

There was a flurry of activity on the train steps, and Ada came down, followed by Laura. The wind caught Ada's enormous hat, and she held it on with both hands. "Well, we certainly are home." She laughed, making her way over to Pearl. "I still had my hat pinned to St. Louis weather."

Pearl laughed and kissed her niece on both cheeks. When she broke away from Ada, she bent down to look at Laura. "Don't tell me this is Laura. Why, Jack, you must be an old man. Here she is, growing into a little lady."

Laura bobbed a brief curtsy, her tights still bagging at the knees, which were sticking out from beneath the hem of her skirt. "Pleased to make your acquaintance," she said, her voice clear.

"Darlin' child, no need to be so formal with your aunt Pearl," Pearl exclaimed, gathering Laura in a tight embrace. "I've known you since you were just a wee little thing. You don't remember me, I guess, but I've been your neighbor for years. Ada's my niece."

When Laura extricated herself from Pearl's arms, she gave a brief smile. Her hair ribbon had been knocked askew. She didn't say anything more and stood politely to one side, completely disinterested in her hometown.

Pearl led them over to the waiting carriages, one for her and one for Jack. "Ada, the house is in apple-pie order. I think you'll like it. Y'all want to come to dinner? At least let me help you get settled."

"Should we wait for our trunks?" Ada turned, casting a worried look back at the train.

"I'm with Pearl. Let's go home. I'll send a boy to fetch them in a little bit." He didn't want to wait a moment longer.

"All right. Laura, ride in the carriage with your father. I want to spend some time discussing the household with Aunt Pearl as we go home," Ada replied.

Laura fixed him with a glower that would curdle milk as he handed her up in the carriage. Ada climbed in beside Pearl, laughing and chatting with her aunt.

As he gave the horses their rein, a strange mixture of feelings took hold. He was happy to be home but nervous about bringing Laura into their home. What if she hated it as much as she hated him? Ada wasn't beside him, either, and that contributed to an odd feeling of loss.

"Ada has been working hard to make the house nice for you," he said as he turned the horses onto the main road. "She's got your room all put together. I think you'll like it. Do you remember our house at all?"

"No, I don't." Laura turned away from him and gazed at the horizon.

"You were just a little thing, of course, when we finished building it." It was difficult to talk about the house, or about the past. But if it helped him to find common ground with his daughter, he would press on.

"Your mother had a hand in designing it. She wanted porches that wrapped all the way around, just like they have at Evermore. They were difficult to build, but I made it happen."

"That's nice." Her voice remained sullen, though. She didn't really think it was nice at all if she spoke to him in that tone of voice.

Ada had advised him to remember how difficult Laura's life was right now. He could respect that. Life was difficult for him, too, though. He had gone to battle to bring home his daughter, expecting her to be the sweet baby he always remembered. She wasn't a baby anymore, though. She was a young lady, and an unhappy one at that. Would he ever find a connection with her?

The sooner they were home the better, he decided. He didn't know if he was going or coming any longer.

Ada folded her hands tightly in her lap and concentrated on the thoughts swirling in her head. Over the course of their journey to and from St. Louis, she had worked hard to be the voice of reason and caution. It seemed she had tried to reconcile Jack Burnett with every estranged relative he possessed.

She should be tired. She should be exhausted. Instead, she felt slightly giddy, because she was at last going home, ready to uphold her end of the bargain. How strange it was to think of Texas as home, but so it was. Already it had staked its claim in her heart.

"Jack was mighty pleased with the way you handled Edmund St. Clair," Aunt Pearl said as she guided the horses down the road. "I believe he called you 'incredible.'"

Ada's cheeks grew hot at the unexpected praise. Had she really won Jack's approval? "I don't know if anything I did was incredible," she demurred. "I just tried my best to help."

"Jack is a man of few words." Aunt Pearl settled back in her seat, holding the reins slack in her gloved hands. "If you earn praise from him, it's highly deserved. In fact, I don't think I've ever heard him sound that effusive."

Ada lapsed into silence. What could she say? Part of the strange emotions swirling within her had to do with Jack. She liked being in his company. It was pleasant—when he wasn't in a temper—to have him around, even in the confines of the train car. Once they returned to the ranch, he would be off working again, and she would no longer have the opportunity to stay close. Besides, she had to worry about Laura, focus her attention on the girl's proper upbringing.

"What's Laura like?" Aunt Pearl steered the horses so they were following Jack's carriage at a decorous pace.

"She's upset. Understandably so, I suppose. She was told by her headmistress that I was her new mother. Frankly, that kind of message should have come from her own father," Ada replied, frowning at the memory. "She refused to come home at first. I managed to talk her around, but she is still not happy about being here. She feels St. Louis is her home."

"Well, she probably doesn't remember much about Winchester Falls," Aunt Pearl replied. Her voice was softer than Ada had ever heard it. "She won't recall it with fond memories. Emily traveled back to Charleston with her a lot as a baby, and that's why they have those two train cars, so she and her infant could travel in style. Edmund is a scoundrel and a snob, but he loves that grandchild of his. I do believe his concern for her is real."

Ada nodded. St. Clair really did seem worried about Laura's well-being and not just about exacting revenge on Jack. "I agree. I promised him I would bring her for two weeks every summer."

"And Jack agreed to that?" Aunt Pearl gave a sharp bark of laughter. "You really did make the impossible happen, Ada."

"He was fine with it as long as I travel as chaperone. Also, St. Clair insisted that I provide him with regular updates. He is going to have his man of affairs pay us a few visits at the ranch, too."

"It's a good thing I kept working on it while you were gone, then," Aunt Pearl said with a laugh. If she was surprised that St. Clair would actually poke around the ranch to check on Laura, she didn't let on. "It's in pretty good shape. We have Laura's room completely finished. The whole place is clean from ceiling to floor, with a pretty white iron bedstead and a dove-in-the-window quilt I made when I was first married to R. H. I think she's going to like it here. Just keep being gentle with her as you have been, Ada. You two have a lot in common, if you think about it."

Ada pondered her aunt's words. There was some truth to them. Like Laura, circumstances had dictated that she find a new home. She and Laura had moved because the men in their lives had, in different ways, made it necessary. It was now up to her to help Laura through this difficult transition.

Providing, of course, that she could make the transition possible herself.

Her own personal history of adjustment around the ranch was less than successful, but every day would have to be better than the last.

Chapter Six

Jack drummed his fingers on the dining room table. If Laura didn't hurry up, she would be late for school. He had planned to drive her there. It was her first day at the prairie school, after all. His long-awaited dream had come true. He was finally about to take her to the little schoolhouse and talk to the teacher and get her all set up. It was too far for Laura to walk by herself, especially since she wasn't used to life on the prairie, and it was his pleasure to take her after many years of just dreaming about having his daughter at home. But he also had a cattle ranch to run, and if his daughter didn't hustle, he'd be behind in his chores all day.

Ada bustled in, two maids trailing in her wake. "I want to make absolutely certain that we turn over the earth near the front of the house," she informed them. "I think, if we plant zinnias there, we will get some nice summer blooms. It will be important to have flowers all year long, or at least as often as we can get them. Those zinnias have tough stalks. They can stand up to the prairie wind."

The maids nodded. Ada paused, putting her pencil up to her mouth as she consulted the list in her hand. Then, as though aware of his eyes on her, she flicked a glance his way. "What are you still doing here? You should have left for the schoolhouse already."

He nodded. "Yup. Should have." Then he took another swig of his coffee.

"Oh, dear." Ada rushed over to the stair landing in a swirl of skirts. "Laura," she called up the stairs. "It's past time to go."

"Coming." Laura sounded sulky. He pressed back the annoyance that threatened to overtake him. His daughter was either sour faced or completely silent or both ever since she had arrived. Why couldn't she be happy?

She thumped down the stairs, appearing in her boarding school uniform. Ada straightened her hair bow and bade her to pull up her baggy tights. "I'll see to it that you have new clothes," Ada added. "This uniform is made of wool. You'll be stifling in a week or so." She scribbled a few more notes on her piece of paper.

Laura nodded and turned toward Jack. He tried to give her the same smile he'd used when she was little. Maybe they'd find a connection on the ride to the schoolhouse. "Ready, sunshine baby?"

She nodded, the corners of her mouth turning downward. Ada shooed them out the door after one of the maids pressed a tin pail into Laura's hands.

"What's this?" she asked, looking down at it as they made their way to the carriage.

"I reckon it's your dinner," Jack replied, handing her up into the seat.

"Oh." Laura looked distinctly unimpressed and lapsed into silence again as he turned the horses onto the driveway.

He grew silent, too. Nothing he said seemed to help the situation, so maybe he should not say anything at all. If he spoke, he irritated his daughter. She used to be such a sweet little thing. Somehow, none of this was going the way he had expected it to when he'd first laid his plans. In his imagination, Laura was all too happy to get away from that stuffy boarding school; she enjoyed life on the ranch and doted on her father. She approved of her stepmother and thought of her as family. The way he had planned it, everything picked up where it had left off, with the exception that Emily was no longer with them, of course.

Maybe he could try to interest her more in what he did on the ranch. He cleared his throat. "Well, after I drop you off, I'm going to work the cattle. You've got to count them every day. I check on them to make sure they haven't taken sick or gotten attacked by wild animals."

Laura's eyes grew as round as saucers. "Wild animals?"

"Sure," he replied. "You see, out here we have coyotes and even the occasional wolf. Now, usually they go after the very young, the very old or the sickly. Even so, I have to keep them away. Each cow is worth a lot of money."

"Will the animals attack me?" Laura shrank against her seat.

"Nope." He said it bracingly, as though he could stiffen her spine with a single word. It wouldn't do to have her start being afraid of life out here. She needed to be cautious but not afraid. "Not while I'm around."

"But you said they went after the young ones. Does that mean young people, too?"

She had a point there. He shifted uncomfortably, focusing his attention on the horses. "Nah," he responded after a pause. "Just animals."

She raised her eyebrow at him and then turned her attention back to the road.

He'd have to try again.

"These horses are some of the finest you'll find in Archer County." He waved to indicate the magnificent matched bays pulling the carriage. "One of them is an offspring of the horse I bought when I met your mother. I went to Charleston to get Lady Guinevere, and that one on the right is her daughter, Jenny."

Laura leaned forward in her seat, fixing her attention on the horses. "Really?"

"Yes." Finally, a flicker of real interest from his daughter. He'd talk to her about the horses as much as she wanted if it made her start feeling like a part of things. "Lady G was a fine animal. It broke my heart when she got colic. It was a really severe case, and she didn't make it. Jenny's just as good as her mama, though. I save her and Bets for pulling the carriage. They look so flashy I figured they're the best for showing off."

Laura nodded. "They are very pretty."

His heart warmed. "Yep, they sure are."

Laura turned to face him, her blue eyes pleading. "Can I drive them?"

He laughed. When she wasn't being sullen, she was being cheeky. "No, you may not."

Her face fell. "Why not? I wouldn't let them run away."

"Bets and Jenny may be used to the prairie, but you aren't," he reminded her gently. "What if a jackrabbit bounded out in front of the carriage and you jerked the reins?"

She folded her arms over her chest. "I would not."

"Sorry, sunshine baby," he responded. "It's just too dangerous. You are too young."

She went from defiance to anger in the bat of an eye, turning her entire body away, focusing pointedly on the prairie horizon. Jack lapsed back into silence. He just wasn't going to win anything with this stubborn little girl.

The schoolhouse appeared before he knew it, a small wooden building on land donated by his neighbor, Jacob Stillman. Children of varying ages and sizes were playing outside, and their shouts seemed to force Laura further into her shell. When he pulled the carriage up to the fence, she hesitated before jumping out.

Miss Carlyle, a young woman with brown hair and spectacles, came up to the fence to greet them. She had been boarding with the Stillman family since her arrival in Winchester Falls a year ago. He knew her in passing but had never really spoken to her.

"Mr. Burnett, how do you do?" She shook his hand over the fence. "This must be your daughter, Laura. Mrs. Colgan came and visited me on your wife's behalf while you all were in St. Louis. I believe your daughter will be joining us?" She gave Laura a kind smile.

Laura adopted a half smile in return, digging the toe of her boot in the dirt.

"I'm not familiar with what she learned at her boarding school," Jack began. He didn't know anything much about Laura's education—or anything much about his daughter, at all. He only knew what he wanted there to be. Ada had been the one to speak to Mrs. Erskine before they left. He should be acquainted with her daily life better. She was his daughter, after all, and it was embarrassing to admit he knew so little about her.

"No need to worry, Mr. Burnett," Miss Carlyle responded briskly. "Mrs. Burnett sent me a letter while you were en route to Winchester Falls, and I have also heard from Mrs. Erskine, Laura's former headmistress. I'm certain we can get Laura situated quickly." She turned to Laura. "Come along, dear," she said. "We must get a slate and a pencil and assign a desk to you."

Without so much as a backward glance, Laura walked around and let herself in the gate. Miss Carlyle bundled her off to the schoolyard, and the other children followed them inside.

Well, there it was. His daughter was now in school in Winchester Falls. His wish had come true.

If that was the case, though, why did his stomach feel so hollow?

He turned his steps and his attention back to the carriage. He had work to do. He had hired Ada to do the fundamental labor of helping him to raise Laura to St. Clair levels of distinction. She had already risen to the occasion by ensuring that Laura's transition from boarding school to one-room schoolhouse went as smoothly as possible. It was time for him to head off and tackle what he knew best, and that was raising cattle.

They were a sight easier to raise than little girls, that much was certain.

Ada rose from her knees after her morning prayers. *Please let the first day of school go well*, she added, punctuating her more formal entreaties with a plea straight from her heart. Laura's face had been so white when she came downstairs after breakfast. She was sure to be nervous, but Aunt Pearl had helped by apprising Miss Carlyle of the situation.

As she glanced out the window, she caught sight of Aunt Pearl and another woman walking up the path. Ada dashed over to her mirror to make sure her hair looked presentable—a concern that seemed never ending, even indoors, in the Winchester Falls breeze.

Cathy appeared in her bedroom doorway. "Miz Burnett, Miz Colgan is here to see you, along with Miz Stillman."

"Of course," Ada replied. She must get used to social calling again. It had been so long since anyone had come to see her. When you were on the receiving end of social ostracism because of your father's scandalous political dealings, you got used to isolation. "Did you show them into the parlor?"

The maid gave a brief nod.

Good. The parlor was the prettiest room in the house thus far, especially now that the maids had taken the time to clean the crystal pendants on the chandelier. Receiving company in that room would be a pleasure.

She followed Cathy downstairs and into the room

where Aunt Pearl and Mrs. Stillman were waiting. The woman with her aunt was tall and blond, with skin that showed the effects of living in intense sun and wind. She offered Ada a smile that completely illuminated her somewhat-worn face with kindness and good humor.

"Well, no wonder Jack picked her," she crowed, turning to Aunt Pearl. "What a looker! Jack will be the envy of five counties, that much is sure."

Heat flooded Ada's cheeks, as it always did when people assumed she was his bride in truth and not a glorified hired hand to help him raise his child. "How do you do?" She stretched her hand out in greeting.

"Ada, this is Dorothy Stillman," Aunt Pearl said, smiling. "She is your other nearest neighbor. The schoolhouse sits on her land."

"Everyone calls me Dot. You're welcome to do the same." The woman clasped her hand tightly.

"A pleasure to meet you, Miss—er, Mrs.—Dot," Ada stumbled. Would she ever get used to the free-and-easy manners of Texas? It was so different from what she was used to.

The two women laughed again and found seats on the velvet chairs nearby. Ada also sat. "Would you like some tea?" she asked, looking for the bellpull. There wasn't one. Another thing she would have to remedy as soon as she could.

"In this heat? No, thanks," Dot replied, drawing off her gloves. "Actually, Ada, this isn't a purely so-cial call, though I have been wanting to meet you ever since I got wind that you married Jack. No, Pearl and I need your help. I think you know that our little town lacks a chapel. We've been working with a missionary group to have a preacher sent out here. They've finally agreed to do it, but only if we have permanent structures in place."

"Such as a chapel and a rectory?" Ada inquired. Why, this could be quite helpful. She had been planning to take on Laura's religious education herself. How much better it would be to have a real man of God instructing them all.

"That's right," Pearl replied. "We can get the men in the area together to build everything, but we need more land. Right now, the Stillmans have agreed that the school can have part of their land. I've got a railroad running through the southern edge of mine. We were wondering if Jack would grant a piece of land for the chapel and rectory."

"Of course, he would," Ada enthused. What an excellent idea. She could just picture herself writing to St. Clair. *Our community is growing by leaps and bounds—thanks in no small part to Jack, who donated the land for the new chapel—*

"Good, then you'll talk to him." Pearl rubbed her hands together as though they were plotting together in a melodrama. "I wouldn't broach the subject myself, but seeing as how he thinks so highly of you, I figured you could take the bull by the horns."

She wasn't exactly sure what that phrase meant, but if Aunt Pearl was reluctant to ask Jack something, should she be concerned, too?

No, that was nonsense. Aunt Pearl was just teasing.

"How many acres do you think you'll need?" She had no idea how many Jack owned, but surely he could spare some of them.

"About three would be more than enough," Dot responded. "Though we'll take more if we can get it."

"We need an answer soon," Aunt Pearl added. "They can send a preacher out here to live in a few months when one comes back from ministering in China. I declare, I didn't think we'd ever get a dedicated preacher out here. I figured we'd have to make do with someone riding in once a month or so. But having a minister all the time will mean so much to everyone."

Ada nodded. Her aunt was right. It was not a good idea to bring up a child with no sense of Christian community. In fact, it was downright odd to live in a place with no established church. Jack had mentioned that Winchester Falls was raw and new and only just starting to come into its own. How much better would that process be now that they would have a church of their own?

"Go ahead and write back to them. I'm certain we can spare three acres," she responded, trying to keep the excitement from ringing through her voice. "I'll speak to Jack about it when he comes in for dinner."

The two women looked sideways at each other but smiled and said nothing. After a bit more polite conversation, they took their leave. Ada busied herself with planting zinnias until dinner, for if she thought too much about the chapel, she was ready to dance all through the house.

Jack came in for the midday meal, more quiet and morose than usual. She sat with him in the dining room, fairly bursting with the news. When she had said the blessing and he'd started eating, the story erupted from her in a torrent of words.

"I told them that we could easily spare three acres," she finished, spreading jam on her buttered bread. "Jack, just think of it. A chapel right here in our own town. How exciting that will be!"

Jack chewed thoughtfully, saying nothing. At length, he pushed his plate aside. "You told them I would give my land for a church?"

"A teeny, tiny piece of it, yes." She bit daintily into the crust.

"Ada." His voice held a note of warning. "I'm not a praying man."

Ada glanced over at him. Was he really going to throw a fit about this? "I don't think it matters if you are or not," she responded crisply. "What we care about is having a place of worship and a home for a man of God. Surely you don't object to that."

He drank his coffee slowly, his eyes narrowed. "You don't just agree to something like that. Not without consulting me."

"I'm an equal partner in this venture, or so you told me." She put the bread down and faced him squarely. "Three acres is a mere trifle when you have so much."

"That's not what I'm objecting to," he rejoined. "First of all, you donated land for a church when I'm not a praying man. Second, you didn't even ask. You should have thought to check with me."

"You wanted me to create an environment for Laura that would be acceptable to Mr. St. Clair." She straightened her spine. "One of his biggest objections was that Winchester Falls was too new and too ramshackle a place for a young woman of a certain class to be raised. I can tell you right now that if Winchester Falls doesn't get a church, it won't become a place the St. Clairs will consider suitable."

He sat there, staring at her. She would not look away. At least he was still there, arguing with her. Just a few days ago, he would have flung himself out of the house and into the pasture for hours.

"You still should have consulted me first. As an equal partner." He said the last few words quietly, so faint that she had to strain to hear them.

"You are right." And he was. She was barging ahead without thinking, and if he had done the same to her, she would have been furious. "I apologize."

"Apology accepted." He stuck his hand out down the length of the table. "They can have the land. You're right. St. Clair will be pleased, and I guess it will be good for Laura, too. Do we have a truce?"

She took his hand in hers. His was rough and callused, the hand of a man who worked long, vigorous hours, using reserves of strength and vitality. He was not a man who frequented a ballroom or a gambling den, or who spent his time in political dealings behind closed doors.

Despite his temper and lack of faith, there was a fundamental genuineness about Jack that spoke deeply to her.

She pulled away sharply, suddenly aware that she had let her hand rest in his for longer than absolutely necessary. Mumbling an awkward apology, she rose, nearly knocking her chair over in the process. Leaving the rest of her meal untouched, she hurried back out to the garden.

Jack was not her husband in truth, and their talk of being partners, as though they were embarking on a business venture, reinforced that fact. As a woman who considered herself the equal of any man, she mustn't let herself be swayed by a man's mere touch.

Usually Jack was the one who ran away, but now she was seeking the respite of the outdoors to hide her profound embarrassment—and confusion.

Chapter Seven

Ada pulled the team of bays to a halt before the schoolyard gate. She hadn't gotten lost; nor had the horses startled when she was driving, so that was another small victory. Perhaps she was getting more used to life on the prairie. In truth, she welcomed bringing Laura home this afternoon. Driving out gave her the chance to get away from the house for a little while, which was nice. Being away from home meant she would be able to, perhaps, distract her thoughts from the curious turn they had taken. That afternoon, out in the garden, she kept mulling over her strange new feelings about Jack.

Laura might still be difficult to manage, sulky and stubborn, but her presence would force Ada to think about something other than Jack Burnett's touch, and especially the way it made warmth spread through her, bringing with it a wave of dizzy confusion. However bewildering, his touch was most welcome. In fact, she could almost embrace her stepdaughter for the diversion.

Ada gathered her skirts and jumped down from the

carriage. The horses stood absolutely still, so calm that there was no need to tie them to the hitching post. They weren't going anywhere.

She let herself through the gate and made her way up the path to the schoolhouse. In contrast to the imposing, ivy-covered brick facade of Mrs. Erskine's facility, this school was a humble frame building. The walls glowed a clean white, so dazzling that she had to shade her eyes from the brilliance. A small brass bell hung beside the bottle-green door. All the windows were open, allowing the breeze to blow through the classroom. As she approached, she heard the hum of voices and what must be Miss Carlyle's crisp, clear tones ringing out.

"Class, we will release after we recite the prayer from my homeland I've taught you." Miss Carlyle made a sharp rapping sound, as though she had hit a blackboard or a desk with a stick. "Ready? Let us say it loudly and clearly together."

There was a rattle and clatter as the students rose to their feet. In rhythmic, singsong chant, they recited:

"Christ with me,
Christ before me,
Christ behind me,
Christ in me,
Christ beneath me,
Christ above me,
Christ on my right,
Christ on my left,
Christ when I lie down,
Christ when I sit down,
Christ when I arise,

Christ in the heart of every man who thinks
of me,
Christ in the mouth of everyone who speaks of
me,
Christ in every eye that sees me,
Christ in every ear that hears me."

Ada bowed her head as she listened, and when they finished, a smile touched her lips. What a lovely way to end a school day.

"Good afternoon, Miss Carlyle," the class called out as a body.

"Good afternoon, boys and girls. Class dismissed."

Ada pressed herself against the wall of the school as the door was flung open. Children of all shapes and sizes tumbled out, laughing, calling and joking with one another. Only Laura hung behind, and her normally reserved expression melted into one of sudden relief when she spotted her stepmother.

"Hello, Laura," Ada said, holding her arms out for an embrace. Normally Laura would shun any touch from Ada, but she practically ran toward her, returning the embrace fiercely. "Are you ready to go home?"

Laura nodded vigorously. Behind her, Miss Carlyle stepped out of the schoolhouse.

"You must be Mrs. Burnett. How do you do?" Miss Carlyle extended her hand in greeting.

Ada tucked Laura beside her on the wooden step and shook the teacher's hand. "Miss Carlyle. It's a pleasure to meet you. What a pretty prayer that was. You said it was from your homeland?"

"My people are Irish," Miss Carlyle responded, tilting her chin proudly. "I learned that one from my grandmother when I was a girl in Kentucky. Of course, it sounds much more musical if you have a bit o' the blarney in your voice, as my Gran did."

Ada smiled. "I can imagine. How did Laura fare today?"

Miss Carlyle glanced fondly at Laura, her green eyes twinkling behind the lenses of her spectacles. "She did very well, indeed, especially when you think of the changes she's had to endure in the past few days. She is quite articulate and expresses herself far more clearly than most children her age. She was so far advanced in her studies that I skipped her a few grades. Her boarding school did well by her, and I'd rather her be challenged than bored."

"I agree." Ada's heart surged with hope. "I shall be very happy to tell her father that—and her grandfather, when I write to him."

"She will need time to make friends," Miss Carlyle continued. "Academically, I can say without reserve that she will do quite well. But her social skills are lacking. I imagine she feels isolated from the other children, given her experience."

Ada nodded slowly. She must come up with a plan to assist her stepdaughter in making friends. How did one make friends, anyway? When she was growing up, her chums were her schoolmates, and they were all the same. Everyone came from wealthy or noble families—or both—and were sent to boarding school together. They dressed alike, talked alike and ran in the same social circles. Out here, life was different. Ada scanned the children leaving the schoolyard. Some, like Laura, were dressed in good dresses and wore shoes. Others ran barefoot and had ragged clothing.

"We will work on it together," Ada vowed. "Miss Carlyle, I will be picking Laura up each day. Her father doesn't want her to walk home, at least not until she learns the ways of the prairie better."

Miss Carlyle nodded. "Of course."

Ada bade the teacher goodbye, and Laura did the same, politely and without prompting. Well, that was something. Perhaps going to school would help to ease her stepdaughter out of her sulk.

She helped Laura into the wagon and then got in beside her. Gathering the reins, she started the bays down the road toward home before she spoke.

"How was the first day? Miss Carlyle said you are quite bright. That must make you feel better."

Laura sighed. "I suppose."

"What about the other children? Did you find anyone you might want to befriend?" Somehow, she felt she was prying, peppering her stepdaughter with questions to set her own mind at ease. After all, she had promised herself that she would wait to write to St. Clair until after Laura started school. She had to be truthful in her account, but it would help a great deal if everything worked out beautifully.

Laura shook her head. "Some of the other children smell bad."

Ada gasped and then laughed—more out of shock at her stepdaughter's forthrightness than anything else. Miss Carlyle was right. Laura was quite articulate when she was moved to speak. "Oh, dear. Well, you must remember that not everyone has had your advantages. You know, you are a very fortunate young lady."

"I know." Laura heaved another gusty sigh. "You aren't mad at me for saying that?"

After a pause, Ada shook her head. "No. You were being honest. Although you should never say that sort of thing when others can hear you. You don't want to hurt anyone's feelings. Save that sort of frankness for me, or start confiding in a diary."

Laura gave her a reluctant smile. "Thank you. It felt good to say it out loud."

Genuine curiosity tugged at Ada. "Have you felt you couldn't say things aloud?"

"Not since I told Father that I didn't want him to marry you," she admitted. "I don't want to make anyone angry but—" she twisted her hands in her lap "—life in Texas is so strange! The maids don't seem to know their own duties. The wind blows in gusts like a train. My teacher says things like 'donkey's years' when I suppose she means that something is old." She paused, her eyes wide at her own temerity. "Oh, I am sorry."

Ada pulled the horses over to the side of the dirt road and burst into laughter. She couldn't help it. Everything Laura said was true and very akin to how she had been feeling since she first landed at the Winchester Falls station. "Oh, mercy," she said, drying her eyes with her gloved fingertips. "What refreshing candor, and well beyond your years."

"Are you teasing me?" Laura gazed at her stepmother, confusion written plainly across her features.

"Indeed not. It just felt good to hear someone else say it." Ada experienced the warmth of compassion flowing through her. "I've been feeling much the same way ever since I arrived. If you thought it was strange here, imagine coming from New York. I've been doing my best, I can tell you, but it has been a struggle."

For the second time since they had met, Laura

broke into a genuine grin. It was funny. Even though she was reported to be her mother's spitting image, her smile looked precisely like her father's, especially when he was in a teasing mood. Did Jack know that his daughter favored him? Probably not.

"Thank you for not being angry with me," Laura said with a giggle. "I suppose it's not polite to point these things out."

"No, but I think it's nice to be able to say them every now and then. Just between the two of us." Ada put her arm around her stepdaughter's thin shoulders. "But we won't say it to anyone who might be hurt by it."

Laura returned the embrace, which was another unexpected thing. Ada said a quick, silent prayer of gratitude. Through His grace, she had found common ground with her stepdaughter.

She gathered the reins and steered the horses back onto the road. They lapsed into silence, but it was a comfortable one now. Before them on the road, grasshoppers clicked and jumped. Hawks circled lazily in the bright blue sky, and wind tousled the long prairie grass. The view wasn't as formally pretty as the parks in New York, but somehow, she felt freer here. Back at her father's house, she was all about forcing her father to accept her as a rational creature. Out here, she was trying to keep the peace. It helped, a great deal, that she was no longer as deeply concerned about her own hurts as she had been. She was too busy trying to help Laura with her difficulties.

"Father treats me like a child," Laura said quietly, her gaze fixed on the sky.

"I imagine he still thinks of you as the baby you

were, growing up here. Before you were moved to St. Louis." Ada guided the horses around a bend in the road. "Of course, your behavior of late hasn't helped that impression. It's childish to sulk, Laura. You're bright. You should show how grown-up you are rather than acting like a baby."

Laura's cheeks flushed pink. "I know. I just hated the way he told me about you."

"I agree the entire matter was handled poorly," Ada said in sympathy. "Nothing can be done about it now. Of course, I imagine that if you start being sweet, you run the risk of losing face."

Laura shifted uncomfortably on the seat. "I guess. How did you know that?"

Ada gave a little laugh. "I have two younger sisters and had quite the acrimonious relationship with my own father. It doesn't do to steep in bitterness, Laura. It poisons your soul." She heaved a sigh. That lesson had been hard learned since Father's death. "Even if you can't bring yourself to forgive him yet, well, you'll have to start behaving in a more grown-up manner. You must begin to take responsibility."

"For what?" Laura turned in her seat. A small smile was quirking the corners of her mouth, thankfully. Her honesty had not lost her the common ground they'd gained.

"Where should we start…" Ada murmured. "Well, your journey to and from school is a good example. Your father fears that you can't handle walking by yourself. Would you like to try driving, instead? If he can see that you handle a team of horses, he might begin to think of you as someone who can handle walking by herself."

"May I? Oh, Ada." Laura clasped her hands together. "I want to drive so badly."

"Here you go." She handed the reins to her stepdaughter. "I know you have had training as a horsewoman. Mrs. Erskine told me that you were quite the
competent rider."

Laura giggled nervously and then fell into silence,
concentrating on guiding the horses down the road.
Bets and Jenny were both so gentle they did not need
a heavy hand. But if something happened, she would
be here to help Laura.

She always wanted to take care of her stepdaughter.

The glow that had been kindled when she met the
scrawny little waif in the parlor at Mrs. Erskine's had
continued to grow steadily since that day. While she
had never considered marriage, and did not ever plan
on having children, it was becoming clear that her
preconceived thoughts about both were too black-and-
white.

Laura was her stepdaughter in truth, even if she
wasn't a wife in fact.

Jack walked up the drive toward the house. He told
himself that he needed to come in early after a day of
riding to wash up before having supper with Laura and
Ada. If he were really honest with himself, though,
he wanted to hear about Laura's first day of school.
He also wanted to take a walk with Ada. Since she
was set on the chapel, he would make sure she had
the chance to pick which part of the ranch to deed to
the church. There was a real pretty point just on the
other side of the hill, one that had a rugged and yet

spectacular view of the valley below. Perhaps he could convince her to come and see it.

The clip-clop of horses' hooves made him turn, and he spotted his carriage. Ada and Laura were sitting side by side, pretty smiles on both their faces. They drew closer, and he saw that Ada was not driving. Instead, Laura held the reins.

Fear paralyzed him as they sailed down the road, raising a cloud of dust behind them. Grasshoppers and jackrabbits leaped out of the path before them. If the horses bolted…if the horses shied…if Laura dropped the reins and they grew tangled in the wheels—a half-dozen scenarios played themselves out in his mind and he watched their approach, horror-struck.

"Father," Laura called as soon as she spied him. "Look. Ada said I should try."

He forced himself to nod at her, but his head bobbed slowly, as though he were moving through molasses. If he made any sudden movement, he could spook the horses. Bets and Jenny were calm enough creatures, but he had felt the same about other horses before. Occasionally, he had ended up in a ditch or flat on his back in the dirt when he let down his guard.

He waited for what seemed like an eternity until Laura had guided the horses around to the front of the house. After she drew them to a halt, he found the power to walk again. But he didn't walk. He ran as fast as he could, grasping hold of the reins as Laura jumped down from the seat.

His mouth was too dry to permit speech. He busied himself with tying the horses to the hitching post and gave his daughter a tense smile while she crowed about her driving skills. Then he went around to the other side of the carriage and helped Ada down, anger beginning to replace the fear that had struck him.

"Father, you don't seem a bit pleased," Laura said finally when he hadn't responded to any of her victorious cries.

"I'm not." If he didn't pace himself, he'd blow up.

"But, Ada said—"

"What were you thinking, Ada?" He turned to his wife. All the color had ebbed from her face. "Don't you know how dangerous driving can be?"

"It's not—" Ada began.

"All it takes is a second. I've experienced it myself, out on the range," he continued, cutting her off with a quick wave of his hand. "A rattlesnake darts out of the brush, and the horse flinches. My daughter's not old enough to be handling that kind of responsibility."

"Don't shout at her," Laura reprimanded him, her hands on her hips. "She didn't know you had forbidden it."

Ada looked helplessly from angry father to angry child. Then, suddenly, she broke into laughter. "You two look just alike. Oh my. Even your scowls are identical."

Jack looked at his daughter and recognized himself in her expression. He forced himself not to laugh, but a smile crept over his face anyway.

Laura stamped her foot. "Be nice to Ada, Father. She doesn't deserve to be yelled at."

"I'm sorry." He looked at them both in turn. "I was scared, that's all. I don't want to lose either of you."

Ada flushed a becoming shade of pink and turned away briefly. He had said it mainly to quell his daughter's ire, but if he thought about it, it was true. He couldn't lose either one of them now. He had come to rely on Ada in the short time they had been married, and now that Laura was here, he would never let her go back to the boarding school in St. Louis.

"Laura, you can drive, but only when you are accompanied by one of us," he continued. "Ada is a good horsewoman, and I trust her to handle herself well in an emergency. And you can only drive on the dirt lane leading up to the house. I don't want you running off across the prairie, not until you know it better. Is that understood?"

"Yes, Father."

Why did she refuse to call him Pa? He'd have called her out on it, but they had just achieved a tenuous peace. He would have to wait for another time to bring it up.

"I agree, Jack." Ada's color had returned to normal, and she gave him a brisk, impersonal smile. For some reason, that was disheartening. He'd like to see her blush again. She was so pretty when she blushed.

"Well, now that we have the matter of my daughter's driving settled, I want to show you a piece of our land." He emphasized the word "our" ever so slightly. "I think it would work well for the chapel."

"Wonderful." Ada turned to Laura. "Would you like to come along, Laura? You haven't seen much of the ranch."

"No, thank you." Laura bounded up the stairs of the house. "I want to change out of this itchy wool dress. I want a cookie, too."

He nodded, smiling. "Run along, sunshine baby."

It was perfectly fine with him to spend time with just Ada. He wanted her opinion of the land, and, also, he should apologize more deeply for almost losing his temper.

To be honest, the idea of a walk with his wife was very sweet.

Chapter Eight

Something ever so subtle had changed in Jack's demeanor. Ada took his arm as he led her down the drive and out into the pasture. Just recently, he would have been so angry with her for allowing Laura to handle the horses that he would have disappeared. In fact, when they'd first pulled up to the house, his expression had been so thunderous that she'd expected him to leave in a temper and not return for hours. Yet he had laughed with her when she couldn't contain her mirth at the sight of father and daughter mirroring each other. He'd changed his mind and was allowing her to help Laura adjust to life on the prairie. This was a good sign. Things were improving.

"You did a good job back there," she admitted as they crossed the pasture. The grass caught at her skirt, and she tugged it free. "Laura was beginning to feel you still think of her as a baby."

"I do still think of her as I did back then," he admitted after a short pause. "When I see her, I see the little bitty thing she was, being held in Emily's arms. It's hard to admit that she's bigger now."

"A little freedom will be a good thing for both of you, I imagine." The grass snagged her skirt again. For the sake of progress, she gathered a bunch of the fabric in her free hand, holding it so it cleared the ground. "I think you did absolutely the right thing."

"Thank you."

They fell silent again as the wind picked up, blowing against her so hard that she struggled to keep her head up. She wanted to say more. But how could she say, *Thank you for not abandoning us for hours just because you were upset?* How could she imply that she was grateful he had held his temper in check without admitting she found his usual method of dealing with anger off-putting, to say the least?

Growing up, she'd had a governess who would always say the same thing after she and her sisters fought: *least said, soonest mended.* That proverb might work well in this matter. She had already praised him, so now it was better to not belabor the point.

They crested a small hill, and as they reached the top, Jack pointed out across the land. "We could build the chapel here. It's a high point in some otherwise flat land. It's got a pretty nice view, too."

Ada gazed around them. The hill was just the right size for a building. It was high enough that everyone could see the chapel for miles around, given how low the surrounding area was. On the other hand, it was low enough that getting up and down the hill would not be a struggle.

She dropped her skirt, shielding her eyes with her hand. The view from up here was spectacular, a patchwork quilt of varying shades of green and brown fields, crisscrossed with fences. The sky seemed to touch the land at a distant point on the horizon. The wind still blew fiercely, but you expected that from a hilltop. It was more surprising to be buffeted about by the wind in a low-lying valley, but that was simply how it was in Winchester Falls.

"Oh, Jack," she breathed, taking it all in. "It's beautiful."

"If you want it, it's yours." He spoke quietly. "I'm sorry I raised such a fuss."

"Don't be sorry. Besides, we already talked about this," she reminded him. *Least said, soonest mended.* "Aunt Pearl and Mrs. Stillman will be so pleased. I'll be able to write to Edmund St. Clair and let him know that we are getting a home church. That, coupled with the fact that Laura is going to do very well in school, should help our cause quite a bit."

He nodded, gazing at the horizon. "You've helped out with everything so much. I don't think I've done much for you."

Ada pondered his words. Actually, according to the terms of their agreement, there wasn't much he had to do. The bulk of the work of change had rested on her shoulders, for it was crucial that she create a home environment for Laura that would please the St. Clairs. Yet somehow, she could not deny that she was a different person now than when she had stepped off the train onto the station platform.

"You've shared your family and your home with me," she replied slowly. "I appreciate that more than you can guess."

He didn't say anything but squeezed her arm more tightly against his side. As they stood together, looking out over the rolling pastures below, her curiosity was roused. Why would a man who was, for all intents and purposes, a good man, turn away from God?

"Why aren't you a praying man, Jack?" She said the words softly, doing her best to keep any tone of judgment out of them. She really wanted to know.

"God played me a trick." He wasn't angry, but his words were terse.

"How?" She would match his tone unless he grew angry. Anger would not help anyone or any situation.

He shook his head and sighed. "Ada, I don't know how to say this without sounding bitter. I've never said any of it to anyone, not even to Pearl. And Pearl has been like a mother to me. But you are different. You're helping me out above what I've asked you to do. I don't feel I can pay you high enough wages."

She demurred, but he rambled on.

"I fell in love with a pretty little lady, Emily. Laura's mother. I knew our life together was going to be perfect. Everything seemed right. Then we moved out here and our marriage fell apart. She yelled all the time. She cried. Emily hated life in Texas. I was stubborn, because I reckoned she had signed on for all the hardships as well as the fun. She was only thinking of the troubles we faced."

Ada nodded, but stayed quiet.

"When Emily and I were first married, I thanked God for bringing her into my life. Later, as things got worse, I began to harden my heart toward Him. Emily got to the point that she didn't even trust me to help raise our child. She turned to her father for help all the time. She spent months in Charleston. I don't know that we would have ever divorced, but she was planning to leave me and take Laura with her when she caught that fever. She passed away, and even as she was dying, she had no kind words for me." His voice, though still bitter, reverberated with sadness, as well.

Ada flinched. What a horrible situation to live in. Day in and day out, the one person who was supposed to be your partner would instead drag you down into the mire of hatred.

"I'm not proud of turning my back on God. I just felt so beat down," he continued, his head bowed. "I didn't understand why the Lord would bring Emily to me only to have us suffer so greatly. I figured my life didn't matter that much to Him. Then, when Emily's father took over guardianship of Laura, it didn't seem that God was listening to me. And that's why I am not a praying man."

She didn't know what to say. Her heart ached for Jack. In a way, too, she hurt for Emily. His first wife was likely spoiled and pampered, as Ada had been before her own life's circumstances forced her to change. Emily had probably been bewildered. Jack had likely been stubborn. It was terrible that such a wedge had existed between the two of them.

Without pausing to think, she turned and placed her arms around Jack, resting her head on his chest. She wanted, more than anything, to infuse him with strength and love. Beneath the surface of his shirt, she could feel his heart beating against her cheek. He smelled of saddle leather and horses, comforting smells that reminded her of the stable back in New York.

He stood still for a moment, as though surprised by her sudden embrace. Then, slowly, he folded his arms around her. She closed her eyes. If only this moment would keep going forever, if only she could make him feel the warmth and the truth that she felt by resting in God's word.

"I'm sorry," she whispered. It was all she could think of to say.

"It's not your fault," he replied, his voice tight with emotion. "You didn't do anything. If anything, you've been fixing everything that was broken."

"We've been working on building your home," she replied softly. "If this chapel comes to fruition, perhaps we can work on building your faith."

Jack didn't say anything. He didn't want to speak and say the wrong thing. If he did, he might break this wonderful closeness with Ada.

She was so small compared to him, and, yet, when she put her arms around him, he felt an incredible strength flowing into him. He breathed deeply. She smelled like starched linen and lily of the valley, two scents that were both pure and utterly feminine. Even with Emily, he hadn't enjoyed intimacy on this level, a communion of spirits.

He lifted his gaze over the horizon, and as he did so, he spotted a line of cows playing follow-the-leader, heading toward the shed he had built to house their feed. Was it really time to feed them already? He glanced up at the position of the sun in the sky. Yes, it was already late afternoon. It was time to come back to earth, and the realities and responsibilities of life.

"Ada, I have to get back to work." He heaved a disappointed sigh. "Thank you for listening to me."

"You haven't answered my last comment." Her voice was muffled against his shirt. "May we begin working on your faith, too?"

For a moment, he hesitated. It was all so much change. Since meeting Ada, his life was transformed. Before she came, he had lived in a house that echoed with loneliness. He had taken his dinner plate and eaten out in the barn so he wouldn't be reminded of how starkly isolated he was. His daughter had been far away in a boarding school. His wife had been dead for years, but her bitter last words still reverberated in his head.

"Why do you care?" He couldn't hold back the question. Unexpectedly, the pain and anger of his long isolation seared through him.

"Because I can't bear to see you so hurt." She tilted her head back and looked him in the face.

Her eyes held a tender light. She cared for him. She cared *about* him, rather. That was not a look of love, which was just as well. He couldn't love anyone yet, either. Not until his wounds had healed completely.

Ada Westmore Burnett cared about him as a friend. After years of exile from any kind of warmth or welcome, that was enough for him.

"Okay," he replied, the pain and anger ebbing to the back of his mind. "If you insist."

She gave him a final squeeze and pulled away. As she stepped back, the sudden loss of her sweet embrace was disconcerting and left him yearning for more. He'd have to impose a rule—no more hugs. After being alone, he was overreacting to a simple touch, and he needed to get used to that kind of thing slowly. It probably hadn't meant half as much to Ada as it had to him.

"I do insist," she replied firmly.

He chuckled. He couldn't help it. Ada was decisive in every little thing she did.

"Do you want help with the cows? Or shall I return to the house and begin my report to Edmund St. Clair?"

For a moment he thought over her offer of help. If he allowed her to help him, he'd be lengthening the amount of time they spent side by side. Given the rawness of his emotions and the sweetness of her presence, that could lead to trouble. Namely, he might start letting go of feelings he'd held in check for years, and that could lead to doing something absolutely stupid, like falling in love.

He wasn't willing to put himself in that position. Based on his experience, marriages went sour and love was fleeting. It was time for him to get back to what he knew best: working in the field. The brief moment on top of the hill was over, and he must return to work.

"You go write your letter," he responded easily. "I'll be back in time for supper."

"All right." She smiled and waved as she headed back down the hill. He watched her until she was a miniature figure heading across the pasture to the house. Then, and only then, did he trek down the hill to get the cows.

His pair of cattle dogs, Jud and Ed, were nowhere to be seen. They must be back at the barn. Sometimes they did that—heading back for an afternoon siesta and quick bite to eat before helping him herd the cows at dinner. He could go back to the barn and get them, but that would easily waste half an hour. He didn't want to break his promise to be home in time for the evening meal, so he would just herd them himself.

The cows lowed as he came closer. They knew that it was time to eat. He gave a whistle, and they began to follow him, organizing themselves single file in a long procession behind him. Perhaps Jud and Ed would hear his whistle and come loping along to help.

The sun was sinking lower in the sky. He'd have to hustle or he'd be late. The moment they reached the shed, he shook grain out of a waiting tin pail into a long trough. The cows lined up, as well trained as dogs, and starting eating. He checked the water trough. There was plenty of water and it was still running clear. All was good. Time to go home. The quickest way to get there was to cut across the pasture.

The sun trimmed the horizon with one last blaze of orange, and the fields out beyond the pasture turned a dusky purple. He breathed in deeply. This was God's country, no doubt about it. The wind was so free it made him feel as though he had wings, just like the hawk circling overhead. How could anyone prefer the rigid confines of city life to this? He had been born and raised in Louisville, Kentucky, but he never missed it. No, Winchester Falls was about as good as it got.

Up on the horizon, the house stood out in all its glory. A sense of pride filled his chest. This was his house. His family's house. The house Emily had refused to name. His enthusiasm ebbed when he recalled what she had said. "Why would we name something like that?" And then she had laughed in her harsh tone, as if the house wasn't worth her energy to think of. "It's nothing like Evermore."

After that, he had given up trying to make it home. If he referred to it at all, it was simply *the ranch*.

Lights came on, one at a time, throughout the house. It was captivating to see it light up little by little. Almost as if it were slowly coming to life as a living, breathing being.

He was about to turn toward the gate when a noise stopped him. He halted; the hair on his neck rose up.

The bull. That snort could only come from Asesino, the massive bull that belonged in the lower pasture. Someone, either him or one of the hands, must have forgotten to shut the gate in Asesino's field this morning. Now he was here and, like any bull, he considered everywhere he went as his territory. The animal wouldn't suffer an intruder gladly, and Jack was definitely an intruder.

Jack's mouth grew dry, and his heart hammered against his ribs. He slowed his movements down to a crawl. If he could slowly mosey his way to the gate, he could make his escape. He could shut the gate quickly and be safe. If Asesino hadn't noticed him, he would be all right.

There was nothing to do but edge along the pasture. He would be quiet and controlled. Even though his heart pounded like an Indian drum at a gathering of the tribe, he would make it.

In the pasture behind him, one of the cattle lowed louder than the others. The sudden sound startled Jack. He stepped clumsily, swaying a little as he tried to keep his balance.

Asesino caught sight of him and, with a mighty bellow, stamped his hoof.

If Jack had any spit left in his mouth, he would swallow. But he didn't. He couldn't even breathe.

Asesino charged.

With the instinct borne of many years as a cowboy, Jack bolted toward the gate. His boots pounded on the short-grass prairie. There was no way a man, unarmed and unprotected, alone and without any help, could do anything other than run. If he could make it to the gate, he could vault over it and be safe. This would then be a silly story he could regale Ada and Laura with later.

The bull's hooves pounded along behind him. There was no other sound on the prairie than his boots thumping against the earth and the bull's hooves hammering along behind him. He was going to make it. In just a few yards, he would be safe.

The bull slammed into him, knocking him off his feet. He landed against the fence, clutching it for dear life. He could not draw a breath. His back went hot and then cold. The rough barbed wire caught on his hands, sticking to him, pricking him mercilessly. With his last ounce of strength, he managed to pull himself over the fence. He somersaulted onto the earth, landing with a smack that reverberated through his body.

There were more stars in the sky than he had ever seen before. Stars swirled and twirled around him. The prairie was silent save for a strange buzzing sound in his ears. His mouth tasted like metal.

He closed his eyes. The swirling stars made him dizzy.

He thought of Laura. Would she be sitting at the dining room table, waiting for him?

plain old pants and a shirt. This was Ada's special request, though, and she deserved a proper wedding. "Can't make a silk purse out of a sow's ear," he muttered. "I'd do anything for Ada, though."

"I know you would." She reached across the table and patted his hand. "I think Ada would do the same for you. You both had so much love within yourselves. You had your love for Laura to sustain you, and she had her love for her sisters. Gus, her father, was never much in the picture. Ada cared for Vi and Delia as if she was their mother, not their older sister. It just made sense to me that two folks with so much love in their hearts, and so much loneliness in their lives, should be together."

Jack smiled, cradling his coffee mug in his hands. "I'm glad Vi and Delia are coming to visit. I guess I'd better go pick them up from the station in a few hours."

"No, indeed." The old woman grinned. "I haven't seen Vi and Delia in ages. I'm going there to pick them up by myself. I suppose the house is going to be crowded, what with Laura, Vi, Delia and me."

"I wouldn't say it is crowded." Jack was overwhelmed with feelings of love and gratitude, yet at the same time, he was struggling to say them aloud. It was hard to go from stubborn silence to open chattiness in the space of a few weeks. "When Emily was alive, I always wanted folks to visit. I wanted to share our home and offer generous hospitality to anyone who came to see us. But Emily didn't want that. She was ashamed of our home, of our lives together." He sighed. "Marrying Ada and gaining a family who wants to be at the ranch is everything I wanted."

She nodded, placing her coffee cup on the table.

"I used to feel kind of sorry for Emily. I could tell she was a sweet child, but one who had been used to getting her own way in everything. When she had to compromise or when things got tough, she cracked. You've been through worse with Ada than you faced with Emily, and you see how well she came through? The Westmores are made of sterner stuff than the St. Clairs." She chuckled.

"I agree. Thank you for having a hand in the matter—for arranging our marriage," he replied.

"It wasn't me." She gave him a wry smile. "I asked Ada that first day if she had faith, and she has grown in faith just as rapidly as a zinnia in the sun since her arrival here. So have you, for that matter. After being so badly burned by love the first time around, I could kind of see your perspective on the Lord. Mind you, I said kind of. I was always a little appalled by it, but I also understood how very bitter you were. It was God who brought you two together, and it's been a real pleasure to sit back and watch your faith and love grow. I'll be mighty happy to dance at your wedding today."

Jack didn't know what to say. It was a little discomforting to know that he had scandalized Pearl Colgan with his lack of faith and that she had loved him anyway and had entrusted her niece to his care. "I reckon you knew what was in me the whole time," he admitted at length.

"I reckon I did." She turned her attention back to her coffee, her eyes bright with what looked suspiciously like tears.

Laura bounded into the dining room, her long blond ringlets topped with a wide pink bow. "Oh, Pa," she exclaimed cheerfully, holding out a handful of flowers. "Pick one of these for your boutonniere. Reverend Caussey says that the groom should have flowers just like the bride."

Jack plucked a white zinnia from her offering. They were hardy flowers that would stand up to a day of wearing without looking wilted in just a few moments. "Have you been pestering Reverend Caussey already today?" Laura had been at the reverend's house weekly since his arrival, spending hours with the reverend's wife over lemonade. Already the Causseys had become an integral part of life in Winchester Falls.

"I was not pestering. I was helping." Laura fixed him with a gravely injured look. "Someone had to help decorate the chapel. Mrs. Caussey says I have a natural gift for tying ribbons."

"I'm sure you do." Pearl patted the chair beside her. "Would you like to go with me to pick up Miss Delia and Miss Vi from the station? They are going to be your aunts, you know."

"I'd love to." Laura squealed with glee. "I can't wait to meet them. Are they just like Ada?"

"Not exactly. They're younger, but they look like her. They are both concerned with politics, just like your stepmother, but they are more concerned about the conditions for poor people. Violet is a writer, and Cordelia used to assist in the slums of New York as a relief worker."

Jack inadvertently let out a long, low whistle. The Westmore gals sure were in possession of social conscience—that much was certain.

Laura fixed him with a sassy look. "What'd you whistle for?"

Pearl laughed. "I suppose he just understood what he was marrying into."

"To be real honest, I'd rather marry into a bunch of people who are ready to take on the world and change it than a bunch of people who are happy to just be in their own small corner of it," he admitted. It was true. Bring him all the suffragists and social workers in the world rather than a bunch of snobs.

"C'mon, let's go." Pearl rose, a little stiffly. "We'll be cutting it close as it is. As soon as we fetch the girls, we'll need to make tracks for the chapel. You don't want to be late, since you're the bridesmaid."

"All right." Laura followed Pearl out of the room and then paused on the doorway. Turning back, she gave her father the broadest, most genuine smile he had ever seen. "Bye, Pa."

He waited until the door shut behind his daughter before allowing the full weight of that cheery little goodbye to take effect. He had been so sure he had lost her to the St. Clairs. He'd felt the love she had for him that day when she told St. Clair that she would stay in Texas. She had called him Pa.

The richness of the blessings being showered upon him this day was truly overwhelming. Not only was he marrying, in truth this time, the most fascinating and wonderful woman he had ever met, he was also gaining a family. Some members of it, like Pearl, he had known and trusted for a long time. Some members, like Vi and Delia, he had never met. The most important inclusion, the one that made his heart leap with joy, was his own daughter. She was his little chickadee once more.

"Father, make me worthy of them all," he pleaded

aloud to the Lord above, his fervent voice echoing through the empty dining room. "Make me worthy of them all, I pray."

Ada turned to look at her veil in Mrs. Stillman's mirror once more. Her neighbor had provided her own bedroom as a dressing room prior to the ceremony, so that Ada wouldn't run the risk of accidentally seeing Jack before they made it to the chapel. "Are you sure I look all right?" Her reflection showed someone distinctly bridal, her hair arranged in careful swirls and her eyes bright with a heady combination of nervousness and joy. "I think the flowers are too much. I look silly."

"Nonsense," Mrs. Stillman replied heartily. "You look lovely, honey."

"Don't you dare touch them," Violet snapped, fanning herself briskly. "You'll spoil my handiwork."

Ada smiled at both of her sisters in the mirror. That they were here, before the ceremony, was a surprise. Aunt Pearl had not been sure they would be able to fetch them and get them to the chapel without being late. The train had been early, however, and Aunt Pearl had not spared the whip.

Delia sprawled across the settee. "You look bridal because you are a bride," she replied sensibly. "Aren't you happy to be so?"

"I am." Ada looked down at the silver-backed hairbrush on Mrs. Stillman's dressing table. Somehow, she didn't want anyone to see the depth of emotion on her face at this moment. It was too great to hide and yet too private to share.

"Good, because I'd hate to walk in there and tell

folks the wedding was off." Mrs. Stillman gave a chuckle. "Pearl Colgan would give me a talking-to, no doubt about it."

Ada smiled wanly at this jest, and at the same time, found it profoundly unfunny that anyone would joke about calling off the wedding. Not after all the time she had fretted about whether or not Laura would be staying with them and whether or not Jack would want to still be married to her. Of course, Mrs. Stillman didn't know any of her struggles. In fact, that worthy lady didn't realize that this was her first real wedding to Jack. She merely thought it was "kind of cute" that Jack and Ada were insisting on renewing their vows in the chapel.

Mrs. Stillman shooed them all out of the room and down the stairs. Laura met them in the vestibule, her entire face glowing with joy. Ada stopped to embrace her.

"Your veil," Vi moaned. "Please don't wreck it."

Ada fought an irresistible impulse to stick her tongue out at everyone and skip to the chapel with Laura, hand in hand. Her nerves were merely getting the best of her, and she simply must calm herself.

They were bundled into the Stillman carriage, with Ada squeezed between Vi and Delia, and Laura sat up front with the Stillmans. Aunt Pearl was meeting them at the chapel. Nervousness claimed Ada as it never had during even the most daunting feminist marches or even the day of the tornado. Was she really worthy of Jack and Laura? They were such treasures. How could she ever have felt against marriage or worried about having children? She couldn't imagine life without them now.

Ada. Where was Ada? If only he could shout loudly enough for her to hear.

"Ada."

Chapter Nine

Ada gave another quick, furtive glance out the dining room window. Darkness had fallen, and Jack still hadn't returned from feeding the cattle. No light glimmered outside. Surely if he had been delayed, Jack would ignite a lantern and carry it with him. The prairie was too vast to wander around without some kind of illumination. The moon was too new to shed much of its pale light onto the pasture.

She gave Laura a strained smile. She mustn't worry her stepdaughter, especially when their relationship had started to improve. "Let's start eating," she announced in a cheerful voice. "Your father must have been detained." She bowed her head and murmured a quick prayer.

"Amen." Laura helped herself to a roll. "Do you think Father is all right?"

Ada nodded. Her voice would likely betray a tremble if she spoke aloud. Jack must be upset. Even though she had grown closer to him when they spoke out on the hill, he must have been angered by her prying. She should never have meddled in his spiritual life. Now he would be gone for hours.

"I hope he comes home soon," Laura continued. If she felt disturbed by Ada's silence, she didn't show it. "I liked being able to laugh with him this afternoon. I don't remember much about what life was like here when I was a baby, but I imagine we laughed a good deal more."

Ada smiled and sipped at her tea. Not likely they did, because Emily wouldn't have had it. But, of course, she could never say that to Laura. Let the poor child imagine her parents as happy. It was kinder for her to picture them that way even if it wasn't true. In fact, the more she heard about Jack's miserable first marriage, the more she could see why he would have a skeptical view of the institution as a whole. As she knew all too well, marriage could wind up as a terrible trap.

She pushed her food around on her plate to make it look as if she was eating, but she could not bring herself to taste a single bite. It had been wonderful, for that brief moment, to experience such a kinship with Jack. Never had she felt that close to anyone, including members of her own family. Yet it must not have meant anything to Jack. At the very least, he was perturbed about it to the point of doing his usual thing—roaming out on the prairie until his anger abated.

She flicked another nervous glance out the window. It was terribly dark outside, though. Wouldn't Jack come in when it was so late? He did seem anxious to keep his promise to Laura to be home.

There was a sudden pounding on the back door. Ada rose so quickly she knocked her chair to the floor.

Cathy, seemingly unperturbed by the noise, wandered over to the door to answer it. There was a murmur of voices, and then the dining room door swung open.

"Miz Burnett, this is Mr. Burnett's hired hand, Johnny Macklin," Cathy announced, ushering the man into the room. He was slightly shorter than Jack and had a rugged, unkempt quality about him. His face was so weathered he could have been anywhere between thirty and fifty years old.

He ducked his graying head and lumbered into the light, where she could see him better. "Miz Burnett, I sure hate to disturb you while you are having your supper, but I need to speak to the Boss."

She shook her head regretfully. "I'm sorry, Mr. Macklin. Mr. Burnett hasn't returned from feeding the cows. Something must have kept him." Her cheeks flushed warmly as she attempted an expression of casual disinterest. Did Mr. Macklin know that her husband had a tendency to wander off, fuming, when upset? She raised her eyes to look at him.

He jumped, as though her words startled him. "How long has he been gone?"

"I'm not sure. I suppose we expected him half an hour ago." She smiled politely. "Would you like to join us until he returns?"

"No, ma'am." Mr. Macklin's craggy face now reflected a strange sort of alarm. "I need to find him right away. If he's not here, then something is wrong."

Ada's heart thumped painfully against her ribs. "What makes you say that?"

Mr. Macklin looked pointedly at Laura. Ada glanced over at her stepdaughter. She was staring at both of them with her mouth open, the dinner roll she had been eating now crumbling from her fingers. "Has something happened to Father?" she asked, her eyes wide with fear.

"I'm sure everything is fine," Mr. Macklin replied, his voice calm and friendly. "It's just that, well, our bull, Asesino, has gotten out of his pasture. I don't want the Boss to try to herd him back alone. That animal is too large and too ornery for a single man to handle."

He was being calming for Laura's sake, but Ada sensed the underlying trepidation that radiated from him. "Of course, we wouldn't want that." Ada tossed the words off as breezily as if they were contemplating a picture together in a museum. "I'll come help you. Laura, finish your supper. When you are done, I want you to change into your nightgown and ready yourself for bed."

Laura nodded, her face drained of all color.

Ada snatched her shawl from the back of the chair, more out of habit than any real need. The night air blowing through the open windows was cool but not chilly. She wrapped the length of silk around her shoulders and followed Mr. Macklin out onto the back porch.

"Miz Burnett, I don't want to alarm you, and I sure didn't want to scare his little girl," the hired hand said as they made their way across the darkened lawn. A feeble beam of light bobbed from the lantern he carried, illuminating their path. "I'll be side-gaited, but she looks like Miz Burnett. The first one, I mean." He cleared his throat awkwardly. "Anyway, Asesino is Spanish for assassin, and that bull lives up to his name. He charges at anyone who gets in his way. I don't know how he managed to get out, but he did. I hope Mr. Burnett didn't try to corner him alone."

"I hope so, too." She scanned the pasture around them, but it was so dark that she had difficulty seeing beyond the weak shaft of light from the lantern. She had no experience with handling cattle or bulls, but Father had briefly owned a stallion, Zeus, that had been a living nightmare. He was a handsome creature to be sure, but nasty tempered. He broke one groom's arm, another groom's leg and destroyed a stable wall before Father shipped him off to a breeder in Virginia. If Asesino was anything like Zeus, then she would remain terrified until she found Jack safe.

She stumbled in the dark, and Mr. Macklin caught her. "Take it easy," he admonished. "We need to slow down. If we get hurt, we'll be no help to the Boss."

She gathered two things from that remark. First, that Mr. Macklin must expect Jack to be injured. Second, that he expected to find her husband. She was horrified by the foremost thought but slightly heartened at the other. Even though every nerve within her strained to press forward quickly, she obligingly slowed her steps.

After a moment, Mr. Macklin said quietly, "I see something." He pointed to an object in the pasture that looked oddly out of place. It must be a pile of fabric, perhaps some rags buffeted about by the wind. But, as they drew closer, she picked out the vague outline of something. Whatever it was, it was not plant life; nor was it an animal. Her breath caught in her throat.

"Jack," she gasped.

"Yep, it's him." Mr. Macklin broke into a run, the lantern bobbing up and down with his stride. Ada struggled to keep up and to maintain her balance without tripping and falling. Jack was lying on the ground. He should not be doing that. Jack was vital, always moving. If he were lying down, he was badly injured. Or—

She grabbed her skirts in both hands and ran, her boots pounding across the tough prairie sod. Macklin reached Jack's side first. He set the lantern down and called, "Boss?" He knelt beside Jack. His face, deeply shadowed, registered concern.

"Is he alive?" Ada gasped, flinging herself beside them.

Macklin put his head close to Jack's, listening intently. "He's breathing."

"Thank You, God." Tears sprang to her eyes. "What happened? Why is he here?"

Macklin shook his head. "I can't tell. He's injured badly. He's breathing, but he's not conscious. You and I are going to have to carry him to the house."

Ada nodded. He was alive. He hadn't died. And there she had been, assuming that he was in a sulk. If Macklin hadn't come tonight, what would have happened? She couldn't think of that now. It wasn't helpful. The only thing she could do was to assist her husband now that she knew he needed her.

"The Boss is a big guy. I don't know how we're going to lift him. I don't know how he's injured, either," Macklin said grimly. "We're just going to do the best we can."

"Wait." Ada unwrapped her shawl. "Would this help? The fabric is very strong."

"Yep. I think we can use that." Macklin held the lantern up so that the fence line was lit. "The gate is closed. He must've been able to get away from Asesino. The old reprobate's probably in the pasture with the other cows." He rubbed his hand across his chin. "There's a couple of extra braces inside the gate. If I can pry them loose, we can make a stretcher out of your shawl."

"Yes." Ada could have cried with relief. "What a brilliant idea."

Macklin took the lantern and went over to the gate. Left alone in semidarkness with Jack, she took his hand in hers. Then she cradled his rough, callused hand against her cheek, as though she could will the strength from her body into his. *Don't die*, she begged. Laura had experienced so much loss and upheaval in her life. She needed her father.

Macklin grunted, and a splintering sound echoed across the still night air. Then he returned, two uneven wooden poles in his hand. Without a word, Ada placed Jack's hand on his chest and busied herself helping Macklin tie the fabric into sturdy knots. Together, they gently rolled Jack onto the stretcher.

Macklin looked from the stretcher to the lantern. "We can't carry both. Do you want to go for help?"

She shook her head violently. What if she left Jack with Macklin when he needed her? What if something even more terrible happened?

"I can go." He gazed down at her as she knelt beside Jack on the stretcher. "Is it all right if I take the lantern?"

"Of course. We won't move. We'll stay right here."

Macklin grabbed the lamp and made his way back up to the house, the lantern making a circle of light as he grew smaller in the distance. She was alone on the dark prairie, but, strangely, she was not afraid. Help was coming. Jack was alive. She would pray until someone came to rescue them.

She took Jack's hand once more. At first she began all the prayers she had memorized since childhood. After a while, though, she began to pray whatever came to her mind.

Jack was motionless on the stretcher, but the faint rise and fall of his chest beneath her hand made her feel more secure.

Could he hear her? She leaned over him and whispered, "Jack, I'm here. Everything is going to be all right."

There was a sound of distant shouting, and this time there was more than one circle of light approaching. Macklin must be bringing several helpers. She squeezed Jack's hand and then struggled to her feet.

Three men, along with Macklin and Cathy, came to her side. The men each lifted a corner of the stretcher, while Cathy supported Ada by placing her arm about Ada's waist.

"I'm quite all right," Ada assured her maid. "We shall carry the lanterns and walk ahead of the men."

The progress back to the house was unbearably deliberate and unhurried, but what could they do? Until they knew just how badly Jack was injured, they couldn't jostle him around. The darkness, even when punctuated by glowing lanterns, made for slow going.

When they reached the porch, Ada set down the lanterns and opened the back door. The men filed inside.

"Should we take him up to your room?" Macklin asked.

Ada opened and shut her mouth, unsure what to say. Jack had his room, and she had hers. Explaining just why they had separate rooms when they were supposed to be man and wife was embarrassing, and now was not the appropriate time.

"We'll put him in the room at the top of the stairs," she said. "In case he needs to make an extended recovery."

If the men found this odd, or if they found the room to be rather lived-in with Jack's things scattered about, they were too polite to say anything. They moved Jack carefully onto his bed, and his eyes opened and shut briefly.

"He might be coming to," Macklin said. "Should I go for the doctor?"

"Yes, please."

The other men filed out of the room, respectfully shaking her hand and introducing themselves as they left. She nodded and thanked each one. They were all cowboys who worked for Jack on the ranch. Thank the good Lord above that they had been available to carry him.

Ada drew up a chair and sat beside the bed, her heart finally resuming its natural beat.

There was a rustling in the doorway. Ada glanced over and beheld Laura standing there in her nightgown, her face pale and her eyes huge.

"Is Father all right?" she whispered.

"He had an accident. We think Asesino charged him," Ada explained, holding out her arms. Laura hesitated for a moment and then stole quietly into the room, accepting Ada's embrace. "Macklin has gone for the doctor."

"May I stay in here until the doctor comes?"

There were so many reasons to say no. Laura had school in the morning, and she would not be well rested if she hovered at her father's bedside. However, it was unlikely that she would sleep if Ada ordered her to bed. This was also one of the first times that Laura really wanted to be in her father's presence. It would be cruel to deny her this chance.

Ada nodded and pulled another chair to Jack's bedside. Then, after Laura had settled herself, Ada reached over and took her stepdaughter's hand in hers.

Thus they sat, silent and at peace together, waiting for the physician to arrive.

Jack drifted in and out of a cloudy mist. Voices spoke and then disappeared. Sometimes Ada was there. When she was there, he reached out to touch her. But he could never accomplish his goal. A sharp pain would stab through his middle, and he would gasp at the searing sensation that tore through his body.

Sometimes Laura was there. He would try to smile at her, because she looked so scared. He would try to say, *Hello, my little chickadee,* or *How's my sunshine gal?* The words were nothing but a dry rasp emanating from his throat. That seemed to terrify her more, so he would lapse into silence, allowing the fog to swallow him once more.

He was drifting. It was pleasant, but he missed his family. He missed work. A good day was a day filled with hard physical labor and the presence of Laura and Ada at supper that night.

He recalled that Ada was with him on top of a hill that night. She was holding him so he wouldn't fall.

The strength from her body flowed through him. She asked him if he would ever have faith again. He looked into her dark blue eyes, eyes the color of the bluebonnets that dotted the pastures in the spring. He said that with her help, he would try anything.

Then he was walking home. Something wasn't right. Something was following him. Whatever it was, it was strong and had no mercy. If only Jack could run quickly enough, he would be saved. So he sprinted for the gate, but he was too late.

Asesino.

Jack sat up suddenly, and the stabbing pain tore through his body so severely that he groaned. His torso was stiff, and he felt as if something was holding him in place.

"It sounds like our patient is awake."

Jack turned to see who that voice came from. The fog was rising, and he could just make out the familiar figure of a man. "Doc Rydell," he croaked.

"Yes, he is definitely awake and with us." Doc Rydell chuckled. "Mrs. Burnett, maybe you'd like to move to where your husband can see you. You are a sight prettier than I am, and he's been drifting in and out of consciousness for too long."

"How do you feel?" Ada drifted into view. She was just as pretty as ever, but she looked tired and drawn. He wondered what had happened to make her look so exhausted. Was Laura misbehaving?

He grimaced. The doctor laughed. "Don't ask a question like that of a man who has two cracked ribs," he admonished. "At least neither of your lungs was punctured, Jack. But you do have a sprained ankle and a few bad cuts on your hand. A man of your age and experience should know better than to take on a bull like Asesino by himself."

Now he remembered. Asesino had charged because he couldn't move fast enough to the gate. He had fallen, and there were stars in the sky.

"Ada."

"Yes, Jack." She moved to sit beside him, pulling a chair close to his bed.

"Is everything…okay?" Speaking was so difficult. He ran his tongue over his lips, but everything still felt parched.

"Yes, Jack. Everything and everyone in this house is doing very well, except for you." She gave him a sweet smile. Seeing her smile made him relax. "Laura has had a splendid few days in school, and I have been working to keep everything running smoothly without you."

He nodded, wincing at the pain even that small movement caused. "Good."

"Jack, you are going to be laid up a while," Doc Rydell interrupted. "The only thing I can do for broken ribs and a sprained ankle is to prescribe bed rest. I've got your bones set so they can knit back together. You need to allow your body time to heal before going back out on the range. Mrs. Burnett," he added, turning to Ada, "I am holding you responsible for him, as well."

Ada gave a weak smile. "I'm not sure he will listen to me. Jack loves to work."

"I'll be good," Jack rasped. He didn't want to cause any more trouble. "Promise, Ada."

She smiled again. "I promise, too."

Chapter Ten

The next morning, Ada pulled her riding habit out of her wardrobe. With Cathy's help, she would get dressed and be downstairs before the sun rose. If Jack was going to be laid up for weeks, he would begin to worry about how the ranch was faring. She knew as much about ranching as she did about running a house, but she had to at least try to help. Perhaps, if she were able to give a daily report to him about the ranch, Jack would stay still long enough to heal.

Her bedroom door burst open, and Laura danced into the room. "Cathy says I may walk to school today. Is that true? May I?" Her blue eyes sparkled.

"If you feel you can do so without getting lost or injured." Ada began to dress. "We are all going to have to be more independent and take on additional chores while your father recuperates. How do you feel about it? Is it something you wish to take on?" Of course, her stepdaughter was fairly quivering with excitement, so the answer was obvious. Even so, she had to make certain.

"Yes, indeed. I'm the only one in school who is

dropped off and picked up in a carriage," Laura mused. "The boys have started calling me Miss Fancy Lady. I don't like it."

"Very well, then. You may walk to and from school." Ada had gotten as far as she could without Cathy to help, so she grabbed her riding boots from the wardrobe.

"Are you going out riding today?" Laura cocked her head to one side. "That's a lovely habit. I haven't seen anything that stylish since we left St. Louis."

"Well, I am not riding for pleasure," Ada admitted. "But I do need to work on the ranch while your father is healing."

"But you aren't a cowboy." Laura flopped across her stepmother's bed. "That kind of work is done by men."

Ada tugged on her boots. "Nonsense," she said with a laugh. "All women are thoroughly competent creatures. I'm a good rider, and I can learn things quickly." Even though she still had trouble distinguishing between baking soda and baking powder and, of course, had nearly set her skirt on fire while lifting the bread out of the oven the day before.

"So...you're going to be a cowgirl?" Laura smiled with glee. "I can't imagine what Father will say to that."

"Your father was amply aware of my independence when he married me," Ada retorted with a smile. She stood, examining herself in the mirror. "Run and fetch Cathy for me. I need her help to finish dressing. You need to dress, too, young miss, especially if you are going to walk to school."

Laura jumped from the bed and trotted obediently

down the hall, calling for the maid. Amazing how little sulkiness she had exhibited over the past few days. Was that a result of gaining a small measure of independence? Had being allowed some agency given Laura the chance to think beyond herself?

Cathy interrupted these new thoughts with her arrival, and Ada's day began in earnest. As her maid finished helping her to dress, Ada reminded her, "I need to speak with Macklin before he starts his duties for the day."

"Yes, ma'am." Cathy stood back, looking at Ada's riding habit. "He is coming up to the main house before he heads out to work the cattle. I got word to him last night. Pardon me for saying so, but that's an awfully formal frock to wear on the ranch."

Ada held the gray worsted wool skirt out to the side as she examined her reflection in the mirror. The habit did seem to belong to an entirely different world—an ancient piece of history from an early part of her life. The gray jacket fit beautifully, revealing a snowy white shirt with a black-and-white striped stock. How she had loved this outfit when she first ordered it from the same Savile Row tailor her father frequented. It had been the perfect outfit for a serious suffragist to wear. Now, however, it seemed like the kind of costume for a masquerade ball, a gross exaggeration of what a wellborn woman with nothing better to do would wear to seem significant and important. "I can't do anything about that now," she said. "It's all I've got. I can't very well borrow Jack's clothes. They'd never fit."

Cathy chuckled. "Will there be anything else?"

"No. I'll follow you downstairs. I'm ready for my coffee."

She looped her skirt over her riding whip and trailed behind her maid, reviewing her checklist for the day. Once Laura was off to school, she would work with Macklin in the morning. Aunt Pearl was coming over to sit with Jack. Or sit on Jack, if he tried to get up. Then in the afternoon, she would stay with Jack so that Aunt Pearl could attend to matters at her own place.

Laura skipped out of the dining room, holding a piece of toast in one hand and her tin pail in the other. "I'm off to school," she announced proudly. "See you this afternoon, Ada."

Ada stooped and kissed her stepdaughter. There were a million things she wanted to say, such as to be careful and watch out for animals. She held her counsel, however. This was a big moment for Laura, and she didn't want to step on it by making her stepdaughter feel like a baby.

If she wasn't home within thirty minutes of school's dismissal, though, Ada gave herself permission to go searching for her. "Have a lovely day." She opened the door for Laura and nearly ran headlong into Macklin, who was raising his arm as if to knock.

"Mr. Macklin, do come in." She opened the door more widely and watched as Laura danced down the path to the front gate. "Would you care for some coffee?"

"Yes, ma'am." He took off his hat and followed her indoors. Ada shut the door behind him and ushered him into the dining room. "I have to say, the ranch is looking better than I've ever seen it. I meant to tell you so the other day, but we were a little busy."

She smiled at this understatement. So many Texans had the gift of phrasing things just so. "The ranch? You mean our home? Thank you. We have been working on it." She poured him a cup of coffee. "Sugar? Cream?"

"Just black." He took the cup from her, muttering his thanks. "Yes, the ranch. They never did name it. Some of the ranches around here have names, but not this one."

Many fine homes had names, come to think of it. St. Clair had mentioned his home, Evermore. Her father's family had lived at Silver Birch. Her mother's people had nested at Aingarth. Was it Jack's democratic manner that had kept him from naming the house? Or his strife with Emily?

"I understand you want to help on the ranch while the Boss is laid up." Macklin sipped at his coffee.

"I do." Ada poured a cup for herself and sat at the table. Once she had settled, Macklin also took a seat. "I think it will be easier for Jack to stay abed if he knows what is happening on the ranch each day. If I help out, even for half a day each day, I can give him a report."

"It's a good plan," Macklin admitted. "I wondered how you were going to keep him off the range."

"We can try it." She smiled and stirred her coffee. "I don't know that it will work, but I'm willing to give it a go if you are willing to have a greenhorn along with you."

"Sure thing." He placed his coffee cup, now empty, on the table. "I'm ready to go when you are."

Ada nodded. She would have liked to linger over her coffee a bit more, perhaps wait until Aunt Pearl arrived, but Jack's day always started early. Hers would, too. She rang the bell for Cathy.

The maid entered. "Yes, ma'am?"

"Is Mr. Burnett still sleeping?"

"He is. I just checked on him a moment ago."

Ada placed her half-full coffee cup down. "Very well. My aunt should be here in less than half an hour to sit with Mr. Burnett. Be sure to be on hand if she or my husband needs anything. I'm going out into the pasture and will be back in time for dinner."

"Yes, ma'am." Cathy smiled. "We'll make a hearty meal for you."

There was nothing to do but jump in. She had her riding gear on, and Macklin had said it would be all right for her to come along, even if she was woefully unqualified. "Well, Mr. Macklin, shall we go?"

"Yup."

Nervous excitement grabbed her. She was going riding, and she hadn't done so in ages. Even though she did not know how to accomplish the job she was setting out to do, at least she would be riding on the range. She would be helping Jack, too, and that thought was nice. When she had found him, crumpled and broken, unconscious on the pitch-black prairie, her first fear was that he was dead. Somehow, if he was dead, she had failed him. It was utterly ridiculous to feel that way, of course, but that persistent thought would not leave her. If she could help him a little every day, perhaps the horror of seeing him so helpless and alone after she had been sure he was off somewhere venting his temper would abate.

She rose, facing Macklin. "All right. I'm ready."

* * *

Jack was drifting down from the ceiling of his room. His nose itched unbearably, like in the spring when ragweed ran rampant and everyone sneezed. Somewhere, in the depths of his mind, he knew his body hurt. But then again, he didn't really care if it did. He was floating along, like a feather on a breeze.

"It's about time you woke up."

Jack's eyes flew open and fixed upon Pearl Colgan, who was sitting in a chair in the corner of the room. He blinked several times, trying to clear the fog from his mind. "Pearl?" His voice was raspy. "Where's Ada?"

"She's out with Macklin and the rest of the boys, learning how to be a cowgirl." Pearl set aside her knitting and rose. "Would you like some water?"

He nodded. It would feel good to ease the fire in his throat. "Why is Ada out on the range?" he demanded. Not that he minded having Pearl here, but it wasn't the same as having Ada beside him.

"She is picking up the slack. Never thought my niece had it in her, although she does have a can-do spirit." Pearl poured some water from a jug into a glass. "Can you ease yourself up a little? I can arrange your pillows for you."

"I've got it." With a mighty effort, he heaved himself so that he was using the headboard as support for his head and back. Pearl handed him the glass of water and then moved the pillows around to accommodate him better.

He drank, savoring the cool water that tasted of the well in the front yard. No other well on the property had water this sweet. Many times he'd considered having that well water bottled so he could carry it with him wherever he went.

"How do you feel?" Pearl drew her chair alongside his bed and took up her knitting.

"Half-past dead, but also as if I am floating on air," he admitted, taking another drink. "What has Doc been giving me? I hate this feeling."

"I'm sure it's laudanum or something like that," Pearl responded, her needles clicking rhythmically. "Two broken ribs—you need something to help with the pain so you can bear it."

"I can bear it just fine." He finished off his drink. "I don't want to be drugged up."

Pearl shrugged. "Suit yourself. You'll have to talk it over with Doc and with Ada. I imagine she'll raise a fuss if you do. Never saw her that white and shaken as the night she found you."

Images of Ada had drifted through his mind while he had been between consciousness and unconsciousness. He had seen her wide blue eyes and longed to touch a lock of her dark, wavy hair.

She was a friend—a good friend. A dear friend. A friend who happened to be a bought-and-paid-for wife, as well. If he allowed himself to think of her as more, he was certainly headed for heartbreak. Most importantly, he would lose the friend he'd found. Just as he had lost Emily once they moved to Texas, he would lose Ada if he allowed himself to think of her in a romantic way. Marriage had a way of doing that.

"I sent off the letter about the land for the chapel," Pearl continued, as though she hadn't spoken of Ada or that terrible night. "I just got the final, official word yesterday that they are willing to send the preacher out when we've built the chapel. So they are sticking to their promise. I guess I need to talk with Ada about getting some men together to build it."

He tried to sit up straighter and winced. "I'd help if it wasn't for these ribs."

Pearl nodded. "I know that. Ada does, too. More water?"

"Please." He was still so very thirsty. It seemed that nothing would quench his burning thirst.

He watched as Pearl refilled his cup. Something else had been bothering him. Thinking of Ada as a bought-and-paid-for wife had brought the matter back to the forefront of his mind. "Pearl," he said as he accepted the glass of water, "how can I pay Ada? It seems seedy to press a wad of bills into her hand. That was our arrangement, though. She has done so much, and I have been behind in taking care of that part of our agreement."

Pearl settled back into her chair. "Ada's main concern is her sisters, Violet and Cordelia. She wants to make certain the girls can finish out the year at their boarding school." She gave him an amused look over the top of her spectacles. "Though we all know how you feel about boarding school, it's a good thing for their family. It gave the girls structure. I imagine their lives with Augustus were pretty chaotic. He sure didn't care very much about watching out for them."

That could, in part, explain why Ada was so good at taking on things for other people. If she had been raised as the eldest in an environment of instability, she would have much practice making other peoples' lives more secure.

"If Ada thinks it's the right thing for her sisters,

then I trust her," he said. "Should I just pay for the boarding school? Send the money for them to finish out the year?"

Pearl took up her knitting again. "I think that would be real nice. I can get you the school's information."

He nodded and then sagged against the pillows. Talking and breathing were difficult. The plaster cast that squeezed his torso made him feel as if he were being gripped by a giant's hand.

Footsteps sounded on the stairs, and then Ada strode into the room. She was slightly pinker than usual, and her hair was disheveled. She had received, likely, the full benefits of prairie sun and wind.

"Jack, you are awake." She smiled at him and put her riding crop aside. "He looks better today. Don't you agree, Aunt Pearl?"

"I do, though I thought it would sound mighty cheeky to say so." The old woman accepted a kiss on her cheek from Ada and went on with her knitting. "Ada, Jack and I were just talking. He wants to pay for your sisters' year at their school. I told him that would probably be just fine. I know you were worried about how you were going to meet that expense."

Strange nervousness gripped Jack. Somehow, speaking of their arrangement aloud was a little strange. "If you want," he hastened to add. "I just realized you've done so much to uphold your end of the bargain and I haven't upheld mine."

"Of course," she replied. Was she blushing, or was her sunburn more readily apparent than he first observed? "I guess I should write and tell them I'm married."

Pearl threw back her head and laughed. "Child! You haven't told them?"

"There was so much to do…" Ada trailed off. "It's difficult to explain, too."

Ada was usually so decisive. Why was she hesitant to tell her sisters about their arrangement? Was she ashamed of their marriage? The old rising distrust of marriage began to well within Jack.

"You better tell them," Pearl scolded. "Tell them you landed a nice, handsome Texan and have a pretty little stepdaughter to boot."

"I'll tell them." Ada turned away and removed her hat. "Have you heard anything more about the chapel?"

Was she trying to change the subject? He wanted to question her about it, to press forward, but speaking was difficult and the medicine was making him too foggy for concise argument.

"I sure did. I was telling Jack that we need to start breaking ground. The sooner we build the chapel, the sooner we can get our preacher. I know that's something you have been wanting."

"Indeed. I wrote to St. Clair about it last week, along with the good news about Laura's schooling." Ada placed her hat on his bureau and turned to her aunt. "I'm here now, if you are ready to leave, Aunt Pearl."

"I guess I'd better mosey." Aunt Pearl began to ball up her knitting, stabbing the needles into it to hold it together securely. "How was your first day on the range, honey?"

"I think I acquitted myself well." Ada gratefully sank into the chair Pearl had vacated. "Macklin showed me how to count the cattle. It's difficult, isn't it, Jack? They keep moving."

They were back on common ground. She was his equal partner in this venture once more. He wanted to laugh with relief, but it would hurt too much. "Yup," he agreed. "It seems like an easy thing, but it's not."

Aunt Pearl patted her niece's shoulder. "You'll get the hang of it, just like everything around here." She waved goodbye to Jack and then promised to return in the morning.

Ada fluffed his pillows. As she bent over him, he caught the smell of horses and hay in addition to her usual lily of the valley.

She smelled like home, only better. Somehow, this made him feel worse. If she was becoming like home to him, then perhaps this wonderful friendship, the only one he had really known in his life, would end. Home was not a place where love grew.

"I don't like you working outside," he growled. Perhaps if she stayed indoors, he could keep her from growing away from him. "That's man's work."

"You don't really have a choice," she sighed. "Come now, Jack. See reason. It's good for me to get to know the inner workings of the ranch so I can help you more as I'm needed. I'm doing all right at managing the house, but we both know it's an effort for me. I am not naturally talented at domestic life, whereas horseback riding comes easily to me."

"Don't get injured, then," he replied gruffly. He had no strength to argue. She would slip away from him as Emily had. There was no hope for it.

"Says the man wrapped up like a Christmas present," she replied tartly. Then, as though unable to suppress her sudden emotion, she leaned forward and caught his hand, holding it lightly in hers as it was still crisscrossed with barbed-wire scratches. "It's wonderful out there. I know why you love it so."

He closed his eyes. Pain pulsed through him. Ada liked the ranch, unlike Emily. But the inner workings of marriage and home life and living together would put strain on their relationship in time. Leastways, he was familiar with that. He was tired, and he hurt and if his experience told him anything, he was going to lose Ada in the end.

Chapter Eleven

Ada eyed the team of men as they hammered nails into place. The foundation had already been laid, just a month after Aunt Pearl received her letter. These men, ranch hands from their place as well as Aunt Pearl's and Mrs. Stillman's, were now preparing to raise the first wall. Ada hugged herself with excitement. It was too bad that Jack was still on the mend and unable to see this sight. Perhaps she would have the chance to tell him about it later, once she came in for dinner.

There was a rustling in the grass behind her and, out of practice, Ada whirled around. Her right hand sought the pistol she now carried with her everywhere she went. Too many close calls with rattlesnakes and other varmints, as Macklin called them, had taught her to come prepared.

"Whoa, there," a familiar but still weak-sounding voice called. "Don't shoot. I come in peace."

Ada's heart surged with gladness as Jack's head, topped with his usual cowboy hat, came into view. Her happiness faded, however, when she recalled the doctor's orders. "Jack, you aren't supposed to be out walking until another two weeks have passed," she chided. "What if you reinjure yourself?"

"I won't." He walked so slowly that Ada made her way down the hill a bit to help him. "I've stayed in bed for a month now. There's only so much of that a man can take."

When they crested the hill, he paused, taking in the view. "They sure are working hard."

"They are, indeed. I think they are going to get all four walls up by the end of the day." She was right. It was better to take this all in with Jack beside her. Even though he wasn't supposed to be here, and even if he ran the risk of reinjuring himself if he wasn't careful. This was a part of his life, as well, and it was good to share in it.

Jack settled himself against a tree stump. "I reckon so. Wish I could help them. It takes all the fire out of a man to be laid up for so long."

"Don't fret," she admonished. "You'll be hale and hearty again in no time." In truth, that had been worrying her since she had found him that terrible night. What would happen when Jack was well again and able to go back to work? What if he had another terrible accident? What if he didn't merely escape with a few broken ribs? She had been working this land for a month now, and while it was beautiful and wild, it was also harsh and unforgiving. More than anything, she wished to lay her head against his chest and beg him to take up something less potentially violent. He should be a bank president or a postmaster. Then he might be safe.

Not that it was any of her business, really. She was

just looking out for him as a friend. It would be terrible for Laura to lose two parents in her young life.

The sudden clanging of the triangle on the front porch broke through her reverie. It was odd that the bell would be ringing now—dinner wouldn't be for another couple of hours yet. Ada turned and spotted Cathy, waving a towel, beckoning her to the house.

"Cathy must need me for something," she mused. "Shall we walk back together?"

"If I won't slow you too much," Jack agreed. He offered her his arm and she took it, marveling anew at his strength. Even after a month of recuperation, he was still far more muscular than any other man of her acquaintance. What would it feel like to have Jack partner her at a dance? He was likely a strong lead.

Ada broke off that train of thought. She must simply overcome her attraction to Jack, for he did not reciprocate. Moreover, as a staunch advocate of women's rights, she mustn't give way to the jellylike feeling in her knees whenever he touched her. It was unbecoming and ridiculous to behave in such a fashion.

They made their way slowly back to the house. Cathy ran to meet them halfway. Worry was etched in the frown on her face.

"What's the matter?" Ada cried with alarm. Never before had Cathy been quite so urgent. Not even the time when Ada allowed the bread dough to rise all over the kitchen counter until it spilled onto the floor.

"It's—it's a lawyer." Cathy panted, fanning herself with the towel. "A fancy city lawyer. He says he was sent here by her grandfather to check on Miss Laura."

"St. Clair," Jack growled. Beneath his sunburned skin, the color drained from his face. "That dog."

"Now, now." Ada used her most soothing and placating voice, even though her mouth had gone dry the moment Cathy had started explaining the situation. "Mr. St. Clair did say he would send his man of affairs to check on Laura. He must have received my letter and decided it was time for a fuller report." Ada turned to Cathy. "Did you show him into the parlor?"

"Yes." Cathy mopped her damp forehead with the towel.

"Did you offer him refreshment?"

"No. I forgot." Tears sprang to Cathy's eyes. "Oh, Miz Burnett," she wailed, "I plumb forgot."

"Don't cry." Ada patted her shoulder. "You did the right thing, fetching us without delay. Go into the kitchen and see what Mrs. H. has to offer. Give us a few moments to settle in and then bring everything in on a tray. Have Maggie help you if you need assistance. I made lemonade this morning. Be sure to serve it."

"Okay. But shouldn't I announce you first?"

Ada shook her head. Cathy needed to calm herself, first. If she appeared flustered, it could reflect badly on the household. "We will announce ourselves. What is his name?"

"Mr. Davidson, I think. Or was it Mr. Robinson?" Cathy shook her head. "I can't remember. Miz Burnett, I'm so sorry."

"It's quite all right." Ada gave her an encouraging smile, even though her stomach was quivering with nervousness. "We shall make the proper introductions."

She sent the maid on her way and then turned to Jack. "Remember, we agreed to this."

"I know." Jack's jaw muscle twitched.

"So we can't be angry at the poor man for doing his job." Ada threaded her arm back through his elbow.

Jack gave a terse nod.

Ada said a silent prayer as they made their way to the house. In the entry, she gave her appearance a quick check, tucking a few strands of hair back into place and smoothing her bodice. Jack looked fine. A trifle thinner than before, but of course the solicitor would not know how Jack had looked before his accident.

Jack led her into the parlor, and she cast quick, searching glances throughout the house. Yes, the furnishings could stand to be updated, but the house itself was much cleaner and nicer than it had been when she arrived.

The lawyer, upon seeing Ada, rose, extending his hand. He was a slight, nervous-looking man with pale green eyes and dark hair. One strand of it stubbornly stuck straight up in the air, despite his liberal use of Macassar oil. "You must be Mrs. Burnett," he said, taking her hand in his. His hand was damp, and Ada resisted the urge to wipe her own palm on her skirts after shaking it. "I'm Donald Davidson, Mr. St. Clair's attorney."

"How do you do?" She smiled and turned to Jack. "My husband, Mr. Jack Burnett."

The two men shook in a polite enough way, but Jack pointedly rubbed his hand on his waistband after greeting Mr. Davidson.

Ada took her place on a low velvet chair with needlepoint cushions. "Won't you sit down?" she queried. "Refreshments will be brought in shortly."

"Thank you, thank you." The man had a curious nervous tic, one that caused his mouth to dart to one side after he spoke.

Jack eased himself into a chair, grimacing as he did so.

"Are you all right?" The lawyer glanced curiously over at Jack.

"My husband had a run-in with a bull," Ada replied, putting on her best socially polite expression. "You can imagine. Broken ribs and a sprained ankle. But he is on the mend."

"How very peculiar," the attorney replied, nervously folding and unfolding his hands. "I always heard that you should stay far away from those animals. Everyone says they are ruthless."

"Yes, Asesino has quite a temper," Ada rejoined. "Unfortunately, he got out of his pasture and caught my husband unawares."

Mr. Davidson darted a glance over at Jack. "How did he escape?"

Jack shrugged. "I guess someone forgot to close a gate."

"Yes, but isn't that a rather large mistake to make?" Mr. Donaldson shook his head. "It sounds to me as though you don't have the proper checks and balances in place to make this a safe environment. Suppose, for example, that Laura had wandered into that pasture. This bull—Asesino—might have killed her. By the way, isn't Asesino Spanish for *killer*? Doesn't that seem like enough warning to be more careful?"

Ada swallowed. Despite the man's nervous gestures and tics, he was quite acute. She glanced over at Jack.

The muscle in his jaw twitched. Jack would lose his temper in a moment if she didn't intervene.

"Laura never goes out into the field alone." Ada gave him a reassuring smile.

"Where is Laura? I should like to speak to her." The lawyer glanced around the room as though waiting for Laura to jump out from behind the curtains.

"She is in school," Ada said reassuringly. "She should be home in a little bit. It takes her about half an hour to walk from the school house."

"She walks?" The lawyer drew back as though Ada had slapped him. "From the school? Across the prairie? Alone?"

Jack turned to Ada. "I never agreed to her walking to and from school by herself. Not until she got to know the prairie better. You were supposed to be taking her and picking her up when I was laid up. I thought Pearl was working with you on that." His expression was dark and unreadable.

Fear leaped into Ada's chest. "You would be amazed at how independent she has become," Ada responded, directing her answer to the attorney. She could not face Jack now. He was furious, surely. "She knows how to drive a horse and buggy, so I decided she was old enough to walk to and from school."

"You decided this without consulting me." Jack's voice was quiet and even, but it still made Ada shake with nervousness. "You knew how I felt about it."

At that moment, Cathy and Maggie burst in, laden with a hodgepodge of refreshments on two trays. With much rattling and clanking, they served everyone. Ada's head began to pound and perspiration broke out across her brow. Could anything else go wrong?

After the maids left, the attorney turned to Jack. "It sounds as though your wife has made a rather important decision about your child without consulting you." He served himself a sweaty glass of lemonade.

"Jack was laid up, and I was helping the ranch hands with the cattle every morning," Ada protested. "I knew Laura could walk to and from the schoolhouse just fine. She has made a success of it every day for about a month now."

Jack folded his arms across his chest and fixed his glare out the parlor window.

"Is this your progressive viewpoint on life, Mrs. Burnett? I heard from Mr. St. Clair that you are a suffragette." Mr. Davidson sipped at his lemonade and then froze. His face contorted, and tears filled his eyes. He glanced about desperately and then ran across the room to a potted plant in the corner. He spit into it, heaving mightily.

"Are you ill?" Ada stood in alarm. "What happened?"

Mr. Davidson gasped. "Salt in the lemonade? Is that your attempt at levity, Mrs. Burnett?" He grabbed his handkerchief from his pocket and wiped his eyes. "I have seen and heard and experienced enough. I will have to make a report to Mr. St. Clair about all this."

"It was a simple mistake," Ada retorted, her head giving a painful throb. "My housekeeping skills lack polish, Mr. Davidson, but I would never do anything like that on purpose."

Jack still sat in his chair, staring out the window. He did not make a move to protest.

"Even if you hadn't salted the lemonade, I would still be making a report to Mr. St. Clair." Mr. Davidson wadded up the handkerchief and stuffed it into his pocket. "It is obvious that this is a dangerous environment to raise a child in. Moreover, you and Mr. Burnett are not in accord when it comes to key points about Laura's upbringing. That would create a stressful environment for her, and my first thought must always be about Laura's welfare."

"But—" Ada stared at him, horror rising within her. "Can't I just—"

"If I leave immediately, I can just catch the afternoon train. Before I depart, though, I will send a wire to St. Clair from the station. Good day." The attorney showed himself out of the room, leaving Ada alone with Jack.

As the parlor door slammed shut, Jack looked over at Ada. She was as white as a sheet.

Served her right.

At best, he was going to get a scolding and a visit from Edmund St. Clair. At worst, he was going to lose his daughter.

Ada had one job to do—to make his home the kind of environment that St. Clair would find agreeable for Laura. He privately thought she had been doing a good job of it, even with her frequent kitchen and housekeeping mistakes. Allowing and encouraging Laura to walk alone to school, however, was an entirely different matter.

"Jack, I'm so sorry." Tears streamed down Ada's cheeks. "I thought I was doing so well."

He wanted to yell with frustration, but he couldn't do that without hurting his ribs. He wanted to hurt

Ada as much as he was hurting now, knowing that his daughter might be lost to him forever.

She sank back onto her chair and began to sob, cradling her head in the crook of her arm. She clearly felt bad. She *should* feel awful. Jack stared at her heaving back and had the oddest sensation of wanting to pat and soothe her until her sobs ceased.

That was a dumb thought. He shouldn't be comforting her. She should be finding a way to fix this problem.

At the same time, the incident with Asesino had started this whole mess. Had it never happened, Ada would not have taken on his chores and he wouldn't have been completely out of it this past month. His accident had been just as alarming to Davidson as the fact that Laura was walking home.

What infuriated him most was that Ada hadn't consulted with him first. She had made the decision on his behalf and given Laura permission. She had overstepped this boundary when she allowed Laura to drive the first time, and, against his better judgment, he had allowed it to pass without making too much of a fuss.

For someone who insisted on equality, Ada certainly did take the lead on a lot of matters dealing with his own daughter. There was no partnership there, even though she asked to be treated as his equal. Instead, she treated him as someone to be kept in the dark while she allowed Laura free rein. For her stubbornness, he might now be losing Laura to boarding school.

"Let's go," he finally said, rising stiffly.

Ada lifted her tearstained face from the crook of

her arm. "Where?" Her eyes widened, as though she were frightened.

He heaved a sigh. "To school," he replied. "I don't want Laura walking home alone anymore, no matter what you say. For the few days I still have her, she will abide by my rules."

Ada choked on a sob but rose to her feet. She reached inside the sleeve of her gown and withdrew a handkerchief, dabbing at the tears coursing down her cheeks.

He led her outside onto the front porch. There was an odd silence across the prairie. Something wasn't right. The sky had turned a strange color of green.

"Ada, we need to make tracks," he said, keeping his voice low and even. "I don't like the look of that sky. Can you hitch up the buggy?"

She nodded. "I'll hurry." She jammed the handkerchief into her sleeve and ran toward the barn, her skirts flying behind her.

He glanced up at the hilltop, where the men had been building the chapel. They had departed, and the hill no longer rang with the sound of hammer blows and men shouting. Against the eerie green sky, the chapel looked exposed, as though its skeleton had been left there by some wild animal after the flesh had been consumed.

He fought to keep his anxiety in check. The men must be on a break. They would go find Laura and bring her home. A storm was brewing, and like all storms in Texas, it would come in with a great deal of fury, then burn away quickly.

Ada brought the buggy around to the front of the house. The horses, normally so placid that they would stand still without being tied, pranced nervously, pawing the ground. He leaped into the seat, forgetting in his haste about his cast. He jerked around awkwardly and grabbed the reins from Ada.

Without a word, he whipped up the horses, giving them their heads. The beasts responded by streaking across the driveway and lurching the carriage along the main road. Ada braced her feet and hands against the sides of the buggy, watching him with eyes that were huge, but she didn't say a word.

They were driving straight toward a towering wall of clouds. The sight of them made the hair on the back of his neck stand up, but there was nothing to do to avoid them. If he were going to get Laura home safe and sound, he would have to drive straight at the storm.

Rain began to spatter, huge drops that hurt as they hit his skin. Then the wind began to slice at them, strange, cold swaths of air utterly unlike the sultry atmosphere that had hung over the prairie all day. Although the temperature was dropping, it was not a refreshing feeling. Instead, it drove him onward, and he urged the horses forward with all his might.

Hail pinged against the carriage, bouncing and rolling all around them. "Get in the bed of the buggy and wrap yourself up," he shouted to Ada.

"No," she shouted back. Then she reached behind them and grabbed a canvas from the back of the buggy. Leaning forward, she sheltered both of them with the canvas as the hail continued to fall.

The horses whinnied and danced sideways. Jack pulled over to one side and urged the horses to stop.

Turning to Ada under the makeshift cover, he admitted his greatest fear.

"I don't think we can reach Laura."

Chapter Twelve

"Don't say that. Of course we can," Ada said and grabbed Jack's arm. Her stomach had grown icy at the realization that this disaster was completely and utterly her fault. She had put Laura in danger. She had no idea that storms on the prairie could be this violent.

Jack whipped up the horses again, and she sheltered him with the oilcloth as he drove. He was urging the horses forward, but they were running against both hail and wind, sliding sideways and causing the buggy to jounce wildly. Ada braced her feet against the floor of the carriage and used all her might to hold the canvas over Jack. If he could see, he could try to drive.

"Maybe her teacher held them at the schoolhouse." Ada was still going to cling to hope. "Perhaps if Miss Carlyle saw this storm coming, she kept them from leaving."

Jack's brow furrowed as he focused on the road before them. "Could be."

Ada's heart lurched. Jack was an experienced cowboy. He was used to life in Texas. If he was concerned and upset, it was because there was good reason to be.

Please, God, just let her be safe. Just let her be safe.
She repeated the prayer over and over in her mind,
scanning the horizon for any sign of Laura.

The schoolhouse was a short distance from the
house, but merely reaching the halfway point was
taking an eternity thanks to the deplorable weather
conditions. Jack had to slow the horses to a crawl as
they picked their way along the road, now slippery
with mud and rivulets of water.

Ada's heart pounded. She squinted as she looked
around. Surely her stepdaughter had stayed at the
schoolhouse. Miss Carlyle seemed too sensible a creature to allow her students to leave shelter when such a
dreadful storm was looming. On the other hand, the
storm had come up so quickly. Was it possible Laura
had left before things looked bad?

Through the lashing rain, Ada peered at the ditch
ahead of them and caught a glimpse of black and gray.
"Laura!" she cried, tears of relief mingling with the
raindrops coursing down her cheeks. "Jack, stop! I
see Laura up ahead."

She dropped the canvas and leaped down from the
carriage without bothering to wait for Jack to halt the
horses. She slipped and slid, twisting her ankle violently and tearing her skirt on a corner of the buggy.
She cupped both hands over her mouth. "Laura," she
yelled with all her might. Then she moved forward
as fast as the storm would allow her with an injured
ankle.

Laura was huddled against a fence post, her
eyes squeezed shut. She looked as though she were
sleeping—or worse. "Laura," Ada screamed again.
"We came for you, darling."

She fell to her knees beside her stepdaughter, catching her in her arms. Laura opened her eyes. "Ada? I didn't think you would come. I thought the storm was too strong. Where's Father?"

"I'm here." Jack slowly lowered himself beside them. "We are safe." He took them both in a strong embrace, and they huddled together. He pulled the oilcloth over them as a makeshift shelter.

As suddenly as it had begun, the rain and hail stopped. The wind ceased to howl, and all became quite still and calm across the prairie. The storm had ended. They would be able to go home now and change into dry clothes, and find some way to get out of the mess Ada had gotten them all into when she failed in her part of the bargain.

Jack pulled away from them slightly, tugging the oilcloth from over his head as he stared intently up into the sky. The wind began to howl anew, making eerie, moaning sounds. Ada shivered.

"Tornado," Jack muttered. He pointed at a patch of dark, greenish-looking clouds. "We're going to have to hunker down."

As Ada watched, a tongue of clouds swirled low and touched the earth. It was the most bizarre, surreal thing she had ever beheld. The howling intensified, sounding for all the world like the train whistle as the train pulled in to Winchester Falls station.

She had never seen a tornado before. She never knew such a thing existed. Jack, however, looked more alarmed than he had on this entire journey. His green eyes were narrowed against the wind, and his complexion was drained of color. Behind them, the horses broke free of their reins. They took off across the prairie, dangling one long strap of leather. The buggy bounced crazily behind them, teetering on two wheels.

"Get down in the ditch," Jack commanded as he jerked Laura up from her huddled position. He grabbed Ada's hand and tugged her down to the watery ditch below. He threw both of them facedown and then covered them, lying between them and draping the oilcloth over them.

"Why can't we run?" Ada demanded. This was all so strange. Surely, even without the buggy, they could outrun that strange mass of clouds.

"There's no time. We are safer in the ditch."

She didn't see how, but Jack knew the prairie better than she did. So she hunched down under the oilcloth and took Laura's hand in hers. Her daughter said nothing, but she shivered violently.

After a few moments, Ada moved forward gingerly to peek out from under the canvas. The tornado had gone back up into the clouds, and she breathed deeply with relief. "We're safe," she cried. "It's gone."

"I don't trust it." Jack didn't budge. "Tornadoes are mighty unpredictable. Stay down, Ada."

Ada followed his directions. She would not argue with Jack, certainly not now when they were facing definite disaster. It was her fault that they were in this mess. Had she gone to pick Laura up in the buggy, they could have sheltered in place at the schoolhouse until the storm passed.

Ada glanced up. The tongue of clouds came back down from the sky, closer than before. The train-whistle sound caused the hair on Ada's neck to stand up. She pulled Jack and Laura into her embrace, holding them as tightly as she could.

Please, God, save us all. She began praying silently, but then spoke it aloud, over and over as a litany. Laura joined in her prayer, her teeth chattering so loudly that her words made little sense. At length, Jack joined in. Ada's heart surged as she heard his strong voice take up her prayer.

Here, in a water-filled ditch, as a tornado barreled across the prairie, they had become a family.

If only, through His grace, they could make it through this together.

She dared not look up. She could only pray. She could only hold on to her small family for dear life. She held Laura tightly and cradled her head against Jack's chest, taking care not to put any pressure on his injured ribs.

The screaming wind died away, and cold dread filled Ada. Before, that silence meant that the tornado was gathering strength. It must be about to touch down again.

Jack rose carefully, fixing his eyes on the sky. "It's over."

Ada brought herself to a kneeling position. "Are you certain?" It was true, this calm didn't feel quite as eerie as the first, but she would never trust her own instincts again. Not after this day.

"Yep. This is the calm after the storm." He helped Laura to sit up.

They remained silent for a few moments, disheveled and rain soaked. Ada glanced down at her hands. They were streaked with mud and bleeding from scratches.

She was here with her family. Of course, she had other family elsewhere. Violet and Delia were tucked away safely in private school. Aunt Pearl had sheltered somewhere, no doubt. This was, though, the first time that she had really considered Jack and Laura to be her kin. It was a strangely warm and yet terrifying emotion.

What if neither of them reciprocated the feeling?

When her nerves had calmed to the point that she could speak without bursting into tears, Ada turned to Laura. "Why did your teacher allow you to leave? Wouldn't it have been safer to stay at school?"

Laura shook her head. "The storm hadn't started when we left. It just looked like it might rain." She stared down at her sodden dress. "I hope my friends were able to get home safely."

Her friends. A sob choked in Ada's throat. Laura was making friends despite her stepmother's anxiety about the prospect.

"It's a good thing we found you before the tornado hit," Jack replied tersely. He pointedly looked away from Ada as he rolled up the wet oilcloth. "This is exactly the reason why I don't want you walking to and from school by yourself."

Ada's heart sank. Now that the crisis was over, they had to deal with the very real problem of losing Laura to boarding school. "Your father is right," she admitted, her voice quavering. "I should not have allowed it. I thought this land was as safe as one of the parks back in New York. I was terribly wrong. I put you in unnecessary danger, Laura. I put your father in peril as we chased across the land trying to find you. I'm so sorry. I can't apologize enough—to both of you."

She could not bring herself to look at either one of them. Instead, she attempted to rub the mud off her hands onto her soaking-wet skirt.

"It's not your fault, Ada." Laura patted her arm.

The gentle gesture made tears spring to Ada's eyes.

She would not cry. Weeping like a baby would not cure any of these problems.

Jack didn't say a word in reply to her apology. Instead, he hefted the oilcloth under his arm.

"We better start walking," he announced, his voice tight. "We've got to see if the ranch is still standing."

She had not considered that. All her energy had been bound up with finding Laura and making sure that they survived the storm as best as they could. What if something happened to their home?

She nodded and held out her hand to Laura. Together, they trudged down the muddy road, slipping and sliding. The horses and buggy were nowhere to be seen. They would have to hike all the way back to the ranch, which was now over a mile away.

Suddenly, marching in a women's suffragist parade didn't seem that brave. The slow steps she had taken that day, proudly holding a banner aloft as she sang "Daughters of Freedom" as loudly as she could, seemed easy compared to plodding along in the mire. Back then, she had been pelted by rotten tomatoes thrown by jeering bystanders. She would relive the humiliation of that fear a hundred times over if it meant never feeling this helpless and frightened again.

What if something terrible had happened to the ranch?

She thought she had weathered the worst of the storm. Living through it, however, was not the worst part. No, what scared her most was the anticipation of what had happened while they were huddled together in the ditch, trying to survive.

What if, while finding each other, they had lost everything else entirely?

* * *

Numbness settled over Jack, wrapping him in several layers of cotton, dulling his senses. Sounds and sensations were muffled. Nothing was sharp or clear, not even the sight of a piece of straw driven through a fence post. Twisters inflicted strange types of disaster. Anyone who had lived through a Texas spring knew that.

Laura was safe. Despite trying to walk home in the jaws of a terrible storm, she had survived. Ada had pulled through, too. The two women of his household had managed themselves very well. Emily would have fainted. Then, in the midst of the calm after the storm, she would have thrown a fit. At least Laura and Ada were taking the event in their strides.

They crested the field that looked over the ranch, and Jack paused. He scanned the entire view for signs of devastation. The Stillmans' tree break had been damaged. Instead of being knocked down all of a piece, some trees had been uprooted and tossed aside like playthings while the ones beside them remained untouched. Fences were down everywhere.

The ranch still stood, though not unscathed. The cedar-shake roof had been peeled back in a couple of places, but the house looked all right beneath the damage.

Ada stood beside him, looking over the view. She gasped, her hand covering her mouth.

"What is it? What's wrong?" he demanded, looking again. The ranch was all right. Why was she so upset?

She shook her head, pointing at the hilltop beside the house. The chapel, a promising skeleton earlier in the day, lay in pieces. From their vantage point, it was as if a bomb had been dropped in the midst of construction. Everything, even the foundation, would have to be rebuilt.

"It will be all right." He couldn't have her bursting into tears now. Yes, they knew that the ranch was all right, but they had no idea if all the people at home were safe. "We'll just start over."

"We promised that we would be done in time for the preacher's arrival." Ada's eyes filled with tears. "I don't see how we can start over and make that time frame."

"Don't cry," he ordered fiercely. He could stand anything but her tears at the moment. There was too much still left to see and determine. "Everything will be fine."

Laura clung to Ada's side, burying her face in Ada's rain-soaked skirts. Both of them likely thought he was being as temperamental as Asesino. This was how a man should face disaster, though. He couldn't just go to pieces because the shell of a building had been destroyed. There were much bigger matters at stake.

He motioned for them to follow and made his way slowly down the hill. The numbness was ebbing, replaced by a stabbing pain that jolted with every step he took. He must have reinjured at least one rib during the storm. That meant more time being laid up, stuck in a plaster cast, while St. Clair and that attorney of his tried to take Laura away. He could have shouted in frustration, but that wouldn't help. He would just have to keep putting one foot in front of the other until they reached the house and, after that, day by day until this whole mess reached its conclusion.

Following a small eternity punctuated only by the

sounds of Laura and Ada sniffling, they made it back to the ranch. Macklin was standing in the front yard, giving orders to a group of hired hands that were gathered around him. As soon as he spotted Jack, a look of sheer relief crossed his rugged face.

"Well, I'll be side-gaited," he hollered. "We wondered what became of y'all. Did you make it to the schoolhouse?"

"Nope." Jack held out the oilcloth. "We stayed under this in a ditch until the storm passed. The horses and buggy are gone. We'll have to send out a search posse to find them."

Macklin nodded. "We'll put a team of men on it. Say, Boss, perhaps you should rest awhile. You look peaked."

Jack waved his hand tiredly. "No. I'm the man of this house." He couldn't resist cutting his eyes at Ada as he said it. Yes, it was petty, but he had been through a lot that day. "Ada and Laura, you two go inside and change out of your wet clothes. Have Maggie start brewing some strong coffee."

Ada nodded, and if she was offended by his jabs at her expense, she held her tongue. She put her arm around Laura and led her inside. After the front door closed behind them, Jack turned back to Macklin.

"Some of Laura's school friends walked home, too. I'm worried those kids ended up riding out the storm by themselves. Maybe the best thing to do is have a bunch of men ride out to see all the damage and look for anyone who was stranded. The storm came up so suddenly, I reckon a lot of people were caught unawares."

Macklin nodded and motioned to the hands. "Grab your horses. We'll meet back here in a few minutes."

Jack watched as the men strode off. "Everything okay here?"

"Lost some part of the roof," Macklin replied, pointing up at the damage. "But everything else seems all right. We haven't checked on the cattle yet, though. We had just gathered up when you all came home. We were going to send a search party after you."

"Thanks," Jack replied. He could always rely on Macklin to stay calm in an emergency. That was why he'd made the man his lead hand when he bought the ranch. "Gotta say, I think I hurt myself. I'm not sure I can ride for the pain. If you have a chance and you see Doc, would you send him up to the house?"

"'Course." Macklin paused for a moment, his brow furrowed with confusion. "Now, didn't you have Pearl Colgan with you?"

Jack shook his head. "Why?"

"Some of the hands saw her go streaking across the pasture on that horse of hers," Macklin replied. "It was after you left, before the storm got real bad. I thought maybe she had gone to find you or to fetch Miss Laura. Maybe she changed her mind. Maybe good sense got the better of her."

"Maybe so." But he doubted it. Like his wife, Pearl would go after someone in distress even if it put her in harm's way. His stomach dropped like a stone. "Y'all haven't seen her since?"

"Naw," admitted Macklin, shrugging his shoulders. "But if you didn't see her on the way home, then I reckon she turned around. You go on up to the house, Boss. I'll send the doctor your way if I see him."

"Thank you." Jack turned to go inside. Then he paused. "You know, I don't hurt so bad. I'll join you."

If Pearl Colgan was missing, then he would help find her. Ada didn't need to know about any possibilities like that. She had been through enough that day.

"If you're sure," Macklin said.

"Sure enough," Jack replied.

Chapter Thirteen

Ada and Laura entered the house only to be engulfed in hugs by Cathy and Maggie. Ada was astounded. Never had she been embraced by servants before. Even the long succession of nannies and governesses through her childhood had been quite strict and standoffish with the Westmore girls. She patted both women's shoulders, marveling at the free-and-easy manner of Texans.

"We were so worried about you," Cathy cried. Her eyes were a telltale shade of red. "I thought for sure you'd be hurt."

Ada's ankle gave a painful throb, a reminder that she wasn't completely unscathed. "It looks like everything weathered the storm, except parts of the roof," she said, wrapping her arm around Laura's shoulder. "Is everyone here all right?"

"Yes, ma'am," Maggie spoke up. "We made it to the root cellar in time. The men were going out to check the animals, and they already told us that the chapel had been hit."

"It was." Ada struggled to keep her voice soft and

even. She had already given in to tears once, and she would not let her anguish show again. There was too much to do. First, they would change into dry clothes. Then she would meet Jack and start making a list of repairs to be done. She would work on organizing the tasks for the hands, the servants and the family.

"Cathy, would you draw some warm baths for Laura and myself? We were soaked to the bone. Maggie, start brewing a large pot of coffee. When I'm bathed and dressed, I shall take a bracingly hot cup of tea. I do not share the Texan love for coffee in the middle of the afternoon."

Both women nodded and scurried off to do her bidding. She turned to Laura.

"Come, darling, let's go upstairs. You can change out of your wet things and wrap yourself in a blanket until your bath is ready."

Laura gave a tired nod. Streaked with mud as she was, and with those large purple rings under her eyes, she looked like a little street urchin. Ada helped her up the stairs and to her own bedroom.

"Ada, do you mind staying with me? I don't want to be alone." Laura paused on her threshold, looking up at Ada with a pleading expression on her face.

"Of course." Ada followed her stepdaughter inside, settling down on a rocking chair in the corner.

Laura changed out of her wet things and wrapped herself in a quilt. She lay on her bed as Ada rocked. The quietness of the room was such a marked contrast to what they had endured that day. It was difficult to believe that the attorney's visit, the storm and the tornado had all happened on the same day—and that the day had not yet ended.

"Ada, I was really frightened." Laura rolled over to look at her. "I thought I was going to die."

"We would never have abandoned you out there to the elements," Ada reassured her, keeping her tone soothing and light. "We would have found you no matter what."

"I know. It's just that—" her lower lip began to tremble "—nothing like that happened to me in St. Louis."

"I never went through anything like that, either, living in New York," Ada agreed. It was important that Laura not feel completely alone and isolated in her experience. "I suppose tornadoes are common on the plains, though. Your father knew what was transpiring and took precautions to protect us."

"It's just—can I just say that I don't like Texas very much right now?" Laura's eyes filled with tears. "I miss St. Louis."

"Of course, you can say that to me." Ada crossed over to Laura's bed and gathered her, quilt and all, into her arms. Laura probably shouldn't say that sort of thing to Jack, for he was likely to take it as a slur on the home he had created for his daughter, but she could vent to her stepmother. "You've been through a lot today, and you are exhausted."

"I hate a lot of things about living here," Laura admitted, her tears beginning to stream down her cheeks, unchecked. "Grasshoppers are about the ugliest bugs I have ever seen, and they are everywhere out on the prairie. Some of the boys and girls at my school still smell bad. It's hot here, too."

Ada patted her stepdaughter's back. "I know, I know," she murmured. A child who had faced a tornado thinking she was about to die was entitled to vent her frustrations about her new life.

"Sometimes I think I'd like to go back to St. Louis," Laura muttered fiercely. "My classmates didn't smell bad. There weren't any grasshoppers or tornadoes."

"But your father wasn't in St. Louis," Ada reminded her gently. "He's created a home for you here. He wants you to live with him so badly. He made many changes in his life so that he could bring you home."

"Can't we all move to St. Louis together?" Laura picked at the fringe on her quilt and gave Ada a hopeful glance. "There are a lot of pretty houses in town, close enough to the school that I wouldn't be a boarder anymore."

"I think your father is a Texan through and through." Ada tried to smile. "It would be hard for him to leave the ranch and go to a city. He loves it here so much. This is his home."

Now it was her turn to tear up. Jack had worked hard to bring Laura to Texas. What he wanted was simple—a comfortable home and his own family. Thanks to her disastrous reception of St. Clair's attorney, he was likely in danger of losing everything he had worked to create.

Then, too, there was the question of what Laura wanted. Was her stepdaughter merely tired and upset, as she had originally suspected? Or was Laura being honest about what she wanted, after giving life in Texas a try and finding it lacking? If she really disliked life here so intensely, would she welcome the chance to go back to boarding school if the attorney pressed for her return?

There was a knock at the door, and Maggie and

Cathy came in, bearing a steaming tub of water between them. "Time for your bath, Miss Laura," Cathy announced cheerfully. "Miz Burnett, we set up a tub in your bedroom, as well."

Ada thanked the maids as they departed. "See if you don't feel a little better after your bath." She gave her stepdaughter a final pat and rose. "I'll check in on you after a while."

She made her way toward her bedroom, and as soon as she closed the door behind herself, she allowed her own tears to flow freely. What a terrible day. What a mess of a day. The tears continued even after she had bathed and dressed in dry clothes. Somehow, it was as though she would never be happy and purposeful again.

Her ankle had swollen to the extent that putting on boots was impossible. She switched to her slippers. There had been no noise of men coming in from checking on the cattle while she was changing, so Jack must still be gone. If she sat on her chaise longue and stared out the window, no one would know that she had slacked off for a few moments. It would do her ankle some good if she rested, and she must compose herself before seeing anyone. Going to cheer Laura up while she had red eyes and tearstained cheeks was not a smart plan.

She rested on the lounge and gazed out over the prairie. The sun was shining, painting the bizarrely trampled fields with light. The complete destruction of the chapel was laid bare. Ada swallowed, blinking rapidly as she gazed down at the ruins of the building to which she had pinned such hopes. She would not cry any longer. Tears wouldn't help repair the damage done both by her actions and the storm.

When she had arrived in Winchester Falls, Aunt Pearl had asked her cryptically if she had faith. Well, of course, she had. Every well-brought-up Christian girl did. Over time, she had come to feel the hand of God working in her life, and in Jack's and in Laura's. Though Jack had brought them together as a family because he needed a proper wife, they had been knitting together as if they truly were kin.

She closed her eyes against the ruins of the chapel and saw Jack's expression when he found out she had let Laura travel to and from school alone. How painful it was to have him gaze at her with such contempt.

She was supposed to have faith that God was still working in her life, but that was difficult to believe. In fact, if anything, she felt abandoned and alone. Was He there with them now? Or had He forgotten them?

Her door opened creakily, and Ada sat up hurriedly, dashing her hands across her eyes. Laura, freshly changed, stole into her room. "You said you were going to check on me," she reprimanded, fixing Ada with a reproachful glare.

"I'm sorry, darling. It's my ankle. I had to put it up for a while." Ada lifted the hem of her skirt so that Laura could see the swelling. She held out her arms. "Shall we rest together?"

Laura nodded and snuggled next to her on the chaise. Ada patted her tousled, wet curls as they both gazed out of the window. Her heart surged with love for Laura. Poor thing. She had tried so hard to do right by her stepdaughter, and how spectacularly she had failed.

As they gazed together out the window, Laura pointed. "Look," she cried. "It's Father."

Ada leaned forward to get a better view. Yes, Laura was right. Jack was riding across the pasture, sitting more stiffly than usual—probably due to his cast. She had not seen him ride in weeks, and the sight of him in the saddle once more made her feel that everything would be all right.

"Is that someone riding with him?" Laura queried. "It looks like there is more than one person on Blue."

Ada squinted harder. "What on earth? There is someone on his horse, riding pillion. They must have found someone injured when they went to check on the cattle." She scrambled to tug her slipper on. Rest time was over. If Jack needed help, she would be there to help him. It would do no good to sit in here and feel sorry for herself because she had made such a hash of things before.

"Come, let us go help," she said, tugging at Laura's hand. "Someone needs us."

"Jack, you're just being stubborn." Pearl snorted, hanging on to the saddle. "I can walk just fine."

"Nope," Jack responded easily. Pearl was alive, and that was all that mattered. He wasn't taking any risks until he had her back at his house, safe and sound. "Keep holding tight."

"If you were my son, I'd give you what for," Pearl snapped. "Seems like you are treating me like an old lady. Well, I'm not. My house might be gone and my leg might be broken, but I could still sit in a saddle better than you. Especially with your busted ribs."

Jack just shook his head. He couldn't suppress the

wry grin that spread across his face as Pearl continued to berate him. When he had seen her house—or to be more to the point, what was left of it—he was certain that if they found her, she'd be dead. Then, remembering that she had ridden away from her house, he searched across pastures for her until he saw her, still clinging to a fence. Though she had been bucked from her mount and broken her leg, she was trying to walk back home by clinging to the fence and pulling herself along, inch by inch.

"I suppose y'all will have to put up with me until I can build a new place." Pearl sighed. "Was there anything left, Jack?"

"Not really," he replied. He could be straightforward with Pearl. In fact, if he tried to smooth things over, she would call him out for bluffing. "It was a pile of sticks. Though the odd thing is, your kitchen table was still standing, with a bowl of peppers on it. The whole house was in splinters around it, but those peppers didn't look like they'd moved an inch."

"Sounds like I get to start from scratch. Well, that's all right. I've always wanted a smaller place, ever since R. H. died." Her voice was crisp and practical, but a thread of sadness ran through it. "I'll never forget when we finished that house. We hosted a barbecue and a dance for everyone in the county. Back in those days, you can imagine how many people that was. Just a handful compared to today. But it was a mighty happy time."

They were nearing the house, and when they arrived, there would be a bustle of activity. He might not have a chance to speak privately to Pearl for a while.

"Seems like it happened a year ago, but St. Clair's

lawyer came to see us today," Jack blurted. It would be better to just come out with the truth. "He took one look at my busted ribs, one sip of Ada's salted lemonade and heard that Laura was walking home—and he lit out. I reckon he's going to tell St. Clair that this isn't a proper place to raise a little girl." The pain in his ribs gave a twinge. "He could be right. After all that's happened, I'm not sure."

"Don't talk like that," Pearl replied sharply. "A girl's place is with her father. If Ada is still having trouble with housekeeping, I'll help her while I'm staying with you."

"Her housekeeping is the least of our troubles," he admitted. "What about the dangerous part of life on the prairie? I've got broken ribs. Laura got caught in a twister on the way home from school—walking home by herself, something I'd never approve. Your house is gone. The chapel is blown to bits. Maybe it is just too rough in this part of Texas to raise a family."

"Now, hold on." Pearl grabbed his arm and shook it to get his full attention, even though she was riding behind him. "First of all, you are a cowboy. Dealing with animals is part of your job. It's a risk you take. If you worked in a city, you'd have to worry about danger, too. Pickpockets might try to rob you. You could get knocked down by one of those newfangled streetcars."

"True," he admitted.

"As for Laura, well, that child is more protected than any other on this prairie. Didn't you and my niece go after her, even in the teeth of a storm? Wasn't I riding out to find her in case y'all didn't reach her in time? Meanwhile, the adults around her are bruised and broken because we rushed to save her." Pearl chuckled.

Why did everything Pearl said make sense? She was the kind of person who should be the county judge. She was just so good at laying out and answering every side of an argument. After all, she had brought a truce between Jack and St. Clair and had come up with the plan of having Ada marry him.

"Thanks, Pearl." Jack couldn't sigh because it would hurt too much. Some of the anger and frustration ebbed away from him, though. They could find a way to make this work.

"Jack, there's danger wherever you go. Poor housekeeping skills can be mended. Laura can start riding a horse if you want her to get home faster. If Ada can learn to use and carry a gun, maybe Laura can, too, when she's older." Pearl tugged at his sleeve. "Now whip up this horse of yours. I'm tired of riding. I want some coffee, and I need to rest this leg of mine."

He obliged. He was tired, too. He wanted to see Laura and Ada and reassure himself that they were still safe. Until he saw them again, he had this feeling that making it back to the ranch as a family had never really taken place.

They arrived home, and as he neared the front porch, Ada and Laura burst out the front door, followed closely by Maggie and Cathy.

"Aunt Pearl!" Ada ran forward, her gait strangely hobbled. "What happened?"

"I had a fresh horse that couldn't stay calm in a storm," Aunt Pearl explained, her tone nonchalant.

Jack rode over to the mounting block. "I think her leg is broken," he told Ada. "She was going after

Laura, too. I found her in the middle of a pasture, clinging to a fence."

"Talking about me like I'm not here," Aunt Pearl muttered, swatting his arm. "This is the second time I've wished you were my son today, just so's I could give you what for."

"He is your nephew-in-law," Ada reminded her with a wan smile. "Will that do for at least one lecture?"

She and Cathy and Maggie huddled together, helping to create a sort of human sling. Pearl slid off the back of the horse and into their outstretched arms. For the first time since he'd spotted her, the color really had drained from her face.

The three women lifted Pearl and carried her up the porch and into the house. He sat for a moment. It was all right now. Laura was safe, and so was Ada and so was Pearl. In a few hours, the men would be back with the cattle count. His house was still standing, even if Pearl's had been wiped off its foundation.

The pain in his ribs returned, and nausea overwhelmed him. It had been a long day, the longest of his life.

"Father?"

He glanced down. Laura stood on the mounting block, smiling at him hesitantly. Then she held out her hand.

A surge of love shot through him as he saw her small hand. She was alive. She might go back to St. Louis, but she was alive. That was all that mattered. Whatever the lawyer said or did, he had his daughter with him for the time being. He should enjoy it while he could.

He dismounted carefully, looping Blue's reins over

the mounting block. After the way the horses had been acting all day, he wasn't taking any more risks. Then he climbed down slowly and took his daughter's hand.

Together, they walked into the house.

Chapter Fourteen

"Miz Burnett?" Macklin called as he entered the front gate. Ada rounded the corner of the porch to meet him. In the few days since the twister had hit Winchester Falls, Macklin had been her primary source of news about the community. With Aunt Pearl laid up with a broken leg and Jack's ribs having to be reset, she had two invalids in the house. Moreover, both invalids were stubborn and hardworking, making it nearly impossible for Ada to keep them still enough to get the rest they both needed in order to heal.

In order to accomplish this, Ada had confined her work to the house and relied on Macklin's twice-daily bulletins to keep the ranch running. Between the two of them, they planned the repair of the house and organized the myriad tasks that had to be completed in the wake of the storm's destruction, from mending fences to felling destroyed trees. They had also planned to have the leftover splinters of Aunt Pearl's house burned and the foundation swept clean.

"Hello, Mr. Macklin," Ada responded. "Are you off to run the cattle?" It was a fine morning for it, nice and breezy, with none of the sultry humidity that had plagued them before the storm.

"What's left of them," Macklin replied, removing his hat as he approached. "The Boss isn't going to like it, but we think we lost about a fifth of the herd to the twister. It took us a couple of days to make sure. We've checked every inch of the ranch now, and we're pretty sure they're gone."

Ada's stomach dropped. "Is that a lot?"

"It's not the worst anyone's ever seen. The Stillmans lost half of their herd. Any loss means hard times for the ranch, though." Macklin sighed. "We still can't find the carriage or the bays, either. That's going to be hard for him to take, too. Those horses were his pride and joy. We haven't seen a trace of any of them—not even a splinter of the carriage. I'm sorry, Miz Burnett. That's just the way of tornadoes. They cause a lot of strange damage."

"I appreciate you telling me," she replied. How on earth would she break the news to Jack? As soon as he heard, he would want to jump on a horse and go investigate on his own. "I'll let Mr. Burnett know." Somehow. Some way.

"One other thing." He held out a piece of paper to her, stiff with dried mud. "I found this letter bound up in the fence along the west pasture. It's addressed to you. When the post office got hit, this letter must have gone flying. Thankfully, the fence caught it."

"Is the post office still standing?" She accepted the letter. So much had been damaged beyond repair that she was afraid to ask. The post office was the heart of the town, though, the glue that held them together. If it was gone, then it would be difficult for Winchester Falls to get back on its feet.

"It spun around on its foundation." Macklin chuckled and dusted off his jeans with his hat. "Craziest thing I ever saw. Its front porch faces back and the back faces front. A bunch of letters must've gotten scattered across the prairie, including yours. But the building is still standing."

"That's something, anyhow," Ada replied. "We'll see you back this evening. Maggie said they are making chili and corn bread for you and the men tonight. Be sure to let all the hands know."

"I surely will." He tugged his hat back on and waved goodbye.

Ada glanced down at the mud-covered letter in her hand. The postmark, as smudged as it was, could still be read. New York. It had to be from her sisters, Violet and Delia.

Her hands began to tremble as she tore at the envelope. Even though she was the eldest and knew what was best for the family, it had still been unnerving to have to tell her sisters she had married and was now trying to raise a ten-year-old on a ranch in Texas. To protect Laura from potential gossip, she had not told her sisters all the details of her situation—they did not even suspect she was a bought-and-paid-for bride, meant only to be Jack's way of securing his daughter.

Which was just as well, for she had—as far as they knew—failed at that task quite miserably.

She sat on the front step and unfolded the letter.

Dearest Ada—

Violet and I are rather taken aback at the news

that you are newly a bride and a stepmother, and yet we know you will be happy. After the breakup of our own family, and the loss of our home, it must be a nice thing to have both family and home again.

Ada, we miss you.

We like school, of course, but a part of us feels lost without you in New York. After Father died and there was no way for us to remain together, it was hard to come back here.

When Mr. Burnett, your new husband, gave our money to the school, he included a note to each of us saying we are welcome to come home anytime. That's how he phrased it—*home*. Vi and I have talked it over, and we may not want to return after the term ends. In fact, we wish to visit you during the Christmas holidays. Life in Texas may be hard, but life without family is even harder.

If we fit in well enough in Texas, we will make plans to stay there at your ranch after the term ends. Maybe you can find cowboy beaux for us, as well.

Vi just cuffed me as I wrote that. She wants me to remind you that her interest is solely in exposing injustice. She wants to study Indian life and culture and write about it. As one who is invested in alleviating poverty, I would be happy to work with her on that endeavor. As we understand it, the Indians endure harsh conditions at the hands of our government.

We should also like to remind you that if Mrs.

Lucy Stone can elect to keep her last name, so, too, can you.

At the very least, as an advocate of women's suffrage, you should style yourself Mrs. Westmore-Burnett. That does sound and look rather distinguished.

We shall see you at Christmas. The school closes on 19 December for the holidays, and we shall take the train.
Much love,
Delia

Ada folded up the letter and placed it in her lap. Then she buried her face in her hands. Part of her wanted to laugh, while the other part wanted nothing more than to cry. Her sisters wanted a home in Texas, rather than a life at boarding school. She had worked so hard to keep them there, and now they wanted to be here, at the ranch.

Of course, it would be wonderful to have Delia and Violet with her again. The only problem was, she wasn't sure that she still had a home with Jack. If Jack lost Laura and she had to return to St. Louis, then there was no need for Ada to stay in Texas and pretend to be his wife. Aunt Pearl's house had been demolished by the twister, so it wasn't as if she could just go stay with Aunt Pearl and invite her sisters to stay there until the situation resolved itself.

What was she going to do?

The storm had disrupted mail service and the telegraph lines were down, so there was no way to tell if St. Clair had been apprised of his attorney's visit. If the man had made it quickly enough to the train and headed out before the storm, he could have already informed St. Clair. He did have enough time, surely. Didn't he?

There really was no way to know for certain. Nor could she write to her sisters and alert them to the situation until the mail service had been restored to Winchester Falls. What if they heard about the twister and began to worry that she had been injured or killed?

Behind her, the front door opened. "Miz Burnett?" Cathy's voice sounded distinctly tired and frazzled.

"Yes, Cathy." Ada grabbed her letter and rose. "What do you need?"

"Mr. Burnett is up and tried to dress himself and nearly broke his ankle in the process. He's back lying down, but fit to be tied. He wanted to speak to Mr. Macklin. Miz Colgan is ordering Maggie around, talking a blue streak. They've both been asking for you. Many times."

"Very well." Ada followed the maid inside. Duty was calling to her. As her governess had taught her, *least said, soonest mended.* She would write to her sisters as soon as she could. They had several months until the Christmas holidays. Perhaps, if she gave everything a few weeks to settle, she would have a better answer for them.

Right now, she had other things to do, chief among them caring for two stubborn invalids.

Jack watched from his window as Ada drove the old, seldom-used gig out of the front yard, the one that had been pressed into service when the carriage was destroyed. She must be on her way to pick up Laura from school. Since the storm, Ada had faithfully taken her to and from school, not once saying a word about giving Laura the opportunity to walk.

Not that Laura would have taken it. She had become much more silent and introspective since then, no longer speaking her mind about things. All of her school friends had been found safe and accounted for, so she could not be sad about an unexpected loss. It was as though the rain and wind had quenched some internal spark of hers.

To be honest, he missed that little fire. Though he had been burned by her outspoken ways and wanted to think of her as a baby still, he had gotten used to knowing what was on his daughter's mind, even if he didn't agree with her at all times.

The same thing had happened to Ada. She was quiet and gentle where before she was a whirlwind of energy with a sharp tongue. Dark circles now ringed her eyes, and the corners of her tender mouth were always turned down, even when she attempted to smile. He had been awfully hard on her both before and during the storm. Had she taken his words, uttered without thinking in the midst of crisis, to heart?

He needed to talk to Macklin. Only by finding out what was happening on the ranch from his own top hand could he begin to understand what was going on within his own family.

"Cathy!" He bellowed as loudly as his ribs would permit. "Get me Macklin!"

"Hush up, Jack, I'm trying to sleep," Aunt Pearl yelled from the next room. "Go and fetch him yourself, if it's such a big deal."

The old woman was right. Ada was gone, so he could risk sneaking downstairs. He made his way to the steps and took them slowly, trying to not bend forward as he did so. The wood floor felt cool on his bare feet. Funny, he rarely walked around the house barefoot. Usually he was in boots, striding through on his way to work on the ranch. It was strange and slightly humiliating to be creeping down the stairs in his bare feet, almost like a kid sneaking out for candy.

At the bottom, he collided with Maggie. "Why, Mr. Burnett, what are you doing out of bed? Miz Burnett would have a fit if she saw you," the maid admonished.

"What she doesn't know won't hurt her," he responded. He was still the boss of this house, no matter how capable Ada was at managing things in his absence. "Where's Macklin?"

"He came out to the kitchen for a snack," Maggie rejoined. "Do you need him?"

"Yep, bring him in the parlor. I don't think I can make the stairs again, just yet." Jack hung on to the wall. He was as tired and limp as a rag doll. "Hurry."

Maggie nodded and went off to do as she was told. Jack inched his way across the vestibule and into the parlor. He had just managed to settle himself on one of the settees when Macklin came in.

"Boss, what are you doing up? If Miz Burnett knew—" Macklin began.

"Aw, hush. How would she like it if she knew you were taking time off to eat snacks in the afternoon?" Jack gave him a withering glance. "I imagine you are just hankering after Maggie."

Macklin turned a telltale shade of red but tried to bluff his way out of his obvious embarrassment by shrugging. "Naw. Cleaning up all the mess is just makin' me hungry, that's all."

A likely story. He'd seen Macklin making sheep's eyes at Maggie for weeks now. He'd better press forward or else Ada might return before he was done. "How bad is it?" Now he could cut to the heart of the matter. "How much did we lose?"

Macklin sat in a nearby chair and put his hat on the floor beside him. "Hasn't Miz Burnett told you?"

"Nope. She's been too busy with Laura," he responded. Why would his best hand ask his wife to tell him what was going on with his own ranch? "Give it to me straight."

"We lost about a fifth of our cattle. The carriage and the two bays are gone, can't find them anywhere. Part of the hay coming up in the west field was flattened, but I reckon we'll still get a good crop. Miz Burnett and I have been working to make sure everything gets taken care of, don't you worry."

Jack sat back for a moment, his ribs sending little shooting pains through his body. "A fifth of the cattle?" That was a lot. On the other hand, if others around them had lost cattle, too, then the price might go up. Scarcity always made prices rise. "As long as we've still got hay to feed them."

"I think so. Miz Burnett came out and looked at the field. I explained to her how it worked—when we harvest, and how we do it, and how we store the hay. She was mighty interested and quick to catch on, especially for a city gal." Macklin shook his head. "If you'd ever told me that a Yankee would come down here and take over running the place while you were laid up, I'd have said you were crazy. But she's as smart as they come, and sensible too."

For some strange reason, it filled Jack with pride

to hear someone speak of Ada in this way. "You think I would pick a bad one?" Jack replied with a chuckle.

"I suppose you learned your lesson," Macklin replied laconically, his eyes fixed on the floor.

All right, that was a direct hit for his crack about Maggie. He should have expected that one. "Yup. I sure did."

They were silent for a moment. Then Macklin, as though he wanted to make peace, spoke up. "Truth is, I'm not the only one who feels this way about Miz Burnett. Folks in Winchester Falls have been seeing how well she's taking care of the ranch, especially while you've been laid up. There's not much to the town to begin with, but what's here has been damaged. When I went up to look at the post office, the postmaster mentioned that maybe we should have Miz Burnett head up a committee. She could sort of gather people together and plan how and when to fix everything."

Jack considered the matter for a moment. Ada had been looking wan and withdrawn the past few days. The twister had taken its toll on her, and so had that attorney's visit. His injuries and Aunt Pearl's hadn't helped. Yet, despite these hardships, life at the ranch remained relatively smooth. Meals were still served. Laura was going to school, and Ada was taking her there. Repairs were being made. She really was becoming an integral part of life out here.

"I think Ada is capable of anything," he replied, running his thumb over the pattern of the fabric on the settee. "If the townspeople believe she should head up any reconstruction, I'm not going to stand in the way. In fact, I think she'd do a good job of it."

"I suppose I oughta ask Miz Burnett if it's something she wants to take on," Macklin replied. A huge grin broke over his rugged face. "People will be happy to hear it if she decides to go for it. All the repairs to the post office and the train depot will go a lot faster if she's organizing things and telling people what to do."

Jack nodded. Ada was doing a great deal of work for other people, helping out with Aunt Pearl's place while her broken leg mended. She had also taken on a huge chunk of running the ranch for him, riding cattle and consulting with Macklin for weeks on end. All of this was done quietly and efficiently, without complaint. She was a true ranch woman, proficient at the things that mattered, and good at bossing others to do the things she couldn't handle as well. She was so good at doing things for others. Wouldn't it be nice to do something for her?

"What's going on with the chapel?" He kept his eyes turned down toward the pattern on the settee. He didn't want Macklin to see any softness toward Ada. He'd never hear the end of it if he let his emotions show.

"Not much," Macklin admitted. "It's going to have to be rebuilt from scratch. I reckon we won't be getting a preacher this year."

"I think we will," Jack responded, keeping his voice even. "I'll pay any man fifty dollars who will work to get it finished on time, as long as it doesn't take away from your time rebuilding the town."

Macklin gave a low whistle. "You sure?"

"Yeah, I am. Mrs. Burnett set great store by that church, and she was real excited that we were getting a preacher here in Winchester Falls," Jack admitted. "It would be good for my daughter, too. Let everyone know. Anyone who is looking for work will find it at the church site. I expect daily reports on the progress."

"All right, then." Macklin rose, putting his hat back on. "Guess I'd better get to work. We've got a lot going on."

"Sounds good." Jack struggled to a sitting position. He needed to get back upstairs now that Macklin was leaving. If Ada caught him downstairs, he'd never hear the end of it. To be honest, he didn't want to cause her any more work or distress. "Try to get Mrs. Burnett involved in the work with the town. I'm getting better, so I will take over more of the ranch work. Since the chapel is on my property, let's try to keep the work on it as secret from her as we can. I want it to be a surprise."

Macklin shook his head, making his way to the door. "I doubt you'll put one over on Miz B."

Jack chuckled. "Maybe not, but I'm gonna try."

It was about time he did something for Ada.

Chapter Fifteen

Ada faced the crowd of murmuring townspeople in her parlor, her pulse quickening. "If I could have your attention, please," she called.

Macklin let out a sharp, high whistle, and the chattering stopped. About thirty people turned to face her, their expressions open and expectant. There were some people among the group she recognized, but none of her own ranch hands. That was odd, but then again, perhaps Jack had too much to do in the fields to spare a man. Macklin was here, and that would have to be enough for now.

What had she gotten herself into? This was far more unnerving than marching in a suffragist parade. However, Jack had asked her to do it. No, more to the point, Macklin had asked her, and Jack had told her that he knew she could handle it. Jack expected her to help rebuild the town. In fact, in complete defiance of Dr. Rydell's orders, he had gone back to ranching. He rode for only a few hours a day, and only in the fields closest to the house, but he still rode out with the sunrise.

If Jack could push forward in the face of his own

illness, then she could work with the townspeople to rebuild the town.

She cleared her throat. "I call this meeting of the Winchester Falls rebuilding committee to order. Do we have anyone here who can take notes?"

Aunt Pearl waved a scrap of paper in the air. "I'll do it."

"Thank you," Ada replied, her heart surging with gratitude. If only Jack could be here. Somehow, she would feel better if he was sitting beside her. Jack, however, was off working the cattle. If he couldn't be here, at least Aunt Pearl was on hand to give moral support. Where should she begin?

"We've all endured a series of hardships on our own farms and ranches," she ventured. The townspeople nodded and muttered among themselves. "We were among those who sustained less damage than others. I believe we should begin by making sure that those people who were hit hardest should receive help from the rest of the town."

One woman, who was very well dressed, spoke up. "I think the families hit hardest were over in the west part of the county. I've heard the shanties in that section were hit hard. Of course, they weren't very sturdy to begin with."

"Is anyone here from that part of the county, someone who can give a report on the damage?" Ada looked over the crowd of people. Everyone shuffled around, craning their necks to see which townspeople were in attendance.

"It doesn't look like it," Aunt Pearl said. "Maybe they didn't know about the meeting. Or maybe they didn't feel welcome."

"I don't think those people care, to tell the truth."
One man shrugged, lighting his cigar. "They're all
the same. Trash, mostly. I hope they never rebuild.
Let them move on to another county."

Ada's blood began to boil in her veins. Oh, if Violet and Delia were here! They would give this oaf
a talking-to. "Extinguish your cigar, if you please,"
she retorted crisply. "I don't allow smoking in here."

The man cast Ada a withering glance and crushed
out his cigar on the fringe of the Oriental rug.

"I've gotta say, I agree with Bill," another man
spoke up, pointing over at the man with the cigar.
"I mean, couldn't we say this was a kind of house-
cleaning? We can start fresh this way."

"No, we cannot." Ada's anger burned white-hot
within her. Yes, she had always been a daughter of
privilege. However, she had also been taught about
"the least of these." Charitable work had been a part
of her life for as long as she could remember. "This
is our opportunity to extend our hands in Christian
fellowship and care for our fellow man. We need to
help the poorest of the poor to rebuild. It's what our
Holy Father taught us."

An uneasy silence settled over the group, but Pearl
smiled bracingly at Ada, her eyes glowing.

"Anyone who doesn't wish to help will, of course,
be given the option of working on other things," Ada
continued, her voice shaking a little at her own bold-
ness. "However, for our community to thrive and to
be the sort of place that welcomes a preacher, we need
to pull together and help those who cannot help themselves."

"I'll head up the repairs to the shantytown," the

postmaster, Mr. T. J. Pollitt, replied, raising his hand. "My folks came from nothing. I'm not ashamed to say it. We had a lot of help in our day, and I'd be glad to help others."

"Thank you." Ada gave him a warm smile. "Anyone else who wishes to help rebuild that part of town, please work with Mr. Pollitt."

Aunt Pearl gave Ada a satisfied nod of her graying head, and Ada felt that same familiar pull of both gratitude and family warmth. When she had arrived in Winchester Falls, she had not felt very kindly toward her aunt. In fact, she thought her aunt had traded her like so much chattel. She was starting to see, though, that Aunt Pearl possessed a great deal of wisdom.

Without her guidance, Ada would never have experienced any of this—the heartache and the sorrow coupled with the love and the friendship. Her life, since coming to Winchester Falls, had been difficult. Yet, somehow, it had been richer and fuller for all the experiences she had lived through.

She wanted to rebuild this town. Even if she had to leave it when St. Clair heard about his attorney's disastrous visit.

"I suppose we should focus on rebuilding the telegraph lines and restoring mail service," she continued. "Without communication to the outside world, we are well and truly stranded."

The postmaster raised his hand. "I'm happy to say that mail service was restored today, and the men from the telegraph company should have the lines repaired by the end of the week."

So soon? Ada smiled, but her heart froze within her chest. She had been hoping to remain in a little bubble, safe from St. Clair hearing and from reacting to his attorney's visit, for just a little while longer.

Obviously, that wasn't going to happen. Somehow, the attorney had made the train out of town before the tornado hit and had communicated with St. Clair about his disastrous visit.

"Thank you," she responded mechanically. "That is good news."

"I'll say," Pollitt replied with a grin. "There's a fellow with a big newspaper out of Fort Worth who's come to town to report on the twister and the damage it did. He's got a photographer with him. Winchester Falls is going to make big news."

A sudden clamor arose at this news, as the townspeople began chatting amongst themselves. Ada furrowed her brow. This could be good or it could be bad. If the reporter only told of the death and destruction, then Winchester Falls would look like a pitiful place, indeed. That would be no way to show off the town she had come to love so much. Moreover, any newspaper coverage would, eventually, make its way back to the St. Clairs. If it seemed that the town had been completely devastated, then that would show very poorly in their favor.

"We need to make sure this reporter sees the good that is being done," Ada blurted, and the commotion from the assembly died down. "If he focuses on the tragic aspects of the aftermath, then we're just going to look like a sad little town out in the middle of nowhere on the prairie. He needs to tell the truth. He needs to show how we are rising from the ashes."

"Hear, hear," Aunt Pearl echoed. "That photographer needs to take pictures of the homes being rebuilt, not just of the ones that have been blown away." Unshed tears sparkled in her eyes, and she slapped her broken leg, still in its cast. "Ada, you need to take that on."

"I don't know," Ada demurred. "Surely Mr. Pollitt—"

"I'm going to be rebuilding the shantytown," he reminded her. "Besides, you speak as though you really love Winchester Falls. Who better to tell our story than you? You came in as an outsider, but here you are, months later, organizing our rebuild."

"All in favor of Mrs. Burnett managing the reporter, say aye," the burly man with the cigar announced.

A tremendous shout of "aye" surged through the room.

"I'll bring them here tomorrow," the postmaster replied. "They are staying just up the road in Sparrow for the night. I just got a wire today. They have to travel by horse and buggy, since the train tracks are being repaired and the train depot still has damage."

"Of course," Ada replied. How on earth was she going to accomplish this latest feat? "Bring them here as soon as you can. I don't want him to photograph anything or interview anyone until I've had the opportunity to start showing him around."

"Let's move on to other business." The burly man pointedly took out his gold pocket watch and looked at it. "Some of us have things to do."

The rest of the meeting was a whirlwind of planning and setting up of committees. One group was working on the train station and railroad, offering to assist the railway company as best as they could. Another committee was going to work on setting the post office back to rights. By the end of an hour, a committee had been assigned to almost every building and portion of the county save one.

"Ada, what are we going to do about the chapel?" Aunt Pearl asked, as the meeting wound down and people began to leave.

"I hadn't really thought about it," Ada said, hoping her voice sounded breezy. In truth, she wasn't sure what to do about the chapel. Rebuilding the entire town seemed easier, somehow, than starting anew what had barely begun.

She had wrapped up so much hope in that little chapel. She had stood with Jack on top of the hill and felt closeness to him she had never known. She was going to help him. They were going to help each other. It was the way a marriage should work, even if this one had started out as a business arrangement. Because of the chapel, they had become dear friends.

"I'll have to write to the missionary group and tell them what's happened," Aunt Pearl fretted. "This will be a difficult letter to write. I surely did look forward to Winchester Falls having its own chapel."

"I'm sure we will someday," Ada replied, placing her arm around Aunt Pearl's shoulder. "We have other, more pressing concerns to attend to at the moment. Once the buildings have been repaired, and everyone has suitable shelter again, we'll see what can be done about the chapel."

Aunt Pearl sighed. "I suppose so."

She made her way out of the parlor, leaning heavily on her cane. Macklin intercepted her at the vestibule, speaking to her in a low voice. He must need her opinion on what to do about rebuilding her house now that the rubble had been cleared away. That was a little disheartening. Not that she wanted to keep Aunt Pearl from having her own place. It was just so nice to have her here. Jack enjoyed her company, especially since they had been invalids together for such a stretch of time. She herself had come to rely on the old woman's salty retorts. Laura enjoyed listening to Aunt Pearl talk about the early days of ranching and Winchester Falls.

It would be a sad day when Aunt Pearl left for her own place. She had become, in a short time, an integral part of life in the house.

The clock on the mantel chimed three in the afternoon. Ada jumped, startled. She must leave soon to pick Laura up from school. "Maggie," she called. "Cathy?"

The two maids clustered in the doorway. "Yes, ma'am?"

"I declare the parlor is a mess," she replied, waving her hand at the cigar butt on the floor and the teacups scattered throughout the room. "We had a good meeting, but I am afraid we've increased your labor for the afternoon."

"Think nothing of it," Cathy replied. "We'll have it cleaned by the time you bring home the young miss."

"Thank you." Ada left the parlor and waved goodbye to Macklin and Aunt Pearl, who were still in deep conversation in the hallway.

"Miz Burnett, I wouldn't go around by the hilltop if I were you," Macklin interjected as she walked past. "Jack is going to be running some cattle through there this week. It's going to be loud and there's a lot going on. Even though it takes longer, you might want to take the other route up to the schoolhouse."

"Thank you, Macklin," she responded. "I'll make sure to avoid the area."

Macklin nodded and turned back to Aunt Pearl. Whatever they were speaking of, it must be rather important.

She made her way from the front porch to the gig, where Blue waited patiently. If only Jack was here. She would love to talk to him about the day's events and ask his help on how to best handle this reporter tomorrow. One of the nice things about his recuperation had been the chance to go and talk to him when she wanted. He was unable to vanish for hours at a time, and she had really come to enjoy his company.

She climbed inside the gig and started Blue on the alternate road to the schoolhouse.

Now that Jack was on the mend, he was back to his usual schedule. That was fine. It was best this way. If St. Clair was going to break this family up, she should get used to being without Jack.

Jack turned to the group of about thirty-five men gathered before him on the hilltop. "We've got about a week to build this chapel," he announced. "If we all pull together, I think we can have it done. Or mostly done. We don't want to delay the preacher's arrival, that's for sure."

The men nodded. "Where's Mack?" one of them asked, breaking apart a little from the crowd.

"Macklin's up at the house. He's sitting in on the rebuilding committee for the town. He'll be joining us later."

"Why don't we just add this to rebuilding the rest of the town? It's gonna be part of the town, ain't it?"

Another man stepped forward, tilting his hat back. "I don't see why we've got to make an extra effort for the chapel."

Jack looked at the hands. Most of them were his own men, but a few were from other ranches, brought in by the promise of the extra pay Jack had offered. They were all strong and tough, and like all strong and tough men, they thought they should be in charge. Well, there was going to be one man only heading up this operation, just like on the ranch.

"It's not the same thing, because this chapel was never finished," he replied, crossing his arms over his chest. "It can't be rebuilt, because it was never fully built in the first place. The rest of the town is going to work on fixing the buildings, the railroad tracks and all the things Winchester Falls needs to be a town. What we're going to work on is building up its soul."

The men shifted a little. It was clear they weren't exactly with him yet. Funny, even the prospect of extra pay wasn't enough to sway some of these stubborn Texans.

"Fact is, Mrs. Burnett has set great store by this chapel," he continued, his voice tighter than he expected. "Her aunt, Pearl Colgan, cares about it, too. Mrs. Stillman and Mrs. Colgan have written letters to missionaries and convinced them that Winchester Falls is a good little town in need of a man of God. The mission folks say they'll send someone here just for us. All we have to do is provide a place of worship."

"All right then." One of his workers, Red Jones, clapped his hands together. "If it means that much to Miz Burnett and Miz Colgan, we'll build it for them."

"Yep. I've seen Miz Burnett out here working those

cattle for weeks. She's a fine lady. Never thought I'd say this about a Yankee girl, but she's one of the best cowgirls I've ever seen."

Jack chuckled. "I agree. Never thought I'd say it, either."

"Miz Colgan helped my family when we first came to Winchester Falls." Chuck Baker, one of the hands from the Stillmans' ranch, stepped forward. "My wife died in childbirth, and the baby died with her. Miz Colgan arranged for their funerals and burial. She never said a word about it. She never expected thanks. To me, she's a real Christian lady. If she wants a chapel, I'll build it. I don't need extra money for it, either."

One by one, the men spoke up, praising Ada's hard work and Pearl's long years of service to the community. These men were rough around the edges and toughened from years in the saddle. Yet they were genuine in their appreciation for those two women and eager to pay respect to them.

That was good. It was gratifying, even. Somehow, though, it wasn't enough. They needed to know the true reason for the importance of building the chapel. Jack gave a loud whistle, which caused a little pain to shoot through his ribs. It was worth it, though. The men calmed down, looking at him expectantly.

"I'm real glad to hear how much my wife and Miz Colgan mean to everyone here," he began. What should he say next? He never talked much, not about anything serious, anyway. "But the real reason for building this chapel is that we need a place to worship. Winchester Falls needs a heart. In a way, we've had a body for a long time—buildings, railroads, mail service, telegraph wires. We've got no heart. I want to take my little girl for Sunday worship. I want to feel the hand of God on my back as I go about my labors.

"I know I'm supposed to feel that anyway. I reckon I have and didn't know it. I suppose I want to thank God for putting up with me all these years I blamed Him for what was wrong in my life, especially all the trouble I caused through my own stubbornness. So if you want to help me bring a heart to Winchester Falls, let's get to work."

Slightly abashed, he looked out over the crowd of cowboys, expecting them to laugh and jeer him. Instead, quiet and stoic as they were, they nodded and walked off, splitting themselves into groups so that they could begin working on the foundation.

Macklin was supposed to deter Ada so she wouldn't be coming past the hilltop while construction was going on. He was going to surprise his wife and thank her for all she had done. Most importantly, he wanted to tell her how she had not just brought family into his life, but had rekindled his love of God. Seeing her work in the community, seeing Winchester Falls band together—it restored the love that had been lost. Without her, none of this would have been possible.

He almost dared St. Clair to take it all away.

Chapter Sixteen

Laura flounced into the dining room the next morning, wearing a sensible cotton dress, and gave Ada a kiss on the cheek. Ada patted her stepdaughter's arm. "Planning on enjoying your day off from school? Saturdays are precious, you know."

"I know." Laura helped herself to a piece of toast and sat at the table. "Where's Father?"

Ada smiled. Laura missed Jack and wanted to know where he was. Surely she was growing closer to him. "Where he usually is every morning, day in and day out," Ada reminded her. "Working the cattle."

"Oh." Laura took a bite out of her toast. "I suppose I should expect that by now."

Aunt Pearl tottered into the room, leaning heavily on her cane. Ada jumped up, ready to help her aunt to the table, but the old woman merely waved her aside with her cane and turned to Laura. "Hey, chickadee. Help an elderly lady out. I need my chair."

Laura obediently placed her toast on her plate and held out a nearby chair for Aunt Pearl. "Thank you, my dear," Aunt Pearl replied, giving her head a pat as she sat.

"Aunt Pearl, you know I would send a tray up to your room," Ada reminded her. "Going up and down those stairs has to be difficult on your leg."

"Nonsense." Aunt Pearl helped herself to coffee. "I need to keep moving. If you rest you rust, so the old saying goes." She turned to Laura. "What are you doing home? Aren't they going to send the truant officer after you?"

Laura giggled. "It's Saturday, Aunt Pearl."

"Oh." Pearl looked over at Ada. "I reckon you'll be working with the photographer and the reporter from that big-city newspaper today."

"Yes." Ada glanced up at the clock on the mantel. "Mr. Pollitt is bringing them here at any time now." The very thought of having to conduct these two men around the county was making her nervous, but it had been her idea. The better the coverage was of the twister's aftermath, the easier it might be to convince St. Clair to let Laura stay.

"A reporter? And a photographer?" Laura bounced around in her chair with excitement. "May I come, too?"

Ada froze. St. Clair would not likely approve of his granddaughter having her picture in the newspaper. He was of that generation, the kind of man who would say that a woman should have her picture in the paper only three times: at her debut, her marriage and her death. "I will show them around the first day," Ada replied with a cajoling smile for her stepdaughter. "Once I know what kind of people they are, I might let you help."

Laura frowned and took a bite out of her toast. "That's no fun."

"Cheer up. You can keep me company," Aunt Pearl replied briskly. "There's nothing a young person likes more than being some old crippled woman's companion." She gave Laura a sly wink, and Laura smiled.

There was a knock at the door, and Cathy showed Mr. Pollitt and two men into the dining room. Ada rose, wishing that Cathy would learn to take everyone to the parlor. The parlor was formal. The parlor was correct. As it was, she could only smile over her half-finished breakfast and offer the men coffee.

The three men took their seats. "Mrs. Burnett, this is Matt Starr, reporter for the *Fort Worth Telegram*. This is Jacob Ledbetter, his photographer."

"I'm sorry to intrude on your breakfast, Mrs. Burnett," Mr. Starr replied. He took off his straw boater hat, and his photographer did the same. "We can wait outside if you prefer."

"Nonsense." Ada rose. "Just let me get my hat. I'll be back in a moment."

She rushed up the stairs and retrieved her beige straw hat with its wide purple-ribbon trim. She tied it on over the dark waves of her hair, which had been subdued to some extent and coiled into a mass on top of her head. Then she grabbed her gloves and went to join the men downstairs.

Mr. Pollitt smiled as she made her way to the vestibule. "I do hope you'll bring the gentlemen to see the west part of the county," he announced. "I went out there after our meeting yesterday and met with some of the residents. We have big plans for rebuilding."

"Absolutely." Ada gave him an encouraging smile.

"We'll drive out in the gig." She turned to Mr. Starr and Mr. Ledbetter. "How long are you two here?"

"Just a day," Mr. Starr replied. "I'd like to stay longer, but my editor wants the story as soon as possible. After speaking to Mr. Pollitt on the way over, I'd like to come back in a few weeks and talk more about the rebuilding process. It's a good human-interest story. But at least we can get started on this trip."

"Very good. Let's not dither any longer. I'll start you on the tour before it gets too hot."

She waved goodbye to Aunt Pearl and Laura, and then led the two men to the waiting gig outside. Mr. Pollitt took his leave, promising to come back for them in the evening.

Mr. Starr helped her into the carriage and then jumped in beside her, grasping the reins. Ada tried not to let her amazement show. It had been months since a man had helped her into or out of a carriage. Jack knew her wishes and applauded her independence to the point that she no longer expected him to try to take over in these matters. She did not really like Mr. Starr taking over, but out of politeness, said nothing.

Mr. Ledbetter climbed in behind them, and Mr. Starr started the horse. "Where should we go first? Lead the way."

It would be a lot easier to lead the way if she was driving, but Ada bit back the sharp retort. She needed this man to write a favorable story about Winchester Falls, and that meant putting her own personal preferences aside.

"Let's drive up to the schoolhouse," she replied. "It sustained the least damage of all the buildings in Winchester Falls, and the children were all found safe. I declare, we all said a prayer of thanks when we heard that good news."

Mr. Starr nodded and guided the horses down the road. She would make certain to avoid the area by the chapel, for she did not want to get in Jack's way while he was running cattle. Then, too, it would be very depressing to show the men the damage the chapel had sustained. They must focus on the positive outcome. If she told them about the chapel and explained what it meant to the community—well, she would burst into tears.

She guided the men all over Winchester Falls the rest of the day. First, they went to the schoolhouse, then down to the western part of the town where Mr. Pollitt and his team showed their plans to rebuild the shantytown. It was no longer going to be an area that housed cheap lean-tos, but a proper little village with stout log cabins.

Then she guided the men down to the post office, where a team of men were working to set the building back onto its foundation, and then over to the train station, where the workers had finished putting shingles back on the roof. At each stop, Mr. Ledbetter unfolded a small, portable camera that looked like a box and snapped several pictures.

While he photographed the area, Ada would explain the buildings to Mr. Starr, who wrote rapidly on a notepad, using the stub of a pencil. He asked intelligent, probing questions that she worked mightily to answer well without sounding like an overeager ninny.

At the last stop, she walked slowly up and down the train platform with Mr. Starr, while Mr. Ledbetter photographed the lingering but mild damage to the tracks.

"You seem to love this place very much," Mr. Starr remarked, pushing back his straw boater. "I have to say, Mrs. Burnett, I never expected to meet anyone like you out here. How did Winchester Falls win you over?"

She smiled. "I owe a great debt of gratitude to Winchester Falls. Had I never lived here, I don't think I would truly understand what it is to be part of a community. Or indeed, how being a part of a community can make you feel free."

"Really?" Mr. Starr opened his notebook, flicking an interested glance in her direction. "Do tell."

She laughed. "No, this is strictly off-the-record. It's just a feeling I have. Winchester Falls is a special place, Mr. Starr. I was a spoiled debutante when I arrived. The few months I've spent here changed me for the better."

He smiled, nodding. "Very well. Off-the-record, then. It helps to know, when writing this piece, how people really feel. It's good to know it's more than just buildings."

"Then you should know that Winchester Falls is a special place," she rejoined warmly, gazing around her. A few workers still clattered about finishing the repairs to the roof, but the station was relatively deserted. "You know, when I was in New York, I thought I understood what friendship and family meant. I can tell you now, I had no clue what those words meant until I came here."

Mr. Starr gave her an appraising glance and began to speak, but was interrupted by the arrival of Mr.

Ledbetter. "I finished my snaps," the older man announced. "I guess we'd better get back to Mr. Pollitt.
He said he'd take us to Sparrow."

"Sure thing." Mr. Starr offered Ada his arm. She
took it reluctantly. It seemed odd to be squired about
by anyone except Jack. Not that this meant anything,
of course. Mr. Starr was of the city and used to being
courtly with all females. There was no need to worry
that his attentions meant anything in particular.

He handed her up into the carriage. "I suppose
we can drive over to Mr. Pollitt's. That would mean,
though, that Mrs. Burnett would have to drive by herself back home, and that would never do."

"But—" Ada began to protest. How ridiculous. She
drove by herself all the time.

"Remember, Mr. Pollitt is meeting us at Mrs. Burnett's home," Mr. Ledbetter reminded him. "No need
to make her drive by herself."

"That settles it, then," Mr. Starr replied, flashing
a winning smile Ada's way. "Our problem has been
solved."

Ada resisted the urge to roll her eyes. She had gotten so used to being treated like a calm, rational creature and one with a brain, to boot. Her husband would
not have ever dared suggest she couldn't drive home
alone. He might voice misgivings, but he never thought
her incapable.

It was nice to be thought competent.

They made it back to the ranch even though Mr.
Starr ignored her directions and went the way he
thought they should go—which, of course, was not the
right way at all. When they finally turned up the drive
to the ranch, Mr. Pollitt was waiting, along with Jack.

Ada started to jump down from the carriage, as was her wont, but was prevented by Mr. Starr, who had already made his way over to her side. With a flourish, he helped her down from the carriage and kissed her gloved hand.

"Mrs. Burnett, it has truly been a great pleasure," he effused. "Thank you for all you have shown me today."

"Of course," Ada replied, struggling to free her hand. "It was my pleasure."

She caught a glimpse of Jack, leaning up against the fence. How much more genuine he was than a slick talker like Mr. Starr. She'd had to work all day to give Mr. Starr the correct impression of Winchester Falls, making sure he understood how hard the town was working to rebuild. Even after all her efforts, though, there was no guarantee Mr. Starr would write truthfully about their town.

She glanced at her husband again. Jack was, aesthetically speaking, a more handsome man than Mr. Starr. In the short time she had been in Winchester Falls, she had come to appreciate a man who worked with his hands rather than a man who made his living behind a typewriter. Jack was taller, broader and more muscular than Mr. Starr, who actually looked a trifle effete in his city clothes and straw boater.

Not that she should be looking at another man when she was married.

Not that she was actually truly married and should be comparing Jack's looks to anyone else's.

Had she gotten too much sun that day? Her head was spinning.

She took her leave and went inside, removing her

hat as she crossed the threshold. She sank onto the settee, ready for a few moments of blessed silence.

Instead, Jack came inside and propped himself against the doorway to the parlor. His hat was in his large, callused hands.

"Ada." He said her name as though it cost a tremendous effort.

"Yes?" She leaned up against the cushions of the settee, trying to look as though she hadn't just been thinking of him and comparing him to other men. Despite her tremendous effort, she knew a telltale flush had spread across her face, heating her cheeks.

"That man kissed you."

The moment he said the words, he wanted to grab them back. Why had he followed her in here? There was no need. The newspaper man was going, along with his photographer. The man talked a big game about coming back to do another story on Winchester Falls once the rebuilding was complete. In his experience, though, city folk who passed through Winchester Falls rarely returned. They had no roots here.

Yet he could not deny the white-hot frustration that had boiled up within him when he saw that newspaper fellow kiss Ada's hand.

Ada was his wife. If anyone should be kissing her, it should be Jack Burnett, not some reporter from Fort Worth.

"He kissed my hand, as any gentleman would," Ada retorted. The flush on her cheeks deepened to a pretty rose red. "There was nothing untoward in what he did."

Of course not. His own father-in-law had treated

Ada in the same courtly manner, but it hadn't aroused the same feelings of jealousy that Mr. Starr had kindled within him. Why?

Starr could have been a rival.

St. Clair was not.

"I trust you." He said the words without even thinking, because they were true. He trusted her with so many aspects of his life that he could not entrust to another human being. He'd had confidence in her ability to run the ranch when he was confined to his bed— something he did not trust anyone else to handle. He'd counted on her ability to be a good mother to Laura. He had come to rely on her opinions and missed her company when she was away.

His feelings for Ada Westmore ran deeper than he'd suspected before. He wanted her good opinion. He desired to prove himself worthy.

He yearned to be her husband.

This last thought knocked the wind out of him. He hadn't wanted to be anyone's husband in years, because marriage meant fighting, disappointment, loneliness and despair. How did Ada feel? Did she like him at all? Did she think of him as anything beyond a friend?

"Thank you," Ada replied quietly. "I can assure you, his attention wasn't something I craved. However, I had to go with him to show him the ways the town has been rebuilding. I wanted to make sure they photographed and wrote about everything positive, so that we could show St. Clair that the town will recover. If the newspaper prints all of that in black-and-white, it might be harder for him to argue that Laura is in an improper environment."

She had done all of this for Laura. Somehow, this didn't surprise him. He crossed the room and eased down beside her on the settee. He had a hankering for her company, and perhaps he could catch just a whiff of her scent of lily of the valley. Ada's eyes widened a little when he turned to look at her. It was invigorating to be this close to her, outside the confines of a buggy or gig. They had not been this close since the moment they had shared at the top of the hill—a moment he had played over and over in his mind while drugged on laudanum.

He would take her hand in his. He would apologize for being so angry with her when the attorney visited. He would tell her that he was a new man because of her.

"Ada?" Laura bounded into the room, her blond curls bouncing. "Are you done with the reporter? I want to talk with you." His daughter stopped short as soon as she spotted him sitting with Ada. "Oh, hello, Father."

"How's my chickadee?"

"I'm fine." Laura nodded briefly, but then turned her attention back to Ada. "Can we speak privately? Please? Only if you are done."

"Of course." Ada rose, giving Jack an absent-minded smile as she passed by. "We can go up to my room. I need to freshen up for dinner, anyway."

Jack sat on the settee for a moment after they left the room, breathing in deeply to savor the trail of perfume left by Ada as she walked past. This was dumb. He should go do something—anything. Otherwise, he'd sit here and pine for Ada like a lovesick fool.

"Jack, you look like a schoolboy." Pearl tottered

into the room, leaning heavily on her cane. "I do believe you've got it bad for Ada. What do you want to do about it?"

He gave her a rapid, assessing glance as she took her seat. "How can you tell? Maybe I just wanted to sit down and relax for a while."

Pearl gave one of her loud, chortling laughs. "Aw, come on, Jack. I've known you too long for this kind of silliness. Let's get down to brass tacks. I heard you talking to her about being kissed by that reporter fellow. I've seen the way you look at her. I don't think I ever saw you look like that at Emily."

He shrugged, toying with the hat in his hands. "So what if I am. That doesn't mean anything. Ada might not like me."

"What's not to like, aside from your stubborn streak and your willful atheism? Are you really building the chapel for her? Macklin said you are. He told me not to write to the missionary group to cancel anything." Pearl smiled at him in a gentle way, with the most tender and sentimental expression he had ever seen on her face.

"Yep, I am." Jack stood. "I'll go check on the progress now."

"Hold your horses." Aunt Pearl hooked his knee with her cane, forcing him to sit down again. "If you like her, you need to court her. Ada might be a suffragette, but she wants to be wooed just like anyone else. She's been working her fingers to the bone for you and for Laura. How're you going to repay her?"

"Never you mind." Jack flashed a grin at Pearl, one of his old mischievous feelings stealing over him for the first time in months. They had been working hard, and there had been too much indecision and fear and pain in their lives. He wanted to show Ada that no matter what happened with Laura, he still wanted her as his bride. "As long as I have your blessing."

"You do." The old woman nodded sagely. "Now run along and plot your wooing."

Chapter Seventeen

Ada closed her bedroom door behind Laura, who immediately plunked herself down across Ada's bed.

"Ada, I've been thinking." She picked at the yarn ties on the quilt.

"About what?" Ada sat at her dressing table and began unwinding her hair, rapidly removing hairpins as she did so. Her hair was a mass of dusty tangles, and it would take more than her customary one hundred strokes to make it manageable again.

"About going back to St. Louis." Laura buried her head on the bed, muffling her voice. "Please don't be mad at me."

"I'm not going to be angry," Ada reassured Laura, even though her mouth went dry at her stepdaughter's words. She reserved the right to be privately hurt and upset, though she would keep those emotions from her stepdaughter. It was better to listen to what Laura had to say than to react immediately. Laura needed to be able to talk to someone. "Tell me why you feel that way."

"I don't know why, exactly," Laura began in a hesi-

tant voice. "I know I told you the same thing after the
tornado came through town. I guess I thought I was
sad. The feeling won't leave me, though. I just get the
impression that St. Louis is where I belong. I liked my
school. I had friends. The weather wasn't so…violent."
She shuddered, and her eyes filled with tears. "I like
being around Father, and I love you. I just hate it here."

Tears trickled rapidly down her cheeks. Ada put her
hairbrush aside and rushed over to the bed, gathering
Laura into her arms. "Oh, Laura. You poor child."

Laura burst into sobs, and Ada held her as best she
could, gently rocking back and forth to soothe her, as
though Laura were a baby and not a big girl.

"I know it's hard here," Ada murmured. "I know it's
a big change. You've done so well with it. I'm proud of
you." If only someone would say those words to her.
They had all been through so much, and they needed
to tell each other how much it meant to be victorious
over adversity.

"Oh, Ada." Laura sniffled. "I want to go, but I don't
want to. I'll miss you so much if I go. I'll miss Aunt
Pearl. She's so funny. She and I laughed so much together this morning."

Ada smiled and kissed the top of Laura's head.
"She's an acquired taste, to be sure. But then, so is
salt or pepper, and look at how much flavor they bring
to life."

Laura laughed and hugged Ada. They fell silent
as Ada searched for the right thing to say. Of course,
they could just send Laura back to Mrs. Erskine's.
That would break Jack's heart, though. Everything
they had done, including getting married, had been to
bring Laura back to Texas. If Laura returned to school,

there would be no need for Ada to be married to Jack any longer. Jack had made it clear he only wanted their marriage for Laura's sake, so if Laura were gone, he would surely want their relationship to end.

That thought caused her more pain than she expected.

What would happen if they weren't married? She would have to try to set up a home somewhere else. Her sisters were already planning on coming and might not return to school if they decided to live with her, instead. Aunt Pearl no longer had a home. Where would they all go if Jack decided that marriage was no longer his desire?

Yes, then there was Jack. How would he feel about it? If Laura left, he would likely be torn between heartbreak and anger. How he might feel about the breakup of their sham marriage was less clear. There were some days when it seemed they cherished a beautiful mutual friendship, the sort of relationship she had never enjoyed before.

Then, other days, it seemed she was nothing more than a nuisance to him, and that he could be happy to be rid of her. It hurt to know that he often must wish that she were gone. She had never wished that Jack would leave. In fact, she spent most of her time trying to make him stay, encouraging him to speak out if angry or upset and not vanish for hours on end.

As complicated as their relationship was, there was another issue to consider—Edmund St. Clair. Laura's grandfather still had the authority to take Laura away from Winchester Falls, no matter what Ada or Jack thought.

"Laura, I spent most of my early years in defiant

rebellion with my father and my place in life," she began slowly. "I did not like being treated like some precious, brainless, spineless creature who didn't have a thought beyond what I would wear to my next ball. So I broke away from his world as fiercely as I could. I didn't become a suffragist to spite him. I became involved with the suffrage movement as a way to mend what I find are fundamental wrongs in the way women are treated by the law."

She paused, wondering if this was at all helpful. Somehow, it made sense in her mind, but was it making sense as she spoke? Laura remained quiet, her sobs lessening.

Ada patted her stepdaughter's back. "I suppose if I had just felt as though my father heard me, just once in my life, our relationship would have been different. Maybe I wouldn't have been so rebellious. I think I still would be me, though, and would still fight for women's rights." She paused. "Perhaps you haven't been heard much, either. After all, you've been moved from pillar to post and had no say in the matter."

She fell silent. Somehow, she wasn't saying things properly, but she felt a kinship with her stepdaughter.

"Ada." Laura hiccuped a little. "I'm sorry. I didn't love you at first. I thought you were trying to be my mother. I hated you for that."

"It's all right," Ada replied soothingly. "I understand how you must have felt."

"I see you taking care of Father every day. I see how much he cares for you. I don't hate you anymore. I don't think I hated you personally as much as I hated...the idea of you."

Ada smiled a tiny bit at that last admission, but

her head whirled a little. Did Jack really care for her, enough that Laura could tell? Her heart skipped a beat as she considered Laura's words.

"There are a lot of people who care about you, too," Ada continued, praying for the right way to say everything in her heart. "Your grandfather is very concerned about you. He allowed us to bring you here on a sort of trial, but he is not convinced that this is the right home for you. I imagine he will have a great deal to say once he hears of the tornado. Shall we wait and see what he says?"

"Maybe." Laura wiped her eyes with her fingertips, and Ada pressed her own handkerchief into her stepdaughter's hands. "I don't know. I don't like him making the decision for me."

"I understand that more than you can imagine," Ada rejoined heartily. "He will, as your legal guardian, have more of a say in the matter than any of us adults. Only you, I think, can convince him to do what you feel would be right."

"Would you miss me, Ada?" Laura blew her nose on the borrowed handkerchief.

"More than you can imagine." It was true. She had never considered herself a maternal sort of person. Growing up, she would get annoyed by her younger sisters' neediness, but what could she do? She was the closest thing to a mother they had, and so she performed her role dutifully if not particularly cheerfully. Her time with Laura had taught her the tenderness and the selflessness of raising a child. She was reluctant to let that feeling go.

But they had to do what was best for Laura. They had to allow her a say in her own life.

"I'd miss you, too," Laura admitted, balling up the handkerchief in her fist. "Thank you for letting me talk about this without getting mad."

"Of course," Ada replied. "But what is the plan? Should we wait for your grandfather?"

Laura shrugged her shoulders. "I'll pray on it. Mostly, I wanted to talk to you."

She blew Ada a kiss before leaving the room, closing the door firmly behind her. Ada sank back against her pillow, her hair rippling around her in waves. In some ways, she wanted to press everyone for an answer right away. Her life was now inextricably bound up with so many other people's lives and she no longer had the autonomy she had once craved. If only she could stamp her foot and force other people to make decisions now, without delay.

Least said, soonest mended, indeed. That counsel was becoming ever harder to bear.

Jack stood a ways back from the men, gazing up at the chapel. It was remarkable how much work they had done in just a few days.

The foundation had been laid, and all four walls had been framed. Today the men had worked on the beams for the roof, and tomorrow they would work on the steeple. At this rate, they would have the chapel finished in plenty of time for the preacher's arrival. Watching the men work was like watching faith in action. They were striking out, hopeful of the result, ready to show their love of God through their work. It was a heady, compelling feeling, one he had not truly experienced in years. It both humbled and gratified him.

The sun was beginning to set in the west, causing the clouds in the sky to turn purple. The wind had died down to a sweet, gentle breeze. Out in the pastures, cattle lowed and the occasional quail chirped, "Bob White? Bob White?" Jack whistled back to them, reveling in the feeling of being alive.

This was the perfect evening for a walk with his wife.

"Say, Mack," he called to his hand. "Would you have one of the men feed the cattle in the lower pasture? I need to head up to the house."

"Sure thing." Macklin gave a sharp, shrill whistle. "Quittin' time!" he bellowed, and the men put down their hammers and saws. Laughing and talking among themselves, they put their tools away and walked back down the hill. Macklin followed after giving his boss a quick nod.

Jack waited until the men had disappeared and then made his way back to the house. Pearl's words kept echoing in his mind. *I've seen the way you look at her. I don't think I ever saw you look like that at Emily.*

What he'd felt for Emily had been different. He had fallen head over heels with an ideal. He had wanted a pretty little wife who would hang on his every word. He'd wanted someone with culture and refinement, a lady who would be different from all the other women he met before.

He hadn't wanted Emily for Emily. He'd wanted her for what she had represented to him.

Ada was different. She was as cosmopolitan as Emily, but more gentle and tender. She was warmer and more mature. Most important, she made him a better person. He wanted to earn her regard, and he wanted to consult with her on everything that came up in his life, from managing the ranch to raising his daughter.

Ada was a true wife, even if their marriage was a sham.

He had to tell her that. He had to make sure she understood it.

He grew as nervous as a schoolboy when he approached the house. How was he supposed to ask her for a walk? Would she want to go?

Stop it. He would not turn into a bowl of jelly over Ada, even if he suspected he was in love with her.

Ada was outside in the yard, watering the zinnias. He paused for a moment just to look at her. Her dark hair, usually twisted and piled on top of her head, was now loosely tied so that it hung in waves to her waist. She wore a lavender dress, and its simple lines suited her. Before, he had always thought of her as a really pretty girl. Now, seeing her there as she tended the flowers, she was beautiful.

"Ada," he rasped. His voice was getting caught in his throat. He cleared it and tried again. "Ada, honey." He had to tell her the truth. He had to tell her how much she meant to him.

Ada dropped the watering can she was holding and looked over at him, her blue eyes wide. "You frightened me," she gasped. "I had no idea you were there."

"Sorry." He took off his hat, holding it in his hands as though it would give him strength. "I thought maybe we could go for a walk."

"Certainly." She paused for a moment. "I suppose I should go inside and get my shawl and pin my hair up."

"No," he replied. He wanted her with him as she

was, naturally exquisite. If she went inside, there would be maids and aunts and stepdaughters vying for her attention, too, and he wanted to share this moment with just her. "The sun is setting over the hill and it looks so pretty. I thought you might like to see it before dark."

"That sounds lovely." She gathered her skirts and walked to the gate.

He opened it for her, and she passed through. He caught a whiff of her familiar scent coupled with the earthy smell of the zinnias and garden dirt. He closed his eyes for a moment. *Lord, make me worthy of her. Help me to say and do the right things.*

Ada took his arm, and they walked side by side across the pasture. The last time they had come here was just before Asesino got out and he broke his ribs. On that evening, she had asked him to allow her to help him. He had. "Are you done with running the cows?" Ada asked, her voice quivering a little.

What was she talking about? He glanced down at her in confusion. Then he remembered Macklin's excuse for keeping her out of the pasture while they worked on the chapel. "Oh, sure."

"Are we…are we going to the hilltop?" She bit her lip distractedly. "I don't think I can go there."

"It's all right," he soothed. "We'll go together."

"I just mean… I can't bear to see how badly the chapel was hit," she replied, her voice still quivering. "Honestly, Jack. I don't think I am strong enough."

"Part of being married is being strong together." He drew her a little closer to his side, trying to keep a silly, telltale grin from stealing over his face. "Besides, the view of the sunset is magnificent up there."

Ada said nothing but turned her eyes downward. He led her up around the back of the hill, where it would be more difficult to see the framework of the chapel. Then, as they crested the top, he nudged her. "Look at that sunset."

Ada lifted her eyes and gasped. "Jack."

The sun was glowing, its last rays touching the wooden frame of the chapel with streaks of gold. Ada shook her head as though she couldn't quite trust her own vision. "What happened? Is this the chapel? I mean, of course it is, but—"

He could not contain his joy any longer. "We've been working on it for days now," he replied, taking her hands in his and pulling her over to the building site. He wanted to thank her for all she had done and apologize for being hateful in the moments leading up to the twister.

Because of her, he was ready to accept God as the only guiding force in his life, and he wanted her to bear witness.

"Ada, I guess I have been a fool. Not entirely without reason, because I've got to admit that Emily broke my heart. I was in love with her, in my own way. I think I was too young and too green to understand what love really was."

He drew her a little bit closer, and her hands trembled in his.

"When I first married you, it was because I needed someone to care for Laura. But what happened just kind of knocked me sideways. You cared for me, too. While I was recovering from my busted ribs, you took over hard work on this ranch. No one asked you to do it. You did so because you cared. You always wanted us to be a team. You even bore my insults when I got angry about Laura walking to and from school."

Ada looked away from him. "It's all right, Jack. No need to feel you should apologize."

"This isn't just an apology." He gave her hands a gentle squeeze. "This is an expression of gratitude, and it's a truthful confession. I started building this chapel because I felt I owed it to you. As the men pulled together to make it happen, and as I saw the whole town working hard to set Winchester Falls back to rights, it was a humbling sight. Most importantly, though, I watched you living out your faith in the way that you cared for others—even me. It brought me back to God."

She returned the pressure on his hands. "That is good, Jack. I'm so happy."

She did not look happy, though. Her eyes were turned stubbornly toward the ground, and the glow that suffused her earlier had disappeared.

He had to recapture that glow, somehow.

"You should know something—I just can't hold it in any longer." She spoke so quietly that he had to lean forward to catch her words. "Laura told me today that she wants to go back to St. Louis. She is unhappy here. If St. Clair hears enough about his attorney's disastrous visit, then she may not even have a voice in the matter. As it is, if it were her choice alone, I think she'd leave today."

Her words knocked him back a pace. He'd been too busy to notice what Laura was up to. Too preoccupied with his own recovery to observe his own daughter. Ada had, though. Laura felt close enough to Ada to tell her the truth, even though it was hard for Ada to hear.

"Well, I am glad she told you," he began slowly. "It means she trusts you."

"Yes, but if she does leave, there is no need for us to be married any longer." Ada pulled her hands free from his and turned away.

He fell silent. If he was losing Laura, would he lose Ada, too? He couldn't lose them both. Not when he had just found them.

He was caught unaware by the knowledge that Laura actually wanted to leave. He'd been thinking all this time that she had grown to love the ranch and the people on it, including himself.

How could he save all that he had built with Ada?

How could he make Ada love him and stay with him and fight for Laura?

"Try not to worry, Ada. I haven't been a praying man most of my life, but you've brought me around to it. I'm going to pray on it." He hesitated for a moment, unsure how to proceed. If he said what was in his heart, would she consider it weakness?

Well, she had seen him laid low by a bull and then survived a tornado with him. There wasn't much he could say that would be more tumultuous than those events.

He took her hand in his.

"Pray for me, too, Ada."

Chapter Eighteen

Jack awoke the next morning after a few precious hours of sleep. For the first time in his life, he knew what it was to pray on something. Over the years he had heard that saying, for it was something the adults in his life would say when faced with a crisis. "I'm gonna pray on it." He had never fully grasped the meaning of it and had always assumed it was the nice, polite thing to say when faced with tragedy. Just as he would say "Bless you" if Ada sneezed, so, too, would he say "I'll pray on it," when faced with the possibility of his daughter leaving.

If he lost his daughter, he also faced the probability of losing Ada. She blamed herself for St. Clair's anger, and she had convinced herself they could stay married only if she could care for his daughter. It was as if she was blind to the truth. He loved her, and he meant to stay married to her no matter what happened.

He needed to talk to his daughter. He needed to keep his wife. So he had prayed on it.

Only this time, he really meant it. He had prayed

all night for wisdom and guidance. He knew what he should do.

He glanced out the window after dressing quickly. The first faint streaks of dawn were lighting up the sky. If he hurried, he could catch Laura before Ada took her to school. No, he would talk to her before school, and then he would be the one to take her. The cattle could wait for one morning. This was far more important.

He hustled down the hall to Laura's room and rapped gently on the door.

"Yes?" Laura's voice was still slurred from sleep.

"Put on your riding duds and meet me outside," Jack whispered urgently. "It's about time you saw the sunrise while riding, like a true cowgirl."

Laura's answer was a low groan. At first, anger surged through Jack, but he fought it back. She was only ten years old, after all. Very few youngsters would be excited about riding out at dawn.

"Hurry up." He eyed Ada's door. If she wasn't up already, she would be soon. Though she would surely understand his need to have a father-daughter chat, he didn't really want to explain everything to her. This moment, this entire morning, was borne on the impulse of prayer. He didn't want to slow down for anything. "I'll be out front with the horses."

He made his way out to the barn, but not before stopping at the kitchen to snag a few biscuits and a tin mug of coffee. Then he got the horses ready and brought them around to the front of the house. Surprisingly, Laura was already waiting, ready for school, with her lunch pail slung over one arm and her hair neatly braided. Had Ada spurred her to rush, knowing that he wanted to have a chat with his daughter? If so, she kept out of sight. He couldn't catch a glimpse of her anywhere in the windows or on the porch.

He handed Laura up onto Blue and then swung into his own saddle, leading her out onto the prairie without saying a word. He didn't really know how to begin. He just had a feeling that after weeks of struggling with his own offspring, it was time for an honest discussion.

After they had ridden out a fair distance over the pasture, he pulled his horse to a halt. They were looking out over the horizon, and the sun was lighting the clouds so that they turned pink. Now was as good a time as any to try to speak his heart.

"Laura, my little chickadee, Ada told me you want to go back to St. Louis." His voice sounded rough even to his own ears. He paused for a moment to gather his strength. He couldn't fall apart right now.

"I wish she hadn't told you." Laura wailed, a sharp change from her sleepy demeanor. "I only meant to talk to her about it. I didn't want to tell you."

"Well, why not?" He was genuinely curious. Why would she want to tell Ada but not him? After all, he was her true father.

"I didn't want to hurt you." Laura sniffled. "And besides, I didn't want to start a fight."

He reached into his shirt pocket and handed Laura his bandanna. She took it, grimacing as she unfolded the bright blue fabric and blew her nose.

"Laura, I don't want to fight about this, either," he admitted. He sighed. "You know, I brought you out here thinking I could recapture what it was like when things were good in our little family. Before your mother died. I wanted to bring you home and raise you here on the prairie. But I never asked you what you wanted. In fact, I just kinda demanded that you come here."

Laura gave a halfhearted chuckle and dabbed at the end of her nose. "Yes, you did."

He smiled ruefully. "Sorry, chickadee. You know, I had your best interest at heart. I made a lot of changes and promised your grandpa a lot of things in order to bring you back to Winchester Falls. You wouldn't believe everything your stubborn, headstrong daddy did to spirit you back to Texas." Marrying Ada, changing his house, agreeing to summer visits, agreeing to nosy attorneys dropping by—oh, he had certainly done more than he ever thought he would. "I just assumed you'd like it here, too."

"I do like parts of it," Laura interrupted. "It's not all bad. It's just that sometimes I miss St. Louis."

He'd never understand anyone wanting to go back to that crowded, dusty, highfalutin town, but he let that remark pass for the sake of peace. His role, after all, was to bring her up right, and his responsibility was to love her and to cherish her. That meant that he would have to check his habit of insisting on his way or that his opinion was right, and instead allow his daughter to have a voice every now and then.

"Well, I guess I could understand that," he said.

They sat quietly for a minute. The saddle leather creaked, and the bobwhite quails sounded their calls across the pastures. In this moment, he felt closer to his daughter than he ever had except in the moments after she was born. She had curled her fingers so tightly around his index finger that it had turned purple. Then she had looked at him with those big blue eyes, and he was a father. Just like that. It was an instant, but that fleeting second had made him a father.

He needed to be that father now, and always.

"Well, if it's not all bad, what do you like about it?" He turned to watch her.

"Aunt Pearl, Ada, the sweet well water, the wind blowing across the pasture, being the smartest in my class and the sound the cows make when they are heading across the range," she replied, as though ticking off a list in her head. "Oh, and being here with you, of course."

The last bit sounded somewhat tacked on, and he laughed. "Glad to hear I made it, behind the cows."

"Oh, Father." She giggled and rolled her eyes. "Don't be mad."

He shrugged. "What? I am truly thankful that I am right up there with cattle lowing in your mind." He leaned over in the saddle and patted her arm. "Just kidding, chickadee. Here's what I think we should do. I think you oughta pray on it. I did, and that's what moved me to have a good old-fashioned talk with you about it. Now it's your turn. You need to talk to God and see what He tells you to do."

She nodded at him, her eyes widening. "I haven't heard you talk like that before."

"Well, let's just say that I finally understand the power of prayer," he admitted. "Now, it's important that you know that you don't get a final say, missy. There are grown-ups involved, which means your granddaddy and me. We all get a say, and your grandpa probably has some things he would like to clarify." He held back saying anything more definite than that, but the effort caused him to grind his teeth a little. "Okay?"

"Sounds all right." She sounded uncertain. "Does Grandfather get to have that much of a say?"

"Of course," he answered lightly. "He speaks for your mother, since she's not here to."

"Well, isn't Ada my mother now, too?" Her blond eyebrows drew together over her blue eyes. "Won't she have a vote?"

"Ada confers with me," he responded. "Now, come on. I've gotta get you to school. Let's ride over together, and I'll lead Blue home."

She lapsed into silence and followed him. As they rode, a strange peace settled over Jack. He wasn't sure why he felt so peaceful; after all, Laura hadn't told him exactly what he wanted to hear. If she had, there would be no question that she would stay in Winchester Falls, and he'd dare old St. Clair to try to change her mind.

Even so, it felt good because they hadn't shouted, hadn't yelled, hadn't ridden away from each other in anger. He'd asked Laura for her opinion, and she'd told him. And he had conducted himself as a man should. That was the truth of the matter. Instead of acting like a petulant boy, he had acted as a wise father ought to behave. There was something to be proud of in that.

As they drew to a halt in front of the school, Laura leaped easily from her mount and came over to him. "Goodbye, Father," she said, and reached up to give him a hug.

He bent down from the saddle and hugged her as best he could, given the awkwardness of still being in the saddle. Then, her blond braid whipping behind her, she was gone in a flash.

He sat back in the saddle for a moment, savoring the morning.

This was the first time in forever his daughter had embraced him of her own accord.

He must never lose that feeling. Even if it meant compromising with St. Clair for all eternity, he would never lose his daughter again.

Ada glanced at Jack over the rim of her coffee cup. He was silent this morning, as usual, but there was something deeper going on. He had already accompanied Laura to school, which in and of itself was unusual. Most mornings, he had far too many chores to attend to and could not see his way clear to take Laura to the schoolhouse. That he had arisen and escorted her there was quite odd. Whatever had transpired, though, he was not angry. In fact, he seemed more at peace than ever before.

Jack glanced over and caught her looking at him. He smiled. "I'll ask Pearl when the preacher is scheduled to arrive in Winchester Falls. I was about to head over to check on the work crew for the morning. They might be able to hang doors today. We'll see."

"Hang doors?" Ada looked at Jack, bewildered. "But it's not even finished. The walls are just beams."

"Doors have to be the strongest part of a building, so they're built first. Walls and roof and ceiling come afterward." He drained the dregs of his coffee and rose.

As he stood, the front door banged open and Macklin came striding in. "Mail call early this morning, Boss. Pollitt just came by. There's a telegram for you, and the Fort Worth newspaper just came out with the

article about Winchester Falls. I thought you'd like
to read it."

Ada took the paper from him, nervousness breaking over her like a wave. With trembling hands, she
smoothed the pages out, glancing first at the photo-
graphs. Ledbetter had done a good job with them. The
pictures showed people toiling, repairing damaged
roofs and rebuilding homes.

She scanned the article quickly as Jack tore open
the telegram. Mr. Starr had done a fairly decent job.
He'd made some sneering asides about how small the
town was and about how rough and ready life seemed
on the prairie, but he did not poke fun at the hard work
or can-do spirit of Winchester Falls. She breathed a
sigh of relief. It was all right. Not the best, most glowing article one could ask for, but better than she had
secretly feared.

"Did you read the article, Mr. Macklin?" She
glanced up from the paper. "It's pretty good, consid-
ering how awful it could have been."

"Yep. I read it outside the post office. The papers
came in on last night's train, and Pollitt put them out
this morning. There was a whole crowd of people gathered there this morning. I've got to say, a lot of them
were relieved. It did us all a power of good to see
Winchester Falls portrayed as a hardworking group
of folks instead of a lot of no-accounts to pity."

"I agree." She glanced over at Jack, who was staring at the telegram. His face had lost some of its peace-
fulness. Panic seized her. "Jack? What is it?"

"It's from St. Clair." He handed it to her.

With a shaky hand, she glanced over the scrap of
paper.

HEARD OF DESTRUCTION IN TOWN
STOP ALSO MY ATTORNEY TOLD ME OF
CONDITIONS THERE PRIOR TO STORM
STOP LAURA TO RETURN TO BOARDING
SCHOOL WITHOUT DELAY STOP
ST CLAIR

Ada crumpled up the telegram, her eyes filling with tears. "That's it, then."

Her marriage was over.

She had no way to care for her sisters.

"Yep." He sighed heavily. "I'm sorry, honey."

Macklin cleared his throat. "Listen, I know y'all are busy now, so I'll just take my leave. See you later, Boss." With heavy footsteps, he left the dining room and let himself out the front door.

Ada waited for the door to slam shut behind him, her heart heavy in her chest. "I failed. I'm so sorry. You wanted me to do one thing, and I made a miserable wreck of it. Now you're losing your daughter." And she was losing her husband. A lump rose in her throat, making further speech impossible for the time being.

"You didn't fail." He came over beside her and placed his hand on her shoulder. "You made this house a home. I talked to Laura this morning, and I know she'll be happy with this decision. I suppose it's the right thing to do."

So that's why they had ridden out together? That he had spoken to Laura and still remained calm was absolutely astonishing. "I don't know what to do." Utter hopelessness flooded her soul. How would she possibly flounder her way out of this mess? "It sounds as if

St. Clair wants us to put her on the next train. Should I go to the depot and buy a ticket? Shall we take her there ourselves in the car?" Normally, in moments of disaster, she was the one who did all the planning. She took control and made order out of chaos. The certainty of her own feelings of anguish was too crushing. She could not act. She could only feel.

"We are not going to step lively and break up our home just because St. Clair ordered us in a telegram." Jack's voice, strong and purposeful, broke through her miserable haze. "If you can spare the time today, go by the post office and send St. Clair a telegram that we are making plans. We need more than a few hours to figure out what to do. Besides which, I have a chapel to build and cattle to run, and you've been bringing the whole town together. We're busy people. We'll accommodate him when we can."

"All right." She dried her eyes on her handkerchief.

She gave Jack a tremulous smile as he left the house. Then she sat, slowly stirring her cold coffee. They hadn't spoken about the most obvious problem facing them if Laura left.

They wouldn't need to be married anymore.

What would happen now?

Jack had wed her just so she would be a mother for Laura. If Laura returned to boarding school, the very purpose behind their marriage would be gone. They could split up. She could move back to New York. Maybe she should try to seek work with another family.

Pain and panic seized her. She didn't want to lose Laura or Jack.

She rose from the table and put on her hat with

hands that refused to stop trembling. Jack had asked her to send a telegram, and she would do so without delay. At least in that way, she could be a help to him.

The morning drive to the post office passed in a strange sort of haze. Time slowed to a crawl, and yet everything from the waving of the prairie grass to the jumping grasshoppers in the roadway seemed sped up, like in a lantern show. Tears flowed freely now that she was alone. This felt so wrong. How could she stay married to Jack when she had failed him and Laura so completely? How could they be a family if Laura was away from home, growing up among strangers in St. Louis?

She couldn't stay married to Jack. She had failed him. If there was any hope of Laura staying or of prevailing on St. Clair just once more, she might be able to remain in Texas. But as matters stood, she could not.

As she neared the post office, she dried her tears and struggled to compose herself. There was a small knot of people standing outside, and she couldn't very well say hello and smile and nod pleasantly if she was weeping.

"There she is," someone called as Ada pulled the gig up to the hitching post.

What was happening? Did they know what a sham of a wife and mother she was? Could they possibly be offering sympathy?

She tied Blue to the post and was going to politely brush past the crowd, when one of the women broke away and called her name. Ada paused. The woman was one of the denizens of the shantytown they were rebuilding. She remembered her from the trip around the town with Starr and Ledbetter.

The assembled group broke into a smattering of applause. Ada looked around her in amazement and even a little fear. What was happening?

"Mrs. Burnett," the woman called, beckoning Ada over. "You probably don't remember me, but I'm Stella Cotton. I met you the other day when you came by with those men from the papers."

"Yes, Mrs. Cotton. I remember you. How do you do?" Ada gave the woman a faint smile.

"Very well, thanks to all your hard work." The woman, who must have been her same age or even younger, beamed. "We've all been talking." She waved her hand to indicate the assembled crowd. "You did a mighty fine job handling those reporters."

"Why, thank you." She gave them a pale smile.

"Just about everyone in the town's been by here to get the paper," Pollitt added, stepping out of the doorway. "You worked so hard to get us to pull together as a town after a disaster—and helped manage the press so that our little town got a nice write-up. You are a model citizen." He beamed at her, the morning sunlight reflecting off his spectacles.

"Thank you," she replied distractedly. Compliments were fine and dandy, but she knew how terribly she had failed in her private life. "I need to send a telegram. Mr. Pollitt, can you help me?"

"Sure thing." He motioned for her to come inside. The cluster of townspeople parted so that she could walk inside the post office.

With Pollitt's help, she was able to compose a sensible enough telegram for St. Clair.

RECEIVED YOUR MESSAGE STOP AM
MAKING PLANS NOW STOP MORE TO
FOLLOW
ADA WESTMORE BURNETT

She could have saved money by not signing it, or by
signing it with just her first name. Somehow, though,
she needed to let St. Clair know that she recognized
her fault and that she was seeking to rectify the matter.

She thanked Mr. Pollitt and waved goodbye at the
few townspeople still gathered outside the post office.

How she had changed since coming to Winchester
Falls. A year ago, she would have been thrilled at
the write-up in the newspaper. How often had she
worked to get the cause of women's suffrage, for example, to be front-page news? Reporters had laughed
at her or turned her away at every turn. At least now,
she had made enough headway with the press to help
them write a flattering article about the town she had
grown to love.

Victory was ashes, though. It didn't matter. The article hadn't changed St. Clair's mind, and her life was
headed toward upheaval. She no longer cared about the
press. All she cared about was her newfound family.

Chapter Nineteen

Ada glanced around the Burnett family train car as they prepared to disembark at the St. Louis station. On the last trip to St. Louis she had been a new bride, and they had come to bring Laura home. Just two months later she was returning and bringing her stepdaughter back to boarding school. Through the journey north, she kept a brave face on, but it was difficult. Laura was leaving, and her absence would now throw their lives into uproar.

"What time is Grandfather meeting us?" Laura peeked out of the heavy draperies covering the window. "Is he here?"

Jack consulted his pocket watch. "I reckon so," he said, his voice tight. "It's nearly noon. We arranged to meet for dinner—or lunch, as you big-city folks call it." He reached over and rumpled his daughter's hair.

Laura ducked, giving her father a pouty look as she righted her hair bow. "Really, Father," she scolded.

He chuckled softly, and Ada smiled at them both. Whether any of them was willing to admit it or not, an intense connection existed among all of them. She had not spoken to Jack about what would happen to their marriage since that fateful day. They had too much to do to prepare for the trip. After Laura was safely settled in her boarding school, then she would talk to Jack. Some small part of her kept thinking that if she never mentioned it, maybe he might just stay married to her anyway.

Who would have thought it? She would have laughed at the mere mention of it a year ago. Proud, independent Ada had fallen in love with a cowboy. This would be a stunning moment, if not for the fact that she would surely lose him in the next few weeks. It was far better to focus on Laura and Jack than on her sham marriage.

Perhaps, after she left Texas, she could continue to try to nurture the bond between Jack and Laura. A thoughtful, well-written letter might help.

How profoundly depressing.

After a small eternity, the conductor opened their door, and they stepped out into the milling throng of passengers on the station platform. Jack took both of their arms in his, and they walked together, creating a small phalanx of three to break through the crowds. He steered them along the platform and into the station, where they managed their way at the fringes of the multitude. The tall stained glass windows cast a kaleidoscope of colors onto the marble floor, adding to the hectic, carnival-like atmosphere.

They made it to the restaurant, but not before Laura's hat was knocked off once by a passerby, and not before Ada was jostled by a passing porter with a cart full of luggage. Just as before, St. Clair was standing in the doorway, his ebony walking-stick in his hand. His gray hair gleamed as sleekly as ever, and his mustache twitched when he caught sight of his granddaughter. "Lolly," he called, his arms outstretched.

"Grandfather." Laura broke free of her father's hold and ran to embrace St. Clair.

"My, you've been growing like a weed." St. Clair set her away from him and glanced up and down. "I was expecting you to come back brown as a nut from that Texas sun."

"Don't be silly," Laura rejoined. "Ada and I wear hats. Gloves, too." She pirouetted and then pointed to Ada. Ada gave her a wan smile.

"Ah, yes, Mrs. Burnett." St. Clair bowed low over her hand. "How do you do?"

"Very well," she replied quietly, "given the circumstances." It wasn't going to help matters, but she couldn't resist adding it. Everyone else seemed entirely too cheerful.

"Naturally." St. Clair gave a sage nod and turned to her husband. "Burnett."

"Hello, Mr. St. Clair." He held out his hand and St. Clair accepted it, looking at him strangely. "Thank you for meeting us here. I know it's a long trip from Charleston."

Ada raised her eyebrows. Jack was actually being affable to his father-in-law. Never before had she heard him speak of or to St. Clair with such a degree of cordiality.

If St. Clair was nonplussed by Jack's civility, he was too well-bred—or adept at deal making—to show it. "Anything for my granddaughter. Lolly-doll, Grandfather missed you so much. I know Mrs. Erskine will be happy to see you again."

Laura smiled. "I missed everyone, too."

St. Clair guided them to the same corner table of the restaurant where he had held court before. He held Ada's chair first and then Laura's. He made the same joke about ordering dinner so as to save them all from a luncheon of chili and corn bread. Jack accepted the barb at his expense without showing his temper.

What had come over her husband? Normally Jack would be drumming his fingers on the table right now, itching to escape. Yet here he was, listening and speaking, jesting at himself and offering tense but genuine smiles to his daughter.

"We don't eat chili at home," Laura said. "We eat proper food."

"Good girl." St. Clair gave her an affectionate, indulgent look. Then he turned to Jack. "I'm glad you saw reason, Burnett. No need to have my granddaughter out on the prairie where it is so dangerous. She's much better off here, where she belongs."

The waitress brought the first course of caviar on toast ends. Laura took one bite and spit it out in her napkin. "That's awful," she gasped, her eyes watering.

"Now, Lolly," her grandfather scolded gently, "has living in Texas ruined your palate? Your mother loved caviar. She would have existed on nothing else, if she could."

"Well, I can't. It's disgusting." Laura took a big gulp of her lemonade.

Should Ada restrain her stepdaughter from spitting and gulping in public? Normally, Laura's table manners were quite fine, and her grandfather had just upbraided her for at least one infraction. Perhaps it would be better to fall silent about the whole thing. Very few children would find caviar palatable, anyway.

She glanced over at Jack. The corners of his mouth were twitching, as though he was trying to suppress a grin. It was obvious that he was thinking, "That's my kid."

"We shall work to get you used to it," St. Clair replied smoothly. "When you come home to Evermore on school holidays, I shall have your cousins and aunts work with you to show you the finer points of etiquette. I thought Mrs. Burnett would handle that aspect of your upbringing, but I suppose she had her hands full. It sounds as though Texas is a string of disasters."

Ada was at a loss for words. She had neglected to give Laura any sort of social polish, that much was true. She had been busy attending to Jack and Pearl, and Laura behaved better than any other child she had encountered. There was no need to gild the lily, so to speak. Laura was naturally graceful and would grow into her maturity.

"School holidays?" Jack spoke up, the traces of good humor gone from his expression and his voice. "Do you mean she will either be at Mrs. Erskine's or at Evermore? Is she not to visit the ranch?"

"I don't believe that's a good idea." St. Clair gave Jack a pointed look. "You are, of course, welcome to visit us all at Evermore, or to visit her in St. Louis before she leaves for the holidays, as you had before. You know what Emily's will stipulated. If you were found to be an unfit parent, then I would take over as sole guardian. I find that life in Texas is far too harsh for my granddaughter. She will spend her school days at Mrs. Erskine's and holidays with me in Charleston."

Could she possibly be hearing right? So, Laura would never be allowed to return to Texas? "But, sir," she said, "don't blame Jack for my failings. He is a wonderful father to Laura. Domesticity is not my forte, I'm afraid. I don't want Jack and Laura to be separated merely because I'm a poor hand at house-keeping."

"My dear," St. Clair rejoined, giving her a silky smile. "Your lack of domestic skills is hardly the largest part of this problem. It is merely indicative of the graver situation, one that I suspected long ago. Texas is no place to raise a child."

She dared not look at her husband. If she did, she would burst into tears.

Laura was oddly silent. Ada hazarded a glance at her stepdaughter. Was she all right?

Laura was staring at her grandfather, her normally pink cheeks a bright shade of red. "Texas isn't like that," she began, her voice quavering. "It's not."

"Now, Lolly." St. Clair leaned over and patted her hand. "It's a fine place for rough-and-tumble cowboys like your father, but it's no place for a young lady."

"That's not true." Laura's entire body was quivering—with rage or fear, Ada couldn't tell which. "Don't say that."

"Keep your voice down, Laura." Her grandfather spoke to her sharply for the first time during their meeting—possibly for the first time ever. "You are making a scene."

"I. Will. Not." Laura punctuated each word with a slap of her palm on the table. "Grandfather, I didn't know that if I returned to Mrs. Erskine's, I wouldn't be able to see my family ever again."

"Lolly." Her grandfather's voice was both pleading and commanding. "You can see them if they come to visit us at Evermore. Don't you love it? You've come there so often. Just as we spoke of during your last visit, I'll make your mother's bedroom into your room. It will be perfect. As if this—" he paused, waving his hand at Ada and Jack "—never happened."

Ada was at a loss for words. During their last negotiation, she had taken the lead. In fact, in every trying circumstance she could think of, she had assumed control. Now, however, she was swamped in misery. This was all her fault. Jack was losing Laura, not just during the school term, but forever. And she was going to lose both Laura and Jack.

The waitress took away the caviar and brought chicken broth. Laura sniffed at hers, wrinkling her nose.

"Perhaps it would be best if Jack could visit her at Mrs. Erskine's," she began, tentatively. "I suppose that would be the best way for Laura to see her father. As you say, he could come see her before she left for Evermore." She didn't say anything about the two of them. She couldn't bring herself to lie.

"No." Laura gave a defiant shake of her head, sending her blond ringlets cascading down her back. "I have a room in Texas, you know. With a pretty quilt on my bed." She addressed her grandfather directly.

"That's nice," he began.

"Ada and Aunt Pearl made my room up just for me," she continued. "Ada drives me to and from school every day in the gig. Every single day. No other student rides in a gig." She gave her stepmother a fond look. "And Father saved my life. He saved all of our lives. When the twister was coming, he threw us in a ditch and covered us. He held us tight so the tornado wouldn't get us. He was still hurting from Asesino, but he did it, regardless of the pain he was suffering." She gave her father such a proud look that Ada gasped.

She never knew, until this moment, how much Laura loved her father.

"That's just what I'm talking about, Lolly." St. Clair threw his hands up in exasperation. "Danger everywhere you turn. It's not safe for you, my dear."

"Well, I know something about Charleston." Laura fixed her grandfather with a glare. "I learned all about hurricanes in class earlier this year at Mrs. Erskine's. I also studied geography. I know that Charleston is situated on the Atlantic coast and that hurricanes can be a problem in some seasons."

Ada took a hasty sip of her lemonade to quell the sudden laugh bubbling up within her. Laura was a smart girl, probably far cleverer than any adult sitting at this table.

St. Clair turned an unhealthy shade of scarlet. "When hurricanes occur—if they do occur—we have precautions we take."

"So do we in Texas," Jack spoke up from his side of the table. His voice, no longer strained, sounded distinctly amused. "We have storm cellars for when tornadoes hit. That's how a lot of people on our ranch made it through unscathed. We just happened to be caught while we were out on the prairie, that's all."

He smiled over at Ada, his green eyes twinkling with mischief.

His expression made his intent plainly obvious. Jack Burnett might lose his daughter, but not without a fight.

If Jack was going to go down swinging, then she would, too.

Jack looked around the table. He wasn't going to lose his family. Ada hadn't said anything, but he knew her heart. If he lost Laura for good, Ada would tell him they could no longer be married. Well, he wasn't going to let that happen. He had promised himself that, after Laura was safely settled at school, he would propose to Ada and marry her in truth. He knew a good thing when he had it, and he wasn't going to let her go. He was going to fight for his daughter and for his wife.

St. Clair had gone from smooth self-assurance to visible anger and frustration within a few heartbeats. Ada had moved from abject misery to budding hope. Laura, who had been so excited to see her grandfather, was now furious.

He should be happy that things were going his way, or at least looking better than they had before. He wasn't happy about that, though. He was thrilled that his daughter was standing up for him, voicing her opinions as he had not heard her do before. Perhaps she lacked the social polish that St. Clair demanded, but she was a wholly rational girl who was making a sensible argument.

His heart jumped with pride as he looked at her.

"My little chickadee," he said, keeping his voice gentle and even. "Your grandfather and I have been on opposite sides for years, trying to raise you right and take care of you. We assumed a lot of things. Some

things we decided on your behalf, because you were too young to make decisions for yourself."

St. Clair flicked him a warning glance, but Jack merely nodded respectfully.

"Your grandfather wants what's best for you. So do Ada and I. If you want what your grandfather wants, you'll still see us. We'll come visit at Evermore. But the thing is, we think we know what suits you—we have opinions on the matter—but it's your life. So you think it over. You tell us what you want. We'll abide by your decision."

He was letting her have her head, just as he would a spirited horse. How many times had that proved useful on the range? A horse was usually a better judge of the height of a fence or the depth of a puddle than its rider. If he judged for the horse, more times than not, he ended up flat on his back in a stream or gasping for air on the ground. But if he gave Blue his head, Blue would figure it out for himself and get them both safely through.

Laura needed to make this call. She knew what she needed. The adults gathered around this table would then strive to provide it for her. Well, he couldn't make St. Clair do anything. But, as Ada had pointed out, St. Clair loved Laura. Surely, if Laura told her grandfather what she truly wanted, he would move a mountain to make it happen.

After all, he had done so for his daughter. Laura's mother.

He attempted to drink the chicken broth because his throat was dry, but it was still too hot. So he sipped at his lemonade while St. Clair glowered at him. Laura

toyed with her fork, marking little patterns on her linen napkin with its tines.

"Well, I can tell you right now I don't want to just live in Charleston and at Mrs. Erskine's," she replied sharply. "I never thought I'd have to leave Ada and Father for good." She set down her fork.

St. Clair remained quiet. This silence was nothing short of remarkable. Usually the man had a suave response for every situation.

"I like Mrs. Erskine's, and I miss my school friends," she continued. "But Miss Carlyle is a good teacher, too. I guess I was pretty much set on disliking school in Texas because it was so different from what I was used to. To be honest, I don't think I gave it a fair trial."

Jack's heart leaped in his chest. At best, he had hoped for some sort of compromise, where Laura would come home for alternate holidays, spending the rest in Charleston. Could she really be willing to stay with them year-round?

"What are you saying?" St. Clair hunched over the table, pushing his cup of broth aside. Jack recognized this posture well. This was his full negotiation position, wherein he was finally ready to cut his losses and make a deal. Hadn't the old man looked the same way when Jack and Emily had eloped and then refused to separate?

"Ada is teaching me to be a rational creature," she replied. "No man will grant women the right to vote if they are indecisive."

Ada grinned broadly, obviously pleased that her lessons were bearing fruit.

"I think I should return to Texas and give the school

a real try," Laura continued. "If, at the end of the term, I don't like it, then I should prefer to return to Mrs. Erskine's next year."

"Sounds fair," Jack replied, and Ada nodded sagely.

"I'd like to visit Evermore, as you and Ada agreed," she continued, looking squarely at her grandfather. "Just—not during the summer. That's hurricane season."

Jack chortled—he couldn't help it. Ada laughed, too.

"What's so funny?" Laura demanded. "I think it's a reasonable request. Don't you?"

"Eminently reasonable." Ada gave her stepdaughter a reassuring pat on the arm. "Entirely sensible."

Jack waited for St. Clair's response, his nervousness rising. To get right down to it, he didn't have a right to insist that Laura have a choice. Emily's will put all the decision making in St. Clair's hands. However, the old man did truly love his granddaughter. His actions were motivated by his deep affection and care for her.

St. Clair made the mistake that they all had— fighting for Laura's happiness without stopping to ask her what made her happy.

Then and there, Jack forgave St. Clair for everything he had done, when Emily was alive and after her death. Like Jack, he was a bewildered and yet belligerent father who wanted what was best for his daughter—and later, his granddaughter.

"Very well." St. Clair sat back, defeated. "I suppose I know when I'm beaten."

"You are not beaten." Laura leaped from her chair and walked over to her grandfather, rubbing her cheek against his. "You are just becoming a sensible creature. Like me."

A wave of relief washed over Jack, overpowering him with the desire to laugh. It was exhilarating to feel good after so much pain, so much tragedy and so much indecision. He could even attempt a deep belly laugh now, as his ribs had healed to the point he no longer needed a cast.

Ada merely smiled at him, her eyes bright with unshed tears.

They were going to be a family once more.

St. Clair chuckled, holding his granddaughter close. "I suppose I am. It's about time, too, at my age. I declare, I don't even have an appetite for chicken any longer. After such momentous negotiations, shall we skip straight to dessert?"

Ada made her way back into the drawing-room car after tucking Laura into her sleeping car. Jack was still awake. He had opened the curtains so that the moonlight glowed through the windows as the train sped through the night.

She took a seat across from him and stared out at the moon. "God's in His heaven—all's right with the world!" she quoted softly.

"Is everything really all right?" Jack leaned forward and took her hand in his. She could not suppress a shiver at the touch of his hand on hers. "Tell me the truth. If Laura had left, you would have, too. Wouldn't you?"

A hot flush crept over her cheeks. She couldn't force herself to meet his gaze. "I thought you would have ended it. After all, the reason you married me—"

"You thought that I had married you just to be a housekeeper and mother. Well, I guess that was the original plan. But oh, Ada honey, you are so wrong. I know I am a cowboy with a stubborn streak a mile wide, but you made me a better man. I'm a better father because of you. I'm a better Christian because of you. If you left me, what would I do?"

"Oh, Jack." Tears filled her eyes. "I love you. I don't know what I would do without you. I've become a better person just by being around you."

"Don't cry." He brushed away her tears with the tips of his fingers. "I love you, too. And do you know what we're going to do about it?"

"What?" She was breathless, hanging on to his words. She raised her eyes to his. Jack was looking at her with so much love, so much longing, that it made her heart hitch.

"We're going to get married."

Chapter Twenty

~❧~

"Jack, I never thought I'd see the day when I would attend your wedding to my niece—twice," Pearl called as she walked into the dining room. Her leg had healed in the weeks since bringing Laura home, and now she walked without a cane. Her limp was barely detectable.

Jack rose and poured a cup of coffee for her. "Good morning to you, too," he replied with a laugh. "I already asked for your blessing, so I know I have it the second time around. The first time, I believe you arranged it. Or at least, we all assumed you did."

Pearl settled into a chair, accepting the coffee cup with a satisfied grunt. "Let's just say I smoothed the road for you," she agreed. "At least this wedding will be done up right. You won't be wearing cowboy duds all sopping wet with wash water, for one thing. That's a mighty nice suit you've got on. I don't think I've ever seen you this dressed up."

He glanced down at his new sack suit with a mixture of irritation and pride. It was hard not to feel silly, wearing shoes instead of boots and a suit instead of